How she would continue to obey his curt instru... quick rejoind... know.

Squarely she placed her feet in front of her and crossed them at the ankle, wishing for something to lean against. Still, the chaise longue was softer than his armchair, and she would allow no fault to be found with her posture.

'That will do.'

As he rested on his heels her whole body stiffened under his scrutiny.

'You need to remain still,' he commanded her brusquely.

How could she be still with him staring at her? She dropped her shoulders and puffed out a slow breath.

'Now turn to the right. No, not like that—turn some more.'

'More?'

'Now raise your eyes. Raise your *eyes*! Not move your whole head.'

'I'm not sure what you mean!' Cameo exclaimed, exasperated.

In a ... e her ...

Author Note

A portrait of passion…

Do you love the Victorian era? I do. It was an amazing time, when passion lurked beneath propriety and secrets and scandals were hidden beneath the surface. This story is inspired by the desperately romantic Pre-Raphaelite artists and models of Victorian England. The beautiful and sensual Pre-Raphaelite paintings are some of the most familiar artworks in the world today. I expect, like me, you have your favourites—do get in touch and let me know!

Just like Benedict Cole's, the art and the love lives of the Pre-Raphaelite painters—a group of brilliant, free-thinking young men—were considered scandalous. Their artistic milieu was in complete contrast with the strict conventions of the Victorian upper classes. Ladies like 'Cameo', Lady Catherine Mary St Clair, lived in a controlled, stifling world, and often felt trapped and unhappy. It would have been considered unthinkable for a young aristocratic woman such as Cameo to want to pursue art seriously, and even more unthinkable to be an artist's model.

This story celebrates every woman who ever challenged convention for the sake of art, and for the sake of love.

I hope you enjoy it!

ENTICING BENEDICT COLE

Eliza Redgold

MILLS
BOON

Published in Great Britain 2015
by Mills & Boon, an imprint of Harlequin (UK) Limited,
Eton House, 18-24 Paradise Road, Richmond, Surrey, TW9 1SR

© 2015 Eliza Redgold

ISBN: 978-0-263-24816-6

Eliza Redgold is an author, academic and unashamed romantic. She was born in Scotland, is married to an Englishman, and currently lives in Australia. She loves to share stories with readers! Get in touch with Eliza via Twitter: @ElizaRedgold, on Facebook: facebook.com/ElizaRedgoldAuthor and Pinterest: pinterest.com/elizaredgold. Or visit her at goodreads.com/author/show/7086012.Eliza_Redgold and elizaredgold.com.

Enticing Benedict Cole
**is Eliza Redgold's magical debut
for Mills & Boon Historical Romance!**

For Madeleine, who first listened to the whole story,
and for my sister, the original Catherine Mary.

Many thanks to those who made Cameo's
acquaintance more than once in writing this story.

To the Wordwrights critique group, Janet Woods,
Deb Bennetto, Karen Saayman and Anne Summers,
who read early versions and made such
valuable comments, and to Jenny Schwartz,
an angel of a critique partner.

Thanks to my daughter, Jessica, who played
Yann Tiersen's *Rue des Cascades* on the piano as
theme music while Cameo raced through the streets of
London to find Benedict, and to my husband, James,
who always makes London magical.

Prologue

'Love, A more ideal Artist he than all.'
—Alfred, Lord Tennyson:
'The Gardener's Daughter' (1842)

'On that veil'd picture—veil'd, for what it holds
May not be dwelt on by the common day.
This prelude has prepared thee.'
—Alfred, Lord Tennyson:
'The Gardener's Daughter'

London 1852

Cameo pressed the letter to her lips.

Beneath her carefully crafted, polite phrases would he read her hopes and dreams in each line?

Through the open window she stared out past the silhouette of the ash tree into the starry night beyond, as if by will she summoned him to reply. Beyond, by the light of the moon, she made out in front of the house the darkened grassy garden of the square with its plane trees, the high black wrought-iron railings encircling the snowdrops and daffodils. She felt caged in the house, like a bird who longed to be free. She wanted to be out in the world, to be part of it all. To learn. To paint. *To live*.

With a sigh she closed the velvet curtains and retreated into her bedroom. On her dressing table the candle flickered. The flame leapt high, with its orange, red and yellow tongue, its vivid blue centre. If only she could learn to capture such passionate colours with her paints!

He did.

Benedict Cole.

That was his name. She'd stared it, scrawled in black paint at the corner of the canvas.

She'd discovered his passion and power when she'd seen his painting at the Royal Academy of Art. It had stopped her in her tracks, her breath shuddering.

The work was marvellous. The subject was simple, a woman holding sheaves of wheat. But the subject of the painting wasn't what caught her attention. It was the strokes of his brush.

As if his paintbrush stroked her skin.

As if it touched her heart.

There was a secret in that painting, as if it held a message, as if it spoke directly to her. She…

recognised it. That was it. Somehow, she understood the soul of the artist who had painted that picture. The effect on her had been extraordinary. She wanted to stand in front of it for hours, soaking in the colours, the textures, his use of light. She returned again and again to view it.

Benedict Cole must teach her. She knew it. She needed to learn everything he knew. Only he could free her hands and the emotions locked inside her. Only he could show her how to put them on paper, on canvas, with charcoal, with paint, until the work came to life.

She must find a way.

Now at last she'd gathered up her courage to write to him.

She yearned to pour out all her hopes and dreams in the letter, her longings and desires. But her phrases remained stilted. Draft after draft, pen staining her fingers, she'd tried to find the right words to ask his consent to give her lessons and that she would pay him handsomely for his time.

And she hoped that he would understand. It meant so much more.

Her heart beating fast, she picked up the letter.

Sealing it with a drop of wax, she blew out the candle.

She could only pray for his answer.

Chapter One

'This morning is the morning of the day.'
—Alfred, Lord Tennyson:
'The Gardener's Daughter'

'The answer is no!' Gerald St Clair, Earl of Buxton, threw his newspaper down on the breakfast table. 'Don't ask me again, Cameo!'

Cameo leaned forward. She clutched the carved stone of her necklace so hard it dug into her skin. 'Please, Papa, please.'

The earl shook his head, his whiskers quivering. 'I've had quite enough of this. You're Lady Catherine Mary St Clair. You have a place in society to uphold. All this nonsense must stop immediately. No daughter of mine is going to be an artist.'

She took a deep breath. 'Being an artist isn't so unsuitable. I'm asking for some proper painting lessons, that's all.'

The vein on the earl's forehead popped out. 'It's quite ridiculous. I blame myself. I should never have allowed you take up art in the first place. It's all you talk of, all you do.'

And all she thought of, Cameo reflected guiltily. At that very moment she wished she had her sketchbook and pencil with her, to make a study of her father's irate expression.

'Listen to me, Cameo. Painting may remain your hobby, but nothing more. I've been too lenient with you, I see that now. It's time to think of your future.' Her father's gruff tone had softened. She knew how much he loved her and he always sounded particularly gruff when he was trying to protect her from the outside world. But she didn't want to be protected. Not from the world. Not from art.

'I am thinking of my future, Papa.' She took another huge breath. 'My future is as a painter.'

The earl choked on his bacon and kidneys. 'Your future is marriage.'

From the other end of the long, polished table Lady Buxton spoke in her soft voice. 'You'll forget all about painting lessons when you're married, Cameo dear. Take our Queen Victoria. She and Prince Albert are an example to all those who seek the happy estate. Even though she is queen, she believes the best place for women is home and family.'

Cameo turned to her mother, sat behind the silver coffee pot. 'I'm not against a home and family, Mama. It's just I've discovered there's more to life. There's art. Art is real life.'

'Art! Real life!' blustered Lord Buxton. 'You'll put off your suitors with all this nonsense.'

'Lord Warley asked especially if you were to attend Lady Russell's ball,' the countess chimed in with a smile. 'He's such a lovely young man. So well mannered.'

Cameo shuddered, as if Lord Warley had taken her hand to bow. Even the slightest touch of Robert Ackland, Earl of Warley, always turned her stomach. He came from a similar background to hers. Their fathers held the same rank in society. But couldn't her mama sense what lay beneath Lord Warley's good manners? Perhaps because Cameo spent so much time sketching, always trying to capture character, she had become more attuned to what was hidden behind propriety. 'Oh, no, Mama. Not Lord Warley. Never.'

'Our family has been friends with their family for years,' her papa reminded her. 'I was very fond of my old friend Henry Ackland. I don't know his son well and he doesn't seem much like his father, but Henry was a good man, God rest his soul.'

Her father still missed his old friend. Cameo

gentled her voice. 'I don't want to think about suitors yet, Papa, that's all. Please. I long to learn to paint in the new style, like the Pre-Raphaelites.'

'The Pre-Raphaelites,' her mother repeated in a horrified whisper. 'The way they carry on is shocking, I've heard.'

'But the new style of painting is wonderful. Why, I saw an extraordinary work in the Royal Academy of Art.' Cameo's heart beat faster as she recalled it. 'If I took lessons, perhaps I could learn to paint like that. I'll never be that good, but one day, I might be able to exhibit.'

Her mama almost dropped her coffee cup. 'You couldn't possibly show your paintings in *public*. What would people say? Perhaps you could paint some flowers on the name cards for our dinner parties this Season instead,' she added hopefully. 'That would be lovely.'

'I suppose George could have art lessons if he wanted them?' The question burst out before Cameo could halt it. She gripped her hands together.

'It's different for your brother.' Her mother put her fingertips to her temples. 'And please don't raise your voice.'

Her father glowered. 'Stop upsetting your mama and stop these foolish ideas. I've let it go far enough. I ought not to have allowed it in the first place.'

'Papa…'

'Enough, I said. I won't discuss this matter with you again. Why are you arguing in such a manner? It isn't like you, Cameo. Now, behave like a young lady.'

I'd rather behave like an artist. Cameo choked back the words.

'I'm sorry, Papa.'

With shaking fingers she picked up her cup.

She hated to deceive her parents, but she had no choice.

Alas. It was already too late.

'Cameo?' Maud poked her head around the drawing-room door. 'Briggs told me you were in here. Am I interrupting?'

'Not at all.' Cameo laid down her paintbrush. No matter how hard she tried there was no discernible improvement in her work. 'It's lovely to see you, Maud. It isn't going well this morning.'

Cameo stood at her easel, an old linen sheet spread beneath her. She was fortunate to be allowed to continue to paint in the drawing room, after an incident with some spilt paint. Of course, it had been ochre.

Her easel was placed where the light was best. Through the windows the March sun cast its spring promise. Cameo had asked her mama if she might fling wide the heavy curtains for more light, but at her mother's shocked face the question had trailed away.

Now Maud peeped over her shoulder. 'What are you working on today?'

Carefully Cameo wiped her hands with a rag. She'd promised her mama to try to keep her hands clean, too, after she'd appeared at luncheon with oil paint under her fingernails.

'I'm doing what apprentices used to do when they worked in the studios of the Old Masters,' she explained. 'They copied the Masters' work to learn their technique. It's a good way to learn, though not as good as actually watching a master at work with his own hands. I'm not up to landscapes yet so I'm making a copy of that portrait.'

She pointed to the gold-framed portrait that hung above the fireplace. It depicted her grandmother as a young woman. She wore a white dress and a cameo necklace tied with a black-velvet ribbon, the same black-and-white stone that now hung around Cameo's neck. Set in gold, with a loop as well as a pin, it could be worn as either a brooch or a necklace.

'You're so like your grandmama,' her mother often said. Her grandmama's hair had been dark, almost black, and her eyes, though difficult to discern in the portrait, were the same deep blue as Cameo's, so deep they could appear purple. Violet eyes, her mama called them.

Maud glanced from one painting to the other. 'Your painting will be just as good,' she said loyally.

Cameo slipped off her paint-splattered artist's smock. 'You're being much too kind, Maud, and you know it. I've got so much to learn, but how can I improve when there is always a luncheon or a dinner or a ball we must attend? And we have to keep changing our clothes. Imagine how wonderful it would be to get up in the morning and be able to paint all day.'

Cameo sighed. She tried to keep her spirits high, but it was difficult. More often now, at night, she despaired. Sometimes she lay awake in bed until she threw back the covers, lit a candle and seized her pencil. Then she drew and drew, sheet after sheet, until dawn came. It was the only way to soothe her sense of being trapped, her frustration. Yet she was forced to play at art, to keep it as a hobby, never learning, barely improving. Without lessons, without a guiding hand, she would never become the artist she longed to be.

Maud's round blue eyes were sympathetic. 'Do you really want art lessons so much?'

'So much that I had the most terrible argument with Papa and Mama.' She paced the room, her gown trailing across the carpet. Impatiently she hitched it up. 'I must take matters into my own hands. I've got a few ideas.'

'Oh, no, Cameo.' Maud's curls bobbed in alarm. 'Your ideas are always so reckless. Surely you must obey your parents' wishes.'

Maud would never do anything of which her parents disapproved.

'Art is everything to me,' Cameo said. 'I will even pay for lessons myself.'

Maud appeared bewildered. 'But how would you pay?'

In spite of the luxuries that surrounded her, Cameo had only a little money of her own. All her needs were provided for and she was made a small allowance, but that was all.

Her fingers touched her throat. 'I could sell some of my jewellery.'

Maud's hand flew to her mouth. 'Not your cameo necklace.'

Cameo smiled. 'I've worn it ever since Mama gave it to me. Just as I've worn the name George gave me when I was born.'

'Cam-mee, because he couldn't say Catherine Mary.' The dimple that displayed whenever George was mentioned appeared in Maud's cheek. 'And it became Cameo.'

Cameo's fingers ran over the black-and-white jewel with the woman's profile carved on to its face. She shook her head firmly. 'No. I could never sell my cameo necklace.'

But she would do almost anything for painting lessons.

Benedict Cole would understand. She felt convinced of it. No one in her family or any one of her friends, not even Maud, understood her longing, her need to paint. To try to speak of it, to explain to those who didn't share her passion, was like speaking a foreign language.

In Benedict Cole's painting at the Academy she'd discerned a flame that burned inside the artist's heart, which drove him on to create, no matter what the cost, no matter what the risk. She couldn't describe it but she knew it was there, that flame.

It burned inside her, too.

After Maud left, Briggs, the butler, entered the drawing room, with a white paper square held aloft on a silver tray. 'This has come for you, Lady Catherine Mary.'

'At last!' Cameo leapt up and reached for the envelope. Her name and address was written on it in strong black letters. 'Thank you, Briggs. And—no one saw?'

The merest glimmer of a smile showed on the butler's impassive face. She only ever saw him grin widely at Christmas, when each year she gave him a picture she had painted especially for him, as she'd done since she was a small girl, the results improving somewhat over the years. One could not call the butler family, yet to Cameo he was. All the servants were old friends and allies, people she could trust with her secrets.

'His lordship has gone to Westminster and her ladyship is resting upstairs.' Briggs gave a slight bow and discreetly closed the door.

Cameo's fingers trembled with such excitement she could barely open the seal. At last, to be able to work with a true artist, someone who would understand. Eagerly, she began to read.

Dear Lady Catherine Mary St Clair
In response to your letter regarding paint-
ing lessons, I regret to inform you I will
not be able to fulfil your request. I have
neither the time nor inclination to teach
aristocratic society ladies to dabble at art.
Benedict Cole

'Oh!' She gasped as if a pail of cold water had been thrown over her.

Tears smarted in her eyes. If he knew how hard she'd tried to learn, to teach herself. How hard she'd fought for lessons, of her desperation, her despair. No, he dismissed her, just as everyone else did.

Her heart sank as she crumpled onto the sofa. She'd convinced herself Benedict Cole was the guiding hand she so desperately needed. She dropped her head in her hands, wiped away another tear. Her hands clenched. She might as well give up.

Just the thought of giving up sparked the flame.

Cameo's temper burst into life. Fury burned within her as hot as the coals in the grate. How dared he. *Dabble at art.* The nerve of the man. How dare he presume that simply because of her title she wasn't serious about art? It was insulting.

Jumping to her feet, she crossed to the oval gilt-framed mirror by the door and surveyed her reflection. How could she convince him?

Off came her pearl earrings and the diamond-studded watch pinned to her bodice. She must appear a serious student of art to make him understand, not the kind of society lady about whom he made such infuriating assumptions. She straightened the white-lace collar and cuffs of her grey morning dress and smoothed down her hair with a nod. Yes, that would do.

For a moment she hesitated. Could she, Lady Catherine Mary St Clair, go to a painter's studio unannounced when they hadn't been formally introduced? Her mama would be horrified.

The spark surged inside her.

It wouldn't be a social call.

Benedict Cole must teach her to paint. Somehow, she would change the artist's mind.

The carriage rattled to a stop.

Cameo's fury and determination had built with every turn of the carriage wheel. As they rolled out of the quiet, leafy square in Mayfair, with its large cream houses, glossy black-painted doors, marble steps and iron railings, onto Oxford St and the roaring bustle of the shops and crowds, all she could think about was Benedict Cole. She longed to confront him. How could he make such assumptions about her, the kind she'd been fighting against all her life? If he knew... if she told him...

She leapt up so fast she almost hit her head on the carriage.

Out on the street, Bert, the coachman, had opened the door and put the box down for her. 'Here we are.' He rubbed his forehead and glanced about dubiously. 'Are you sure this is the place you're wanting?'

Briskly, she stepped down into the street and adjusted her skirt. No turning back now. 'Yes, this is it. Will you mind waiting for me, Bert?'

'I'll be here.' He grinned good-naturedly. 'Anything for you, Lady Catherine Mary.'

Tying her bonnet with a firm bow, she set off against the wind. In spite of spending much of her life in London, there were parts of the city she barely knew. She certainly never stopped in Soho. The family carriage always drove through. She had expected the soot and dirt, certainly, but not the vibrant activity sweeping her along the cobbled road. Spread with straw and litter, the busy street echoed with the sounds of carriages and carts, horses' hooves, and vendors shouting their wares. There were shops, too, with people going in and out, tinkling the doorbells. The smell from the fishmonger's window, full of shoals of mussels and oysters, reached her before she saw it and a yeasty odour emanated from empty barrels outside a public house, a sign with a lamb painted on it swaying above the door.

Through the crowd she hurried, past two fighting boys, their mothers with baskets on their arms chatting to each other uncaring of the scuffle, and past a flower seller who offered with a toothless grin to sell her a bunch of daisies. A young woman in a low-cut bodice standing on a corner sent her a brazen glare. With a gulp Cameo hastened on.

In front of a tall red-brick building she checked the number. Yes, this was the address of the infuriating Benedict Cole, yet in front of her stood a bakery, the scent of hot bread and buns wafting out every time a customer opened the door. The artist must live upstairs, but there was no obvious way to get in.

A girl sat on the pavement nearby, shabby and meek, with bare feet and a shawl around her thin shoulders.

'Matches,' she called hoarsely, 'matches.'

Cameo crouched down and smiled. 'Hello.'

'Hello, miss.'

'What's your name?'

'It's Becky, miss. Do you want some matches?'

'I don't have any money with me.' Why hadn't she brought her reticule with her? She normally did, for she kept a tiny sketchbook and sharpened pencils inside, but she'd rushed out in such a hurry. 'I'll bring you some another day, I promise.'

The girl sighed. 'That's all right.'

'I will, Becky. Perhaps now you can help me. Do you know how to get in to where the people live upstairs?'

'You go round the back, miss, down that alleyway. There's a red door.'

'Thank you,' Cameo called, already moving away.

A cat yowled as she entered the dingy alley. For a moment she hesitated before she picked her way through the sodden newspaper, broken glass bottles, cabbage stalks and something that looked like—no; it couldn't be. Edging around the rubbish, she narrowly avoided a puddle of something that looked and smelled worse.

The red door, if the flakes of peeling paint identified it as such, was ajar. At her touch it swung open wider, creaking.

Inside the cramped entrance hall, she stared, half fascinated, half appalled. She'd never visited such a rundown establishment. The walls had been white once, perhaps, but now they were an indeterminate colour, yellow or cream, with water marks at the bottom, where the damp had crept in. A staircase with a worn green runner lay directly in front of her, the woodwork scuffed and dull.

Dust dirtied her white-kid gloves as she gripped the banister. She brushed them on her skirt. Up two narrow flights of steps she climbed, passing closed doors on each landing, checking numbers as she went and up a third flight, which was narrower still.

Out of breath, she reached the attic door at the top. It bore no number, just a name plate beside it, simple and beautiful. She hadn't expected something so unique. Carved from a piece of oak, a pattern of leaves and berries had been etched on to its square edges, and at the centre scrolled the name: Benedict Cole.

Well, now, Benedict Cole. You're about to receive a surprise visit from a society lady.

Her heart drummed as she rapped on the door. No reply.

Under her skirts she tapped her foot. She knocked again, harder.

The door flung open. Cameo gasped and fell backwards at the sheer force of the man who glowered in front of her, his fist gripping a paint-brush. Benedict Cole. She knew it with a certainty flaming inside her belly. Tall, with dark hair that swooped over his forehead, he wore a loose, unbuttoned painting shirt covered with blotches of dried oils in a frenzy of colours. Yet his eyes held her attention. Dark brown, under heavy black brows, they blazed with a fierce inner light that seared into her very soul.

'You're too late.' His educated accent held an unexpected warm burr.

With a huge gulp of air she tried to steady her ragged breathing. 'Too late?'

'I'm too busy to see you now.' He started to close the door.

'Wait! I must see you. You are Benedict Cole?'

He scowled. 'Who else would be working in my studio?'

'Please. Just give me a few minutes of your time.'

Eyebrows drawn together, he studied her. 'You've seen the notice.'

'The notice…?'

'Will you please stop repeating every word I say? Are you dim-witted as well as unpunctual? Yes, my notice seeking a new model. I have a major new work in mind.'

'You're looking for a model. For your painting.'

'How many times do we have to have this conversation? If you're not here to be considered, then why exactly are you here wasting my time?'

In a flash, she realised what had happened. 'Well, actually…'

'Well, actually what?' he mimicked, the corner of his mouth lifting in a sneer.

How dare this man speak to her in such a manner? In person he was just as rude as in his letter, even ruder if that were possible. Cameo opened her mouth to tell him of his mistake in no uncertain terms and then snapped it shut again.

Her mind whirred. He'd made it clear he didn't wish to provide painting lessons to Lady Catherine Mary St Clair. Now, upon seeing him, he appeared to be the kind of man who would never change his mind.

Cameo smiled. 'I'm so sorry I'm late, Mr Cole. You're quite right. I've come to be your model.'

Chapter Two

'As never pencil drew. Half light, half shade,
She stood.'

—Alfred, Lord Tennyson:
'The Gardener's Daughter'

'We'll see about that.' Benedict Cole arched his eyebrow. 'You'd better come in and let me look at you.'

Leaving the door ajar, he turned away. 'Are you coming in or not?'

Cameo followed him into the studio. Was it necessary for him to be so abrupt? He turned his back on her, something that was never done in society. Yet her irritation vanished as she surveyed her surroundings. Why, the studio was exactly the kind of space she had always wished she might have one day. The light that flooded in from the windows was so much better than in the drawing room at home. It glinted on the tools of the painter's trade scattered everywhere: papers, pots of oil paints, rags, bottles and brushes, and canvases propped against the walls. A huge easel, much stronger than her slender folding one, dominated the room. There were no fine carpets to worry about here, just wooden floorboards, scratched and worn.

Her eyes closed. She savoured the smell of oil paint and turpentine permeating the studio. No perfume had ever smelled so sweet. Upon opening her eyes, she encountered the artist's stare.

'Are you quite well?'

A flush heated her cheeks. 'I like the smell of oil paints and turpentine, that's all.'

'That's unusual. Many models complain about it. They say it makes them feel ill.'

'How could anyone not like the smell of paints?'

'It's a point in your favour.' He threw aside his paintbrush and beckoned. 'Come over by the window.'

'Why?'

'Why do you think? I need to see you in a proper light.'

To her surprise her hands trembled beneath her gloves. She walked over to the window on legs that were also unsteady.

'Take off your coat and your bonnet.' His impatience was barely concealed. 'I need to see your face.'

With effort she bit down the sprightly retort that sprang to her lips. Removing her pearl-tipped hat pin, she dropped her bonnet along with her grey woollen coat on to a faded brocade chaise longue pushed up under the window.

He gave a sharp intake of breath.

'Is this what you…?'

'Be quiet,' he snapped. 'I need to look at you, not listen to you.'

He must be the most insufferable man she had ever met. No one had ever spoken to her in such a way. Cameo fumed as he stared at her with increasing intensity.

'Take down your hair.'

Her gloved hands flew protectively to her head.

He responded with an impatient shake of his own. 'How can I see you as you should be when your hair is in that, how can I put it…' He gave a dismissive wave. 'Overdone style? I must see it loose. The painting will require it.'

An overdone style. Her mama's French maid had done it in the latest fashion, with ringlets down both sides, that morning.

'What's the matter now? Did you come here as a model or not?'

His words renewed her purpose. One by one,

she took the pins from her hair and dropped them on to the chaise longue, sensing Benedict Cole behind her watching each move. She slipped out the last hairpin. Curls whispered at her neck as strands of long, black curls loosened from their ringlets and loops, tumbling about her shoulders, foaming down her back.

Twirling towards him she met his dark eyes. She couldn't break his gaze even if she wanted to.

At last he spoke. His voice had become husky. 'This is extraordinary. I've been thinking of a painting for many months now. I imagined a woman with hair and eyes in exactly your colour. I began to think I may never find her and that perhaps I imagined such shades. You're precisely the model I'm looking for.'

Cameo clasped her fingers together as a thrill raced through her. 'You want me in your painting? Me?'

As if she were no longer in the room, he turned away. She heard him mutter to himself, 'Yes, I can do it.'

'Do what?'

He spun around with a scowl. 'You must keep silent if you model for me.'

'I will keep silent when I'm modelling, but I'm not modelling now.' She reached to pick up her bonnet. 'Nor do I wish to do so if you're going to be quite so rude.'

'Wait.' He made an apologetic gesture and sent her an unexpected smile. 'You'll have to forgive the moods of an artist. I'm not one for social niceties when I'm painting. You need to understand that.'

'I do understand that,' Cameo retorted. 'But *you* have to understand. If I am to be your model, I will require them.'

'You require social niceties?' He studied her for a long moment with an expression impossible to fathom. He moved over to the fireplace and indicated a chair. 'Come and sit down. There are a few questions I need to ask you.'

Cameo's stomach lurched. She'd almost given herself away. Her temper mustn't get the better of her.

This was her only chance.

Trying to appear subdued, she followed Benedict Cole to the fireplace. Papers and books lay on each available surface, even on the armchair.

'Just move those,' he said irritably.

She placed the pile of books on a gateleg table and sat. Horsehair poked out in tufts on the arms of the chair and, judging by the hard feel of it beneath her, there wasn't much left in the seat either.

With one hand, he dragged a straight wooden

chair opposite her after dropping more papers on the floor with an easy, casual gesture. No wonder his studio was so untidy. It was unimportant to him. His surroundings took second place to his work, while she spent most of her painting time spreading sheets and tidying away.

His face was half-shadowed and he didn't speak for a long moment. Unnerving enough when he stood staring at her, now he was seated, his closeness became even more alarming.

Cameo's heartbeat quickened.

'So you want to be an artist's model?'

'Ah, yes.'

He gave her another of his long-considering examinations. 'Forgive me. You're different from the other girls I've seen who want to be models.'

He suspected her already, she realised with dismay. 'Different? In what way?'

'Your voice suggests you've been raised a lady,' he said bluntly. 'As does your request for social niceties. As do your clothes.'

'I wore my best to see you.' With trembling fingers she smoothed her foulard skirt, a mix of silk and cotton. Did she dare try to put on an accent? No. She'd never make it work and it seemed horrid, too. 'This is my finest gown.'

His dark eyes narrowed. 'Tell me, why is it you're seeking employment?'

'I have little choice in seeking employment.'

She put her hand to her forehead. 'I've fallen on hard times.'

'Have you indeed?'

'Yes. I'm alone in the world and I have few options for an income.'

Crossing one long trousered leg over the other, he leaned back. 'Tell me more about yourself. First, what's your name?'

There was no way she could supply her real name. She cast a quick look down at her dress. The colour? Too obvious. 'My name is Ashe. Miss Ashe. With an *e*.'

'With an *e*,' he drawled. 'And your first name, if I may enquire?'

Surely it was safe enough to use her nickname. 'It's Cameo.'

His head reared. 'Cameo? I've never heard of a girl named Cameo before.'

'I was a foundling.' She pointed to her necklace. 'I was found with this necklace, so I was called Cameo.'

His intent gaze fell to the neck of her dress, where the stone nestled. He seemed to take in more than her necklace. 'It's a fine piece.'

Her cheeks burned. 'Yes. It is very fine.'

'You say you were found with it. Your mother must have been a person of quality.'

'My mother may have been of quality. She may have been a lady.' Cameo found she was quite enjoying making up a new life story, her indignation driving her imagination. 'Though perhaps my father was a gentleman, perhaps he gave her the necklace. It's often a gentleman who takes advantage of a poor, innocent girl.'

He arched a winged eyebrow. 'Is it?'

'I believe so.'

As he leaned over, a strong masculine scent mixed with turpentine and paint reached her. 'Some people invite trouble, don't you think?'

The horsehair prickled through her dress as she shifted away from him. Suddenly she became aware of the danger of being alone in a room with a man to whom she hadn't been introduced. Her mama would have fainted away. 'I don't know what you mean, sir.'

'Cameo.' He lingered on the word. 'The word is Greek. Tell me more about your necklace.'

'There's little else I know about it. Though I'm sure it was a tragedy. I have a strong feeling my mother never left me willingly. I think she was forced to give me up. Perhaps my wicked father gave her this necklace and she left it with me as a keepsake or perhaps, as you say, she was of quality and owned it herself. In any case, it was found with me.'

'Where?'

'In my swaddling clothes.'

'No, where were you found?'

The question floored her, but only for a moment. 'There's a place near Coram Fields in Bloomsbury. Foundlings have long been left there.' Luckily her mama had given money to help the unfortunate foundlings only a few months before.

Still he seemed suspicious. 'And who found you?'

'Nuns,' Cameo replied wildly. 'Nuns found me. Then a kind genteel lady took me in and raised me as her own.'

'And her name was?'

'A Mrs…' From her sleeve she edged out her lace handkerchief to play for time. 'Cotton. That was her name. Poor Mrs Cotton. She had no family of her own, so she took me in. As I grew up I became her companion.' With a corner of the handkerchief she dabbed at her eyes. 'It's sad. She died close to a year ago. After that I was all alone. It is thus you find me, seeking employment.'

He crossed his arms. 'It's a strange story.'

'Not so strange. There are many others who have found themselves in my sorry position. I cast myself upon your mercy, sir,' she added, with a dramatic flourish.

A smile seemed to play at the corner of his lips and then vanished. 'So you're at my mercy, is that right?'

The sense of danger came back as she swallowed hard. 'Yes.'

He stood and dropped a log on to the fire. With a blackened poker he made sparks fly. Turning back, he leaned casually against the chimney piece and crossed his long legs, the poker still in his grip. 'There's other, more suitable employment than being a model. You might work in a shop or be a governess or be a companion to another lady.'

The thought of Lady Catherine Mary St Clair working in a shop made her duck her head to hide a smile. 'That's true. And it may come to that now Mrs Cotton is gone.' She dabbed at her eyes again with her handkerchief for effect.

Deftly he dropped the poker into a brass pot on the hearth. 'Being an artist's model is not the most respectable occupation, Miss Ashe. Not all the girls are from such a genteel background as yours, raised as you were by the good Mrs Cotton.'

'What's the usual background of models?'

'They're generally girls who work in shops and factories. Have you heard of the Pre-Raphaelite Brotherhood?'

Had she heard of them? 'Yes, I've heard of them… I mean, I think so.'

'One of the Brotherhood, John Everett Millais, has recently been painting Shakespeare's Ophelia. The model for his painting is called Lizzie Siddal and she was discovered working in a hat shop. She's going to be married to another member of the Brotherhood, Dante Gabriel Rossetti.'

'I didn't know that.'

'Not many do. But the artist-and-model relationship is one that often becomes…intimate.'

Cameo's cheeks tinted yet again. How she wished she might stop blushing in this man's presence.

'Lizzie had to lie in water for hours on end in the painting to show Ophelia drowning and she nearly died. Modelling can be dangerous.'

'I'm not afraid of danger.' If only he knew. Just by being here she risked everything.

His brow lifted. 'Is that right?'

'Where else do artists' models come from?' she asked quickly to change the subject.

'In the past it's not been unknown for models to have come from the streets.' An alarming glint sparked in his eyes. 'As I said, modelling is not the most reputable occupation. Fallen women, kept women, mistresses, whatever you wish to call them—many have modelled for paintings.'

Cameo gripped her gloves together. She refused to reveal to Benedict Cole that his mention of mistresses and kept women shocked her, even if she never openly discussed such scandalous topics. 'I'm merely an admirer of art. That's why I seek employment as a model. Many a wet afternoon have I spent looking at paintings in a gallery.' No need to mention that the gallery where she'd spent most time recently was the Royal Academy, where she'd been spellbound by his work.

'I'm not sure you're being entirely honest with me, Miss Ashe. But...'

Her breath caught in her throat.

'But you're ideal for my next painting. You're hired.'

She exhaled. 'Thank you.'

'I'm not sure you'll thank me when we're working,' he warned. 'Being a model is not the easy job many young women think it will be. I shall require you to sit without moving for hours at a time, every day. Do you think you can do that?'

'Yes, of course.' Wasn't half her life spent sitting bored at dining tables and in drawing rooms? 'I'll have no trouble with that.'

'I've already completed a lot of the background work so I don't need you for that. The work is partly complete.' The wooden chair scraped across the floor as Benedict sat by the fire again and pushed his dark hair from his brow. 'Do you have any questions for me?'

'I don't think so.'

'Then you're unusual. You haven't asked the

question most models ask the minute they walk in the door.'

'And what is that?'

'Payment, Miss Ashe,' he drawled. 'Most models are interested in how much they will be paid. Since you're experiencing such—how did you put it?—hard times, I expected payment to be of the utmost importance to you.'

Beneath her layers of petticoats she gave herself a kick. 'Oh.'

'Perhaps it is your preference for social niceties preventing you making mention of the sordid topic of coin? Will a shilling each session be satisfactory?'

'Is that the customary rate?' she asked boldly.

His mouth curved. 'I'm not trying to cheat you.'

'Then that will be perfectly satisfactory.'

'You're most trusting, Miss Ashe.'

She dragged her attention away from him and his sardonic expression. 'I do have a question. The painting's subject—what is it?'

'That's a question I can't fully answer now. I can only tell you it's based on a poem by Alfred Tennyson. You know the poet's work, perhaps.'

'Mrs Cotton was fond of his work, as our dear Queen Victoria is,' she replied, as her mind went immediately to the fine leather-bound volume of the poet's work she kept on her bedside table.

She had read the poems over and over again, revelling in the romance and passion, wishing she could make her paintings speak in such a way.

'Many painters today are drawing on Tennyson's work for inspiration. I must warn you, the painting may not be what you expect.' He allowed a silence to fall between them for a moment. 'How can I put this in a way to suit your delicate sensibilities…?'

Her skin rippled as his all-encompassing artist's stare lingered over her. 'Let me just say the painting will be somewhat—revealing.'

'I'm not sure what you mean, Mr Cole.'

'The painting will not be like your cameo. That is a profile of a woman's face. But my painting will not merely be of your face. What I have in mind will require I make a study of…your form.' Once again his gaze wandered over her.

'I see.' Her stomach gave another of those mysterious lurches. 'To what extent will my… form…be displayed?'

'You need have no fear.' A smile flickered at the corners of his strong mouth. 'I will produce a work acceptable to common standards of decency and at this stage it's a private project. In the painting, you will appear in a simple white gown. But in order to paint you as I wish, you may need to show parts of yourself which ordinarily you do not. But even among artists, I can assure you, there are proprieties we observe.'

'I'm no prude, Mr Cole.' She gulped. 'I will model to your requirements, assuming all the necessary proprieties are observed.'

'Of course. I wouldn't consider proceeding otherwise. Then we are agreed. Can you come tomorrow?'

'Yes.' Somehow, she'd find a way.

'Come in the morning at nine o'clock. The sun will be at the right angle.' He stood, ending the interview.

'Thank you for calling,' he added, with a somewhat teasing politeness.

Cameo got to her feet and replied coldly, 'Thank you very much, Mr Cole. I will see you tomorrow.'

'Miss Ashe. I think you've forgotten something.' His voice halted her as she picked up her coat and bonnet. 'Your hair.'

Why, she'd been sitting there the whole time in the company of a strange man with her hair down! Frantically she found the hairpins she'd dropped on to the chaise longue and began to pin up her heavy mass of hair. How could she restore it to her previous style, without the help of her mama's maid? After a few attempts, she gave up. With a few hairpins, she coiled it into a spiral at the back of her head and pinned it in place. He made no comment, but she knew Benedict Cole missed nothing of her clumsy work.

She seized her bonnet and coat. 'Well, goodbye.'

He gave a mocking bow. 'Until tomorrow, Miss Ashe.'

Chapter Three

'The full day dwelt on her brows, and sunn'd
Her violet eyes.'

—Alfred, Lord Tennyson:
'The Gardener's Daughter'

The studio door slammed and a gust of wind blew through the window. Crossing the room, Benedict heaved down the sash. Miss Cameo Ashe had not yet appeared on the street. She'd still be going down the stairs with that quick light step he'd noticed, in her fine kid boots.

Her boots had exposed her. She'd been dressed in that alluringly simple grey dress, which had all the marks of simplicity that only came from quality, carved ivory buttons all the way down the front, a pristine lace collar and cuffs. Her figure was slender, willowy, her tiny waist emphasised by her corset, yet not in the overexaggerated way he hated, for she was perfectly proportioned. Nestled at the tender point of her throat above her collar was her cameo necklace tied with a black-velvet ribbon, a large stone, black and white, the carving in relief exquisite. But her elegant, obviously expensive boots were the biggest clue. And her ankles, which he'd been unable to ignore as she sat on the armchair, were equally elegant, with the delicate lines of a pure-bred filly.

She was no orphan girl turned out on the street. Certainly there was a strength to her he'd noticed immediately, a determination that suggested an ability to survive, but there was also a vulnerability he found himself unable to define.

The story she had told him. His mouth lifted at the corners. It had so many holes, that story, yet she struggled on, trying to convince him she was a girl who had no choice but to be an artist's model. How did she expect him to believe her when her voice held no hint of the streets? True, she explained that by saying she'd been taken in by a genteel lady, but it hadn't added up.

At his easel he idly picked up a paintbrush, running it through his fingers. Explanations played in his mind. Nothing she told him made sense. Yet she intrigued him, captivated him. He hadn't been able to believe it when she had lifted off her bonnet and eased the pins from her long black hair. As each silken strand was liberated, his heart had drummed faster and faster.

He'd found her. He'd begun to think it wasn't possible, that he might never discover a model for the painting of his dreams. Yet there she was, standing in front of him, slender yet strong. And her eyes. Shaded beneath her bonnet, they had looked grey or blue outside the door when he had first met her. In the light of the studio he'd discerned they were the rare shade of purple he had searched for.

He'd already painted the background of the portrait in painstaking detail. It had been frustrating beyond belief to have an empty space at the centre of the canvas, waiting for the model to appear in order to complete the work.

His grasp tightened on the paintbrush as he visualised her. It would be all too easy to respond to her as a man rather than a painter. Not only did the quickening of his body tell him of his instant attraction to her physically, but also the curious vulnerability he saw in her eyes had touched him. She was no hardened model.

He laid down the brush and ran his fingers though his hair. 'Trouble,' he said aloud. 'That's what you are, Miss Ashe. Trouble.'

A knock came at the door. Was she back again to elaborate on her story? He hoped she wasn't planning to cancel the arrangement. With a frown, he realised just how much he didn't want that.

It wasn't his mysterious new model standing there.

A familiar husky female voice greeted him. 'Hello.'

'Maisie. You'd better come in.'

She entered the studio with the sensual walk that so enticed her many admirers. It was a shame such a movement evaded capture on canvas, he often thought, though its sensuality had long ceased to tempt him. The appeal of Cameo Ashe's awkward self-consciousness, on the other hand…

Loosening the thick cream-coloured shawl she wore, Maisie dropped it lazily on the chair by the fire to reveal her blue dress, cut low at her full breasts. Her thick, corn-coloured hair curled. He'd painted her as Demeter, the Greek goddess of the grain, with her arms full of wheat. The ripe epitome of plenty was young Maisie. But as an artist he knew hers were the type of looks that faded quickly.

Miss Ashe's face flashed into his mind. Hers was a beauty that would stay the years, for it was in her bones and in her bearing. Puzzlement hit him again. Just who was she? And what had led her to him?

'I came as soon as I heard you'd been looking for someone for your new work,' Maisie said. 'Why didn't you come straight to me? Didn't you want me to model for you?' Her arms looped around his neck, giving him a full view of her luscious flesh. 'No one else is as good as me.'

He unlooped her clinging arms. 'You're not right for this painting, Maisie.'

She pouted. 'I want to come back.'

With a smile she traced a teasing line from his chest down towards his trousers.

'You walked out on me, remember?' Benedict reminded her. More accurately, her affections had wandered, he recalled drily as he removed her hand, to another man who'd shown her more attention. Clearly that hadn't worked out.

Maisie moved her shoulders with a flounce. 'Only because you're always painting, painting, painting. It drove me mad. I wanted you to take me out once in a while.'

'Painting isn't just what I do.' He'd tried to explain it to her many times before. 'It's who I am. I paint the way I breathe.'

'But it's so boring sitting here all day!'

'Well, you've been spared that. I've found the model for my next work.'

From the flare of jealousy in her eyes he

judged she didn't like that news. 'Who is she? Annie? Jenny?'

'It isn't anyone you know. It's someone quite new.'

Maisie thrust out her chest like an indignant chicken. 'Why's she muscling in on our patch?'

That was indeed the question, Benedict brooded. Just why did Miss Ashe want to be his model?

'Never mind.' He picked up Maisie's shawl and gave it to her. 'I have to work.'

'What a surprise,' she snapped crossly.

At the door she turned and let the shawl fall away from the front of her dress. 'You know where to find me, Benedict.'

The door closed behind her and Benedict let out a sigh of relief.

Models. He'd not let himself fall into a relationship with one again. When an artist painted a woman posed before him, he created an idealised version of her and, sometimes, that ideal enticed him into bed. But he wouldn't be tricked that way again. He needed to concentrate, stay focused. He smiled inwardly. It was easier to paint without live models, but he was no landscape artist. Views weren't enough for him.

Yet Miss Cameo Ashe, with her mysterious mix of spirit and beauty, stayed in his mind. He picked up his pencil and began to draw.

* * *

Cameo lit another candle. The flame flickered, sending shadows dancing on the walls of her blue-and-white bedroom, newly papered in a flowered print, for her mama liked to keep up with the times. Just recently she had installed a water closet down the hall, exactly the same as Queen Victoria's.

It was the window seat in her bedroom Cameo loved most. The blue chintz curtains were open tonight, letting in the cool air. Through the windowpane a full moon outshone the fog, silvering the dark grey trunk and slender boughs of the ash tree outside. Sometimes, she heard the call of a nightingale in the square as she sketched through the night. Trying again and again, always aiming to improve. Attempting to make her hand recreate what was in her mind, in her heart. It was so hard, working alone. There was no one to share it all with, the triumphs and the failures. No one who understood that hidden, passionate part of her. No one who sensed the heat of her flame. Now, at last, even though it was a secret, she had a chance. To watch and to learn from a real artist.

From Benedict Cole.

She clasped her pencil. As his model she would spend hours in his studio, watching him as he worked like the apprentices of old and yet he had no idea of her true identity. There was so much she'd be able to learn, incognito.

So you're at my mercy.

The sense of danger returned as his words reverberated in her brain. He suspected her, but she had to take the risk.

Taking up a fresh sheet of paper, she stretched. She'd sketched for hours perched on the gilt chair in front of her dressing table with her blue-and-white china jug and basin, silver hairbrushes and bottles of scent pushed impatiently aside.

A muffled voice came from outside the door. 'Cameo? Are you still awake?'

'Come in.'

'What are you doing up?' George entered in his black-tailed dinner jacket, his bow tie loosened. 'I saw your candle. You ought to have been asleep hours ago.'

'So should you. Where have you been? At your club, I suppose?'

'Got it in one.' With a yawn he stretched his legs out on the window seat and propped a chintz cushion behind his brown hair. 'What a night. I've been playing cards. I say, I ran into Warley. He's coming to the ball. Frightfully keen on you, isn't he?'

Cameo grimaced. 'Unfortunately.'

'He lost a lot of money tonight, I believe.'

George craned his neck to look at her. 'And what have you been doing? Painting?'

With her pencil she pointed to the pile of discarded paper. 'Just drawing, trying to improve.'

He shook his head. 'You're a strange sister for a fellow to have, Cameo, with all this fuss about art. Why can't you just be interested in gloves and bonnets like a girl ought to be?'

'Like someone we both know, is that it?'

To her astonishment George coloured bright red. 'Actually, there's something I wanted to tell you.' He grabbed another cushion and tossed it in the air, catching it neatly. 'The thing is, I've decided to ask Maud Cartwright to marry me.'

'Finally!' Cameo wanted to leap up and hug her brother, but they never did such a thing in their family. 'I thought you'd never ask her.'

'Well, it takes me a while to come to a decision, but once I've made it I stick to it. That's my way.'

'Have you decided when?'

'I thought I'd pop the question quite soon if I can get my courage up. Maybe at the ball.' He tossed the cushion up again but she wasn't fooled by his nonchalance. 'Not sure she'll have me.'

'How could you possibly think Maud doesn't want to marry you?'

'I haven't been entirely sure.' He flushed redder and added, 'Whether it's more than friendship. We've all known each other so long.'

'Since we were children and used to play in the square together.'

George grinned. 'You were constantly in trouble for climbing trees.'

'Nanny always shouted at me about the dirt and grass stains. You scaled trees as well, George, and you never got into trouble for it but Maud never wanted to climb. She always looked perfect in her pinafore and curls. Do you remember how she clapped when you got up on to the top branches?' Cameo laughed softly. 'Maud always loved you, I think. Oh, I'll be so happy to have her as a sister.'

'I expect it's mutual.'

'Everyone will be delighted.' She mimicked their father's gruff tone: '"You've made an excellent choice for your future wife, George."'

They both laughed.

'I'm so pleased for you,' she said simply.

'I'm rather pleased myself.' He stood and tousled her hair on his way out the door.

How lucky George and Maud were to have each other, Cameo thought, as she stared out the window.

Benedict Cole's mocking expression flashed into her mind. *Until tomorrow, Miss Ashe.*

There was no doubt he suspected her. Her

temper red-hot, she'd grasped the opportunity to learn from him, but there was a deeper part of her that disliked being forced to deceive him, the same way she was deceiving her parents. It troubled her even though she didn't want to admit it.

With a sigh she blew out the candle. Somehow, she had to keep his suspicions and her own doubts at bay. She wanted—no, she needed—to learn to paint.

Yet as she lay in bed, the sudden recollection of the artist's sardonic gaze gave her stomach a sharp twist.

Cameo had to wonder if she would learn more than she'd bargained for from Benedict Cole.

Chapter Four

'And stirr'd her lips
For some sweet answer…'

—Alfred, Lord Tennyson:
'The Gardener's Daughter'

Cameo hitched up the skirt of her blue-poplin gown, avoiding the puddles in the alleyway. She'd dressed with care, avoiding her finer gowns. Benedict Cole mustn't have any more clues as to her real identity.

In Soho, amidst the morning bustle, she made sure her family's crested carriage stayed out of sight. Bert obligingly agreed to collect her later. For a moment she stood and watched as the shopkeepers rolled up their awnings and opened their shutters to reveal their goods on display in the windows, the apprentices washing down the windows and stoops. How she wished for time to sketch the lively scene. She wasn't often out so early and she certainly had never seen the fresh fruit and vegetables being delivered in old carts pulled by heavy horses and one small cart pulled by a donkey.

Outside the bakery she stopped to pass some money to Becky, sitting with her matches forlornly laid out in front of her on the cobbles.

'Thank you, miss. I never thought you'd remember.'

'Of course I remembered, Becky. I promised.'

The girl sighed. 'Lots wouldn't, what if they promised or not.'

Becky would have the money Benedict Cole had promised her for being a model, Cameo decided, as she ascended the narrow staircase to the studio. It seemed deceitful to take payment from the artist when she knew she received a fair exchange, with the painting lessons he was unsuspectingly providing. It wasn't as if she needed the pin money. It would be shoddy, as though she were cheating him.

On the attic landing Benedict opened the door wide. 'Ah, Miss Ashe, you're on time today.'

Cameo swept by him. As Lady Catherine Mary St Clair she would have made a spirited response. As Miss Ashe she must keep her temper.

'I'll endeavour to be punctual from now on, Mr Cole,' she said with assumed meekness, as she removed her bonnet and cloak.

He seemed to hide a smile as he appropriated them from her and dropped them over the armchair by the fire. He hadn't fallen for her obedient act.

Retreating to the window, she raised her arms, curving them above her. 'Do you need me to take my hair down again?'

Her movement held his brooding glance. 'I ought to paint you like that. No, leave your hair up for now. I wish to focus on your face. I need to get that right first.'

And she'd styled her hair in a simple knot to ensure she might easily put it up again. Vexed, she dropped her arms.

As she glanced out of the window at the rooftops and chimneys, towards the clouded sky, it struck her again how wonderful it was to have no curtains. What a contrast with the thick-cut velvet cloths of the drawing room in Mayfair that constantly felt as if they stifled her.

An acid voice broke her reverie. 'If I might have your attention, Miss Ashe.'

Biting her lip to prevent a retort, she queried, 'Where do you want me?'

He paused for a moment before he pushed out the shabby gold-brocade chaise longue. 'Here. Sit down. Don't go slouching into the side. Keep your spine straight and face me.'

How she would continue to obey his curt instructions without a quick rejoinder she simply didn't know. Squarely she placed her feet in front of her and crossed them at the ankle, wishing for something to lean against. Still, the chaise longue was softer than his armchair and she would allow no fault to be found with her posture.

'That will do.'

As he rested on his heels, her whole body stiffened under his scrutiny.

'You need to remain still,' he commanded her brusquely.

How could she be still with him staring at her? She dropped her shoulders and puffed out a slow breath.

'Now, turn to the right. No, not like that, turn some more.

'More.

'Now raise your eyes. Raise your eyes! Not move your whole head.'

'I'm not sure what you mean!' Cameo exclaimed, exasperated.

In a single swift movement he vaulted beside her. He clasped her chin. 'Raise your eyes, but hold your chin straight. Like so.'

Cameo jumped as he cupped her face. His fingers were strong, with a sensitivity that told of his artistic temperament.

He trailed his fingers lightly against her skin.

'You won't be able to jump like that when I'm drawing you.'

'I didn't jump! A draught must have come in from the window.'

'I haven't yet opened the window.' Still scrutinising her, he backed away and pulled a stool into position behind the easel.

'That's it.' He crossed his legs in front of him in an easy, practised manner. 'Now you must hold still while I do my initial drawings. Can you do that?'

'Yes.' Why, from now on she vowed not to move an inch. She'd keep her attention on the reason why she'd come.

Painting lessons.

A chance to see a real artist at work.

A thrill ran through her whole body.

From where she sat with her head towards the interior of the studio she had a perfect view of exactly what Benedict Cole was doing. He wore no paint-splotched cover shirt today, just a loose white shirt with the neck open and a paisley waistcoat carelessly buttoned down to dark brown woollen trousers, his feet clad in well-polished boots.

Taking up a large sheet of paper, he propped it against the easel. Holding a stick of charcoal, he flexed his muscled arm and made strong, bold strokes, glancing back and forth at her all the while. Soon she became transfixed by the way he held her in his sights, put his head down to draw, then came intently up again in a single movement, like a breath. More than once he impatiently pushed back the black lock of hair that fell over his forehead, down towards two lines that creased between his eyebrows as he frowned in concentration.

You think you're watching me, Mr Benedict Cole, when in fact I'm watching you. She smiled inwardly.

How fast he drew. Perhaps lack of speed was her first mistake with her own work. She was too tentative, too slow. She considered each line before she put it down. He sketched with an assurance she envied, rapidly completing one drawing, putting it aside and just as quickly picking up another piece of paper, skimming across the page with a strong sweep of his arm.

On and on he drew. How long she sat there she wasn't sure, but surely one hour passed, then another. Her neck locked and ached. She hadn't realised how difficult it was to hold one position without moving. The muscles of her tight neck wanted to roll, her stiff legs to stretch.

To keep her mind off it she continued her survey of the studio. There were things she hadn't noticed yesterday. The canvases propped about the room appeared to be in various stages of progress. One seascape looked particularly good, but most of them were faced to the wall, their subjects hidden from her assessment. There were frames and odd pieces of wood, too, stacked to one side. It appeared chaotic at first glance, but she discerned an order beneath the chaos. He seemed to know exactly where to find what he needed with speed and ease. He reached for his tools on a cluttered painting table beside the easel without a sideways glance. There were strange objects on the table, too. A pile of stones, a bird's feather and some oddly shaped shards of smooth glass.

Peeking to her left without moving her head, she spotted a huge bed with a carved wooden bedhead in the corner of the room. She hadn't really noticed it yesterday. Why, she'd come not only to Benedict Cole's studio, but also to his bedroom. Her cheeks felt hot.

He had left the bed unmade, she noted in amazement. The white sheets were rumpled and the pillow dented. The thought of him lying there sent an unexpected thrill through her body. Hastily, she focused on the carved bedhead above, with its intricate patterns of blackberries and leaves engraved into the glowing dark wood.

Next to the bed stood a washstand with a mirror, a thick white-china jug and bowl on its veined marble top, his brush and razor lying carelessly to the side. She pictured him shaving, the sharp blade sliding through the soap along the skin of his strong jaw. He'd use the same smooth strokes as when he drew, she imagined.

Would he be bare-chested? The question popped into her mind, startling her. *Why, Lady Catherine Mary*, she reproved herself in her old nanny's voice. *What a thing to think*. But the intimate image of him shaving persisted, the muscles of his shoulders rippling beneath his olive skin as he leant over the water basin, his face dripping with water as he splashed off the soap.

Unable to hold still, she wriggled on her seat.

Benedict's voice shot across the room. 'Don't move.'

'I'm sorry.'

'I told you that you'd have to hold still for long periods of time,' he snapped, not raising his head.

'I will be quite able to if you give me a moment to rest.' The man was a tyrant. She had no intention of being bullied by him.

He tossed down the charcoal. 'Yes, of course.'

With relief Cameo stretched her taut body. She knew Benedict Cole kept watching her as he leaned against the edge of the stool.

'You've done well. Not every model can keep up with me.'

'Thank you.' Surprised at how much his praise pleased her, she stepped towards the easel.

'Have you always painted?'

'I can't not paint.'

At last. He did understand. 'I know just what you mean,' she said impulsively, then bit her tongue. She momentarily forgot he must never suspect she, too, was an artist, or wanted to be. How wonderful it would be to reveal her true self and all her secret longings. But she had to pretend at home and here in the studio, too.

'Watching you draw, I can see that it's part of you,' she said at last. 'It seemed to come from somewhere within you.'

He studied her closely. Too closely. Had she revealed too much? 'You're observant. Yes, when I paint or draw it sometimes feels as if there is another hand guiding me. I'm doing what I'm meant to do. I'm driven to do it. There's no alternative.'

'May I see the sketches?'

'I don't show most of my models my first drawings. They're not always flattering.'

'I'd still like to look at them.'

'If you insist,' he said eventually, though she suspected he'd been about to refuse. 'I started some of them yesterday.'

'You drew me straight away?'

Collecting the sketch papers from the easel, he

made no answer, just passed them to her before leaning back again, his arms crossed.

Cameo held up the first drawing, then the next and the next. They were simple head studies. Yet in each sketch was the mark of a true artist.

'You—you've seen me.' Her gasp escaped from her lips. 'I mean, you've really, really seen me.'

He uncrossed his arms. 'When an artist looks at his model he's not just seeing the exterior. He must discern more.'

The smell of turpentine, soap and another more masculine scent she'd noticed the day before reached her as he moved closer and pointed to the drawings. 'When I look at you it's the line of your chin that reveals the determination of your character. But there's something else. There's wistfulness in your eyes, as though you're longing for something.'

Instantly she dropped her lashes. 'You saw this in my eyes?'

'Yes. Your chin says one thing, but your eyes say another. It's as if part of you is waiting to come to life. I perceived it immediately.'

Why, in a few hours this man had learned more about her than most people who had known her all her life. He had spotted what she tried to keep secret, contained within her body, all the passion and desire always threatening to brim over. And she thought she'd had his measure, watching him as he drew!

She forced out a laugh. 'I have no such longing.'

'Don't lie to me,' he rasped. 'I'm an artist. I know what I see.'

Impatiently Benedict seized the sketches. 'Let's return to work.' After a moment he cast down the charcoal. 'It's no good.'

'What do you mean?' Cameo asked indignantly. 'I haven't moved.'

His eyebrows knit together as he scowled at the paper in front of him. 'It's not that. I have the angle right, but I need—'

'What is it?'

Impatiently he ran his fingers through his hair. 'Your determined chin, Miss Ashe. I'm afraid it leads to your neck.'

Her hands flew upwards. 'I don't understand.'

'I told you I won't merely be painting your face. I'll also be painting part of your body. I did make that clear.'

Cameo's heart raced. Of course she understood what he'd said to her, but she hadn't considered which parts of her body needed to be revealed.

'I expected that, Mr Cole,' she forced herself to reply with feigned unconcern. 'What exactly is it you ask of me now?'

He pointed to her blue gown. 'Unbutton the collar of your dress.'

A gulp of air rose up from her lungs. It was no more than she revealed in a dinner gown or a ball dress. In such evening attire her neck, even her shoulders and décolletage were bare. Yet her fingers became clumsy as she reached for the tiny buttons that held the collar tight, her heart beating so loudly he surely heard it.

She undid the top button. He made no sign to stop her. She undid the second. She ought to feel shy with her throat bare in front of him, yet she didn't at all.

'Is—is that enough?'

'Almost.'

Cameo undid the third button.

His eyes darkened with an unidentifiable emotion. 'Wait.'

With long strides Benedict crossed the room and reached for her.

Her body gave an instinctive jerk.

'I'm not going to hurt you.'

No muscle moved in her body as he lifted her cameo necklace from where it had been lying on the soft fabric of her dress and dropped it down into her open collar. It fell against her skin towards the crevice between her breasts.

The cooler stone met her warm skin and she gave a sharp intake of breath, but the necklace wasn't the cause of her sudden ragged breathing. His closeness, the heat from his body emanating through the thin cotton of his shirt, did that. He moved his hand away, but his powerful vision stayed transfixed upon her throat as if he were actually touching her skin.

His lips came down at the exact moment she raised hers to his. They moved together as one, his strong arms lifting her from the chaise longue as she stood on tiptoe to reach him while a greater force thrust them together. Nothing stopped her seeking the hardness of his lips in that moment, causing an explosion within her that dived to the depths of her stomach and flamed up again as a deep sigh opened her mouth. She let his cool tongue probe, meeting his hunger with hers, longing to taste him. She flung her hands around his neck as he wrenched her body even closer in his fierce embrace.

With a groan, Benedict heaved himself away from her and ran his hand through his hair. 'Goodness.'

Cameo sank on to the chaise longue, clutching her bodice. Her heart felt like a bird beating its wings against the cage of her chest.

Benedict retreated behind the easel. 'I warned you the relationship between artist and model can all too easily become intimate.' Harsh lines bracketed the mouth that just moments before had so passionately searched hers. 'That was… regrettable.'

She couldn't reply. She could only gasp for breath.

His glance flew to his easel as though it were a powerful magnet. 'This painting may be my greatest work. I can't have anything interfere with my focus. I must complete this. It's what I'm meant to do.'

Silence fell between them, except for the gasps that continued to escape her lips.

'Some people don't think artists have any rules.' He spoke again, his voice husky. 'But they do. They must. To be able to paint each day without fail there must be the kind of self-discipline that cannot be broken.'

Words evaded her as her body continued to shudder.

'Do you understand? I cannot allow this between us. If you're to remain my model—it must be as if what just happened never occurred.'

With shaking fingers Cameo touched her tender lips. 'I see.'

'I can assure you there will be no such lapse again.'

He coiled away from her and thrust his taut hands against the chimney piece. When he rounded on his heel, his expression appeared unfathomable.

'I think we've had enough for today.' He ran his fingers through his hair again. 'We'll continue tomorrow, Miss Ashe.'

Shocked to her core by her response to him, Cameo buttoned the bodice of her dress right to the top of her neck. In a trembling grip she grabbed her bonnet and cloak and rushed from the studio as fast as her shaking legs could take her.

Chapter Five

'Ah, happy shade—and still went wavering
down,
But, ere it touch'd a foot, that might have
danced.'

—Alfred, Lord Tennyson:
'The Gardener's Daughter'

A hand parted the fronds of the potted palm
tree. 'What are you two whispering about?'

'George!' Cameo dropped her fan. 'You startled me.'

Her brother gave his easy smile. 'You look
quite panicked. Just what is it that you have to
be so guilty about?'

Retrieving her fan, Cameo pretended to study
the ballroom, with its huge white pillars, gilt-
painted cornices and ferns in huge tubs. The
chandeliers scattered their rainbow reflections on

the shimmering polished floor, challenging the dazzle of the women's bright jewels. 'Nothing.'

'Hmm. Why is it I don't believe you, little sister?' George turned to Maud, standing beside Cameo, who peeped up at him from beneath her lashes.

'Hello there,' he said with a smile that Maud returned adoringly with added dimples. 'Now tell me what is it you're both so intent on discussing here in the corner that keeps you from dancing?'

'Oh, well…' Maud fluttered.

'Are you telling each other secrets?'

Cameo had considered telling Maud all about her visits to Benedict Cole's studio. How she wanted to pour out to her friend everything that happened. But she didn't want to put Maud in such a position. It would be unfair, even though she longed to tell her all about it.

'I don't think you could keep a secret from me, could you, Maud?' George asked. 'How would I get it out of you?'

Maud giggled.

'Blast.' George's teasing expression changed. 'Look who's coming towards us. It's your new beau, Cameo.' He raised his voice and gave a nod. 'Good evening, Warley.'

'St Clair.' The man who approached them gave a stiff bow in return and then bowed to

Cameo. 'I hoped you might do me the honour of giving me the next dance, Lady Catherine Mary.'

As she bent a reluctant curtsy in reply her skin crawled, as it always did when she came close to Lord Warley. Still, there was no way to refuse the son of her papa's oldest friend a dance. She loved her father too much for that.

'I'm sure she'd be delighted,' George said with a straight face.

The orchestra struck up another Viennese waltz. Cameo tried to avoid instinctively pulling away as Lord Warley pressed her up against him.

His tongue wet his lips. 'Delightful evening.'

'Delightful.' Cameo dodged his feet landing upon her toes in their white-kid slippers, which offered no protection. He made a sharp turn and she stumbled.

'Watch your step.'

It had been his fault, not hers. She fumed as he spun her again, nearly bumping into the couple next to them. George gave her a grin as he expertly swept Maud past.

From over George's shoulder, Maud sent her a look of sympathy. They had made a list of dance partners once, ranked from best to worst. Lord Warley with his groping hands was at the bottom of both their lists. George, of course, was at the top of Maud's.

Oh, Maud had to say yes to her brother's

proposal tonight. Her friend looked so sweet in her ruffled white ball dress trimmed with pink roses, staring up at George's smiling face.

From under her lashes, Cameo studied her own dance partner. Often she heard Lord Warley called handsome, but for Cameo his sloping chin spoilt his dark good looks. His eyes were brown, his black hair brushed from his forehead. He had similar colouring to Benedict Cole and was almost as tall.

Benedict Cole.

She was imagining him everywhere.

That kiss. All she thought of was that kiss, that explosive, passionate kiss. Her lips tingled at the memory. Surely such a kiss was something real and rare. Why then had the artist rejected her so coldly and dismissed her from the studio as if she were an inconvenience?

Lord Warley trod on her foot again. 'So sorry.'

The pressure was so hard it seemed as if he had done it on purpose, to gain her attention.

She looked up sharply. There was no clue on his face.

'You look very well tonight.' He glanced down at her lacy white dress and her cameo necklace, tied with a blue-velvet ribbon to match her sash.

'Thank you.' She fought her sudden urge to pull up the lace of her low décolletage.

They swept past the pillared alcoves, half-curtained with heavy cream brocade and the scrutiny of the grand society ladies who sat behind the curtains. Her mama sat at one of the tables, no doubt being congratulated on the fine pair her daughter and Lord Warley made. Wickedly, Cameo imagined dancing by with Benedict Cole. What would they think if they found out she'd been kissed by the bohemian artist in his studio in Soho? What would they think if they'd seen the way she responded?

The passionate touch of Benedict's lips seemed on hers again, the vision so powerful she wanted to close her eyes and just sink into those sensations.

Stop it, she instructed herself. *Stop it*.

The last strains of the waltz finally played out. With relief she escaped Lord Warley's hold. 'Thank you.'

'Would you care for another dance?'

Pretending to consider, she opened her fan and gave it a dismissive flick. 'How kind. But I think that I might appreciate a rest.'

'Just what I was thinking,' he said smoothly. 'The terrace?'

Cameo fumed with frustration as he once again took her arm and steered her towards the French windows which opened on to the terrace. He'd cornered her. There was no way she could be rude to a friend of the family. Still, fresh air was preferable to having her feet stamped on in another dance.

Outside, the garden sparkled with candles. Cameo sank down on to one of the wrought-iron chairs laid out on the terrace.

Warley leaned over her, so close that she shrank back against the cold iron of the chair. On his breath was the faint whiff of claret.

'Can I fetch you refreshment?'

'I am thirsty. Thank you.'

Enjoying the momentary respite, she breathed in the scent of jasmine and roses. There was no one else on the terrace, though perhaps George and Maud were somewhere in the garden. Why, he might even be proposing at that very moment. How lucky they were, while she was here with Lord Warley. Under her skirts she stretched out her painful toes. He didn't seem to have done any permanent damage.

Something near to despair filled her. These evenings were supposed to be enjoyable, but they exhausted her more than sitting for Benedict Cole. Modelling was hard work. But being forced to play a society role was hard work, too. Not the kind of work to complain about. How could she complain about having to go to a ball? It sounded spoilt. Never complain, never explain. That was what her mama advised.

Too soon Lord Warley returned with two glasses of iced punch.

'Thank you.' Cameo took a sip.

He sat down on the chair opposite and hoisted one leg over the other. 'My pleasure.'

Silence fell. It wasn't the same kind of silence as when Benedict Cole painted her; that silence didn't bother her at all.

'I'd love to try to capture those roses,' she said at last, studying the white tea roses that were tumbling down the trellis closest to them.

'Capture them?'

'Paint them, I mean. What do you think of the latest style of painting? The Pre-Raphaelite Brotherhood and the other new painters?'

'Ridiculous.' He shocked her with his vehemence. 'They make far too much of themselves, like all artists. They should get decent occupations.'

'Art's a passion!' Cameo protested.

'Art's a fuss about nothing. Who can't slap a bit of paint on to some canvas, I ask you? Of course I go to the opening of the Royal Academy of Art at the start of the Season, one's got to. And we've got some fine Old Masters in our long gallery at Warley Park. Not that I care for them that much. It's all a waste of time.'

'How can you say that?' She sipped her punch to quench her anger. It didn't help.

'That's right—you enjoy that kind of thing, don't you?' He emptied his punch glass. 'You do a few watercolours, I seem to recall. I'm surprised your father allows it. Well, good for you young ladies to have something to do, isn't it?'

Cameo drank more punch. 'It's more than just something to do for me.'

'Perhaps when you come to Warley Park you'll allow me to show you the Old Masters in our gallery. You haven't forgotten you and your parents are coming to stay at my estate, have you?'

She had forgotten. She'd forced the engagement from her mind. A dance with Lord Warley was penance. A long visit would be intolerable. Yet there was no chance of talking her parents out of it and she had to be polite. 'I'm sure it will be most pleasant.'

'Your presence will make it so, Lady Catherine Mary.'

She didn't remind him that all her friends and family called her Cameo. She'd never invited him to, yet she gave the pet name to Benedict Cole without thinking.

Lord Warley smiled. It was his smile that made her uneasy, she reflected. It never reached his eyes. In contrast, Benedict Cole's eyes had searched her soul.

Would Benedict Cole ever leave her mind?

Lord Warley pulled off his gloves, revealing each of his fingers in turn. Without warning, he leant forward and imprisoned her hands. 'How pleased I am to have this moment alone with you.'

'Lord Warley!' Desperately she tried to extract her fingers, but his grip was too tight.

He squeezed them tighter. 'You must allow me to make my addresses. I'm sure your parents will not object.'

Cameo wrenched her hands away.

'Your addresses?' Her stomach sank. His intentions were more serious than she'd feared.

'Indeed.' Putting his fingers together in a steeple, he said, 'Our families are well connected. You will recall, of course, that your father was good friends with my own, God rest his soul.'

The late Lord Warley, the current earl's father, had died while she was still in the schoolroom, studying under a governess with Maud. He'd been dark-haired like his son. But his eyes had been different—kind, although sad. Cameo remembered that.

'My father thought most highly of yours,' she vouchsafed. If it wasn't for the family friendship she wouldn't be forced to associate so closely with him against all her instincts. It made it all very difficult.

'When I inherited Warley Park—you must

know that it's one of the greatest houses in England—I took on a great responsibility. I shall enjoy showing you the estate on your visit. You will be an ornament to it.' Once more he glanced towards her bare décolletage.

Cameo wished yet again for a shawl to cover her upper body. She didn't want to be an ornament to anything, even Warley Park, that great country estate in Sussex. It was even larger than the one belonging to her family in Derbyshire, which George was to eventually inherit.

'It will be wonderful to see the Old Masters at Warley Hall.' That was true at least. 'I'm sure I'll like them. But you may not find you like me. For a start, I'm most attached to painting.'

His smile became supercilious. 'You'll soon outgrow your childish hobbies.'

'I assure you I'll never outgrow painting,' she said through gritted teeth. Why was it that women's passions were considered so insignificant, as though they could easily be put aside for polite society? Did no one understand the passion that drove her?

Benedict Cole's face flashed again into her mind.

He was a man who understood painting.

And passion.

Down deep her stomach rippled.

'You're young.' Lord Warley licked his lips.

'There's nothing you could be sure about at your age.'

He had only been a few years ahead of George at school. 'I might be young, but I do know my own mind.'

'I appreciate spirit in a girl.'

Before Cameo moved he was on his feet. Looming over her, he pressed her backwards, hard, into the wrought-iron chair, banging her head against the trellis.

No! He meant to kiss her. She couldn't bear it. Not with the memory of Benedict's lips still burned on to hers. In a surge of strength she pushed him away.

Leaping to her feet, she seized her necklace as if it were a talisman. 'I'd like to go into the ballroom.'

'Yes, of course. The moonlight, your beauty... forgive me.'

As he took her arm, his eyes did not meet hers. Sickened, Cameo realised he wasn't sorry at all.

She'd been right to avoid being alone with him. All her suspicions about him had been right all along.

Backed up against the trellis, Lord Warley had trapped her like a bird in a cage. Right where he liked a woman to be.

Chapter Six

'She look'd: but all
Suffused with blushes—neither self-possess'd
Nor startled, but betwixt this mood and that.'
                    —Alfred, Lord Tennyson:
                    'The Gardener's Daughter'

'What have you been doing, Miss Ashe?'

Cameo jumped. From her place by the window she'd been surveying Benedict Cole at work. He'd positioned her in a different pose today, half-reclining, but he hadn't touched her once, just barked sharp commands at her to get the angle right.

He was behaving as if he had never kissed her. Two could play at that game. If he was going to use his artistic discipline, then she would use hers, too.

'What do you mean, Mr Cole?' she asked coolly.

He laid down his pencil. 'It seems to me you have barely slept.'

'How did you…?'

'You're pale and you have the slightest shadows beneath your eyes. They were not there before. What have you been doing all night?'

Did Benedict Cole miss anything? She could hardly tell him she had attended Lady Russell's ball, then stayed up late drawing, desperate to make up for lost time, and when she had at last laid her head on the pillow, memories of their kiss kept her tossing and turning until dawn.

'I was…I was…sewing.' She must think of something. 'I…I do mending for extra money. Luckily Mrs Cotton, the woman who kindly took me in, if you remember, taught me her excellent skills with the needle. It's come in most useful.'

'I had almost forgotten the estimable Mrs Cotton,' Benedict said in a dry voice. 'So she taught you needlecraft, how fortunate. I shall have to take up your services.'

'My…services?'

'Alas. As I am a bachelor, I find many of my shirts require attention I cannot give them.'

In a few long strides Benedict left his easel and went to a chest of drawers near his bed. It seemed bigger than ever today, with its great carved wooden headboard. All too clearly she pictured him in that bed. Her neck and cheeks flushed hot again.

From a drawer he retrieved a white shirt, similar to the one he wore beneath his dark red waistcoat. He came across the room and passed her the shirt, brushing her skin. At his touch, Cameo gave a jolt he surely couldn't mistake.

If he, too, felt the current that flared between them he revealed no sign. 'There's a seam gone, there. Can you fix it?'

Holding the shirt up to the light of the window, she saw a seam had indeed torn across the shoulder, given way in what must have been a powerful stretch.

As she lifted the shirt closer the powerful masculine scent coming from the garment made her giddy. She suppressed her unexpected primitive urge to bury her face in the linen.

'Well?'

Her head bent, she examined the rip with what she hoped appeared a professional air. 'This is quite easy to mend. I've repaired similar garments.'

'Have you indeed? Is that your trade?'

'My trade?' She was echoing him once more, unable to string a sentence together.

'Yes, your trade. You mentioned Mrs Cotton brought you up. But what do you do now to earn your keep?'

'Oh. My keep.' For a moment her mind went as empty as a blank canvas. 'Well, I, well, I'm a...governess.'

'You don't sound too sure.'

'Oh, well, what I mean is, I'm usually a governess, but the family, the children, they're away at the moment. In the country. Derbyshire. Yes, Derbyshire,' she babbled. 'That's why I can come here and model for you.'

His expression remained dubious.

Cameo coughed. 'And while they're away I take in sewing, too. For extra money. I can certainly fix this. Would you like me to do it now?'

'No, I'm not expecting you to mend it instantly,' he said, with an impression of amusement. Relief flooded her. If he insisted, he would soon witness her poor performance at plain sewing. Her fancy embroidery stitches would look most out of place on his shirt.

'Perhaps you can add it to your mending basket in your lonely nursery, with your young charges away. But I must ask you to promise not to do any more sewing too late into the night. If I'm to complete this painting I must have you fresh-faced.'

As if pulling on her cloak, she assumed the meek manner of Miss Ashe. 'I'm sorry.'

His sharp glance made her realise he suspected her meekness as much as her mending.

Benedict returned to his easel. Yet another story she'd told him. Part of her was pleased she'd come up with something so quickly; part of her felt sick at having to tell more lies. It was beginning to be hard to keep track of them all. She'd told her mama she was taking extra riding lessons. That explained her absence at home. But all the lies troubled her.

It soothed her mind to watch Benedict at work. He'd moved on from drawing to painting now, using a fine brush tipped with black paint. He painted more slowly than he sketched, more deliberately. His strong fist clasping the paintbrush moved powerfully yet lightly across the canvas. His hands... She recalled the firm yet gentle way Benedict had held her, when his lips had met hers, so different from Lord Warley's attempted grab at Lady Russell's ball. The way he'd trapped her...nausea rose in her stomach. If only their fathers hadn't been such good friends.

Benedict's irate voice shot across the room. 'Now you're making a face. Your mouth is all puckered up as if you've tasted a lemon.'

Cameo tried to resume her previous expression and put the interlude at the ball from her mind.

'You don't need to pose any more just now, Miss Ashe.' He sent her a fleeting but intense glance. 'Sit down by the fire for a moment.'

'Don't you need me?'

Reaching for his brush, he dipped it into the black paint pooled on the palette. 'I just want to get this right.'

Eager to watch his technique from another angle, she crossed the room and hovered behind him.

'I can't paint with you at my elbow,' he snapped without turning his head.

The man was infuriating. Cameo sat down with a thump on the armchair by the fire and cast her eyes around. A book lay on the table among all the papers. The red leather binding appeared new. *The Stones of Venice*, its gilt lettering spelt out, by John Ruskin. She knew the author's name, of course, for Ruskin was the famous champion of the Pre-Raphaelite movement who was able to make or break a painter's reputation with a single review. She flicked the book open and found herself immediately held by the magnificent illustrations. She began to read.

'I didn't realise you were a reader, Miss Ashe.' Like a prowling cat, Benedict had silently moved beside her. 'But as you are a governess, I suppose it makes sense.'

At his sardonic drawl Cameo glanced up from the pages. She wasn't sure how long she had been reading as he continued to paint, a companionable silence seeming to settle over them both. 'It's a wonderful book.'

He studied her for a moment before he reached across and retrieved it. 'It's the first volume.' He flicked it open with his thumb. 'It's only just been published last year. It's a masterpiece, as is Venice itself.'

'You've been to Venice?' She was relieved he'd dropped the topic of her role as a governess.

'You sound surprised.'

'It's just the expense.'

'How can an impoverished artist living in a garret afford it, is that what you mean?' Benedict's voice remained light, but his face shuttered closed. 'I received an inheritance of a sort.'

She didn't press him on where such an inheritance might have come from. A look of pain, quickly hidden, caused by her innocent query halted any such enquiries.

'It wasn't a Grand Tour as such.' His mouth twisted. 'But all artists must see the works by the Renaissance Masters, such as Titian, Bellini and Giorgione, who are among the greatest of the Venetian school. It's an essential part of our training.'

'My bro—' She had opened her mouth to tell him her brother, George, had indeed travelled on a mandatory Grand Tour as did all young men of means. With a snap she shut it again. She possessed no brother George as the orphaned Miss Ashe.

'The family I work for have travelled to the Continent. Will you tell me what you saw in Venice?' Quickly she tried to cover her mistake.

'How can I describe it in words, instead of paint? You must see it to understand the beauty of the city, with its canals and the palaces reflected in their waters, each a work of art in itself.'

'I'd love to see it.'

He sent her his unexpected smile. 'Perhaps you'll go there one day.'

Her parents would never consider such a thing. Young ladies did not go on Grand Tours, at least, not the kind of tour Cameo dreamed to take, any more than they could be painters. 'I don't think so.'

'You never know what might happen,' he said lightly.

A silence lengthened between them.

Finally, she was unable to take the tension. 'Do you need me to pose any more?'

'No, Miss Ashe. I'm making excellent progress, especially with all my preparatory work before you appeared. I think that's enough for today.'

Feeling strangely light-headed, she buttoned on her coat and replaced her bonnet, sensing his usual awareness of her every movement. 'You'll still want me again?'

He made no reply but just folded his arms and nodded.

'Until tomorrow, then.'

The door slammed.

Benedict waited a few moments, then pelted down the stairs, keeping a safe distance behind Miss Cameo Ashe.

There she was on the street ahead of him, that determined, slim figure, her bonnet bobbing as she hurried home.

But to where? He'd tormented himself speculating about her. Did his model live alone? Or with someone else? With a man? Those thoughts had kept him awake at night. Her claim today to be a governess helped ease his aching suspicions, but something still didn't ring true about his model.

His model. Wryly he noted the possessive pronoun as he followed her down the street.

Ahead she rounded the corner, just as a woman carrying a basket of fruit and vegetables pushed towards him.

'Fancy something ripe, love?' She winked.

'I'm in a hurry.' Benedict raced past her.

As he turned the corner he stared down the street in astonishment.

Cameo Ashe had vanished. A crested carriage was pulling away and Becky the match girl stood alone. He gave her a wave. He often gave her food as she sat outside the bakery shop. He slipped her money when he had it; more often he gave her warm bread rolls. It must be torment to smell the baking bread.

Becky waved back. But of his model, there was no sign. As if she was a character in a fairy tale or a creature of his imagination. Gone.

Benedict ran his hand through his hair.

With a suppressed groan he made his way back up to the studio and strode over to the washstand, pouring the jug of water into the basin with an unsteady tilt. Glancing up into the mirror, beyond his reflected face he caught sight of the chaise longue Miss Ashe had just vacated. The scene echoed with presence, like a good still-life painting. So clear was her remembered image it seemed as if she still sat there, that slim upright figure, the sunlight bringing out unexpected glints in her dark hair.

Finishing this portrait was too important. Already his gut told him how good it was going to be. There must be no distractions. Cameo Ashe must not become more to him than a model. He vowed not to go chasing after her again, trying to find out more about her. No. Better that she was an apparition who appeared from nowhere. The flesh-and-blood woman, he must resist.

But he'd almost weakened. He wanted to show her the sketches he had made of Venice, see the curve of her neck as she studied them, to take his paintbrush, and take his finger...

Biting down an expletive, he leant across and pushed back the mirror. It swung like a pendulum. Her image he could surely erase, but the unexpected feel of her in his arms, the touch of those soft lips, the face lifted up to his like a delicate flower... The kiss they had shared, the one he sensed they were both trying so hard to forget, had been a promise of passion that ran deep.

What was it about her? he reflected as he unbuttoned his waistcoat, shrugged it off in a way he wished he could shrug off his persistent thoughts of Miss Ashe. She seemed different from any other model he had ever employed, but in a way he couldn't put his finger on.

Was it her complete stillness as she posed? She only made tiny breaths. Other than that she hadn't moved a muscle. Even the involuntary opening and shutting of her lashes seemed slow, as though not to disturb him, while his meticulous nature drove him on to sketch her over and over again, seeking to capture the exact lines of that chin, the shape of those lips. All his other models became bored, unable to hold positions for more than an hour or so. Miss Ashe sat there on the chaise longue unmoving for longer than that, her spine straight, apparently able to hold her pose unendingly.

Something else bothered him. He swore she was watching *him*. As intently as he sketched her, so she studied him in return, observing the slightest movement he made, taking in each step of the process, each sweep of his hand across the paper. He felt as if she were drawing with him in a strange fusion that bound them together.

Therein lay the difference. His other models, Maisie in particular, wanted him to stop working as soon as possible. Miss Ashe seemed to want him to go on, whilst drinking it all in with those violet eyes.

He'd sensed her complete focus as he finished drawing her mouth, with its full upper lip, and at last began to get her pointed chin right. Then he'd known he could go no further. The high blue collar of her finely woven woollen dress was tight around her neck and he'd only been able to guess at the exact shape of her collarbones that, even beneath her dress, hinted at being delicate and fine. He'd had to see her bare neck, that beautiful slender neck. And then the delicate scent of violets had risen up as he dropped the cameo necklace against her pale skin of her throat…

Damnation. He tore off his shirt and thrust his hands into the basin of water, splashing it against his face. He would resist her. Foundling, seamstress or governess, he had to subdue his curiosity, his need to know more. When she came for the next session he'd continue to paint her, but that was all.

Time to get to work. It would be another long night.

Chapter Seven

'Brothers in Art; a friendship so complete
Portion'd in halves between us, that we grew.'
—Alfred, Lord Tennyson:
'The Gardener's Daughter'

Cameo turned the corner. Above her head the sign for the Lamb public house creaked as it swung in the breeze. The street was becoming so familiar to her: the crowds of people buying and selling their wares, the carriages and carts, the busy butcher's shop, the bakery with the smell of warm fresh bread wafting from inside.

Becky, the match girl, sat on the cobbles with her wares laid out beside her.

'Good morning.'

'Morning, miss.'

'Do you have any brothers and sisters, Becky?' Cameo asked as she passed her a pocketful of coins.

'Five, miss. And one more on the way.'

'Five! You can share these with them.' In a paper bag she handed over the buns she'd bought at the bakery. The girl looked thinner than ever. No wonder, with so many siblings.

'Thank you, miss.'

'See you tomorrow, Becky.'

Cameo sighed as she climbed the stairs with their shabby green runner up to the studio. How many more times would she come here to Soho and to Benedict Cole? She didn't dare ask him for how many more sessions she might be required, in case he told her he didn't need her. Her stomach sank at the thought. She would miss it more than she ever dreamed possible. It seemed as if she belonged here now, but that was fanciful.

For the past two weeks, every morning except Sunday, she had faithfully appeared in the studio. So far, no one at home had discovered her deception, but she couldn't keep it up for much longer. Her mama had begun asking why she needed riding lessons instead of receiving callers. All too often the caller was Lord Warley. Since Lady Russell's ball, he'd begun sending flowers and notes, too, that she dropped instantly in the wastepaper basket.

She forced her worries from her mind. To her

surprise on the attic landing, at the top of the stairs, the door was ajar. She pushed it open.

'Mr Cole?' Her voice echoed in the empty studio. Perplexed, she frowned. Where was he? She'd come at the usual time. Slipping off her bonnet and gloves, Cameo sat down next to the table by the fire. It was still smouldering in the grate. He hadn't been gone long.

The studio was as untidy as ever. Paints and papers were everywhere; on the easel the canvas was shrouded in a sheet. With ease she conjured an image of him standing in front of the easel, how he looked when he painted; his jaw like granite as he concentrated, his hair wild, his movements fierce. Her heart skipped a beat.

Unthinking, she reached for a sheet of paper lying on the table. A piece of charcoal—she took that, too, and began to sketch furiously, trying to capture the image of him in her mind, the way he looked when he worked. Soon there was only the sound of the clock ticking on the chimney piece as her hands tore across the paper, using the same strong strokes she watched him make when he sketched her.

How much she had learnt by observing him. She had never drawn in such a way before. At home in her bedroom, or in the drawing room in front of her easel, she'd been so tentative. Now it was as if all the emotion inside her had been released to live and breathe in her art.

'Miss Ashe.'

The charcoal clattered on to the table.

Benedict stood beside her, unloosing a red scarf from his neck. It ruffled his hair. 'I'm sorry I wasn't here. I worked all night. I had to get some supplies.'

He crouched to check the fire. As he straightened his glance fell to the sketch on the table. She tried to cover it, but he was too quick for her.

'What's this?'

A trickle of perspiration formed at the base of her spine as he picked it up and studied it. She was merely an amateur. What would he, a professional artist, think of her work?

'Who taught you? Who taught you to draw?'

'You did.'

In amazement he threw back his head. 'I did?'

'Yes. I've done some sketching before, but I've learnt so much more from watching you.'

His brooding expression held hers for a long moment and then dropped down to the sketch in front of him.

'But you're good. You're very, very good.'

He moved behind her, enclosing her body in his as he leant over her shoulder. He lay the paper down on the table and picked up the charcoal, replacing its length in her shaking fingers. 'You're going wrong here. Let me show you.'

Cameo held her breath as he pressed closer, the charcoal in her fist within his strong grasp, drawing together as if they were one. His movements were gentler than she'd expected, slow and steady.

His closeness made her light-headed. She forced herself to concentrate on what he showed her, tuning into his smooth rhythm. Tense at first, she started to sense through his grip a powerful force, a certainty about where to place each line, each curve. She knew such sureness existed, she saw it in him, but she had never experienced it. Her fist easing in his, she curved back into his broad chest, into the security of his embrace, turning her liquid.

'You need to be easier here.' His warm breath was on her neck. 'You've got the perspective right, but your lines are too limited.'

In a broad sweep he lifted her arm as if it were a wing. 'Can you feel that? Can you stretch the expanse of that?'

'Yes.' Her breath came in choking gasps.

'That's the sense you need to have even if the drawing is on a small scale. You need more movement, more passion.'

More passion! She dropped the charcoal as if it burnt her. If only she could tell him how the rest of her life faded to black and white, like a cameo stone, while the hours in the studio with him blazed with colour.

He came to the other side of the table, looming over her, his brow darkening. 'Something's wrong.'

'No! I think I've had enough of sketching, that's all.'

A fierce glance told her he wasn't fooled. He picked up the charcoal and passed it to her. 'You must sign your sketch. It's good.'

She smiled, her mood lifting. He meant it. She hadn't been wasting her time, all the hours she'd spent trying to improve, all the times she'd argued with her parents that it was worth giving her a chance. She began to write her name. Lady Catherine Mary...

Petticoats twirling, she leapt up and seized the revealing paper. With wild fingers, she tore it across the bottom where she'd started to write her telltale signature.

'What are you doing?'

Whirling around, she threw the paper into the blazing fire. 'It isn't good enough!'

'No! Don't destroy your work!' He grabbed at her, but it was too late. They watched as the paper curled and blackened, turning to ashes in front of them.

He seized her by the shoulders. 'There was

nothing wrong with that sketch. What's the matter with you?'

Her lips quivered. She couldn't explain.

His eyes went to her mouth and stayed there.

Her breathing quickened.

His head came closer.

'Am I interrupting?'

'Trelawney.'

Cameo spun around to see a short, round-bellied man enter the studio.

'Indeed it is.' A pair of twinkling eyes alighted on her with interest. 'And who is this vision of loveliness?'

'My new model.' Benedict fell back, away from her, leaving her chest heaving. 'This is Miss Cameo Ashe.'

Trelawney smiled and bowed. 'How appropriate to such beauty. Delighted to make your acquaintance, Miss Cameo.'

Cameo smiled, too. It seemed impossible not to instantly like the man, with his bald smooth head, pixie ears and pointed beard, a red-spotted cravat tied jauntily at his neck. He looked like a wicked faun.

'I,' he said with a bow, 'am Nicholas Trelawney, sculptor. You've heard of me, I presume?'

'Well, no…'

'Of course she hasn't heard of you, Trelawney. Why would she?'

The sculptor put his hand to his heart as though fending off a dagger. 'Oh, wounded, wounded! You will hear of me one day, I am certain of it. My work will live and breathe for ever!'

'It will live and breathe if you ever finish anything,' Benedict commented. 'You've started and stopped more sculptures than I can count.'

Cameo supressed a smile. 'I'm pleased to meet you, Mr Trelawney.'

'And I you, my dear. Ignore this painter's disparagement of my work. His bark is much worse than his bite as no doubt you have discovered.' He turned to Benedict. 'Now then, admit it. I don't imagine you've remembered. You get caught up in your painting. I've come to remind you of my soirée next Friday evening. You've forgotten, haven't you?'

Benedict spread his hands. 'It's true.'

'It's not healthy,' Trelawney protested. 'Stimulating company is essential for the artist. That's why I hold my soirées. It's a service to you all.'

He turned to Cameo.

'I hold the most marvellous soirées, you see. Everyone who's anyone in the art world attends. Help me to persuade him to come. In fact—' he glanced from one to the other '—why don't you come, too, Miss Cameo? I'm sure you'd enjoy it.'

Benedict broke in. 'I'm sure it isn't Miss Ashe's kind of affair.'

'How can it not be? Other artists' models will be there, too. She'll be among friends.'

Cameo lifted her chin. 'Thank you. I'd love to come.'

'Marvellous. Benedict will bring you or just come along as you like.' He gave his address.

'Until the soirée, my dears!' With a wave of his hat, Trelawney disappeared down the stairs.

Glancing up, Cameo witnessed Benedict's scowl.

'Is there any difficulty if I attend the soirée with you?' she asked. 'Mr Trelawney has invited me, has he not?'

The expression in his eyes made her quake. 'Yes. But I don't think you should come, Miss Ashe. I prefer our relationship to remain purely professional.'

'This is professional, Mr Cole. Mr Trelawney said other artists' models will be there, along with other artists. Are you denying me the chance to meet painters who might also wish me to model for them?'

The corner of his mouth lifted. 'You wish to ply your trade, is that it?'

'If that's how you wish to put it.'

For a moment his challenging regard held hers. Then he shrugged, freeing her arm. 'In

that case I suppose I will have to take you,' he
said, then added with a warmth in his voice she
hadn't sensed since he'd kissed her. 'There's not
much I can do when you point that determined
chin of yours at me. Would you like me to collect you?'

'Oh, but I'll come in the carriage,' she replied
without thinking.

A terrible silence fell. She refused to meet
his eyes.

'Your employers make the carriage available
to you, do they? How unusual.' His voice remained flat.

'Not all the time. I mean, only by day. I mean,
by night. I mean, the driver is a good friend of
mine. In the servants' hall,' she added wildly. 'I
can make my own travel arrangements, thank
you.'

'I see.' His expression told her he didn't see
at all.

He knew she lied.

'Shall we get back to work?' he said at last.

'Yes, Mr Cole.' As she took up her pose,
Cameo tried to ignore the way his eyes stared
into her soul.

The earl clapped his son on the back. 'You've
made an excellent choice for your future wife.
Well done!'

Cameo and George burst into stifled laughter.

'Why are you and George so amused?' Maud asked them plaintively.

Cameo hugged her. 'Don't mind us. We knew what Papa would say. Everyone is so pleased. Tell me, are you happy?'

Maud, in a rose-sprigged dress, gave a radiant smile. 'How can you ask? I can't believe it. Of course I'm happy. I always dreamed I'd marry George one day.' She threw a proud glance in his direction, not dissimilar to the looks she used to bestow on him when he climbed to the top of trees, as George received congratulations from the earl and from Mr Cartwright, his future father-in-law. 'And we're really to be sisters!'

'I couldn't have hoped for a nicer one.'

'You'll be my chief bridesmaid, won't you?'

'Of course I will. I'll be delighted. When is the wedding to be?'

'I'm not sure yet. That's for Mama to decide. I think perhaps next June. She's already fussing about arrangements.'

Maud's mother, Mrs Cartwright, sat beside Lady Buxton on the leather chesterfield sofa, their heads bent together. Both were clearly delighted by the match between their children.

Who would not be pleased for George and Maud? Cameo sighed. Their love for each other lit up their eyes and brought an even rosier pink than usual to Maud's cheeks.

Benedict Cole's image appeared in Cameo's head. Just for a moment she pictured him standing beside her in the drawing room among them. In spite of his bohemian lifestyle he wouldn't appear out of place with his height and broad shoulders, his dark good looks and an innate gentlemanliness.

How she wished there was no deception between them.

Briggs popped a cork on a champagne bottle and brought the silver platter around, offering them each a delicate, rounded glass.

'May I offer my best wishes to you, Miss Cartwright,' he said with a bow. 'We're all delighted below stairs.'

Once again Maud revealed her radiant smile. 'Thank you, Briggs.'

Briggs gave Cameo the faintest flicker of a wink as he glided away.

'Oh, Cameo.' Maud laid her hand on Cameo's sleeve, her huge new diamond betrothal-ring dwarfing its small size. 'I hope you'll fall in love next. It's bliss!'

For a moment Cameo longed to confide in her about Benedict Cole. But she couldn't ask Maud to keep such information from George.

No. It must remain a secret, no matter how it tore at her.

Deceiving Benedict Cole was the only way.

Chapter Eight

❦

'And up we rose, and on the spur we went.'
—Alfred, Lord Tennyson:
'The Gardener's Daughter'

'My dears!' Nicholas Trelawney flung open the door. 'How delightful. Now I know how to get you here, Cole. It's by bringing the charming Miss Cameo with you. Come this way,' he called over his shoulder. 'Welcome to my humble abode!'

Untying her cloak, Cameo followed their host into the crowded drawing room. The walls were covered by a bold red-and-gold-flocked paper that would surely astound even her fashionable mama and there were books, paintings, stuffed birds in glass domes and other strange objets d'art crammed everywhere. Coloured-glass gas lamps balanced haphazardly on wooden chests and tables and a merry fire blazed in the grate beneath an oversized marble mantelpiece, which was topped by a fat gold clock, clutched on either side by a pair of Cupids. Smoke emanated, not only from the hearth, but also from pipes being smoked by more than one gentleman in the room and, she noticed in amazement, by a woman who was talking animatedly by the fire. In one corner an artist sketched madly; someone else tinkled on the piano. A pair of men were arguing with a woman laughing as she stood between them, her palms on each of their waistcoats.

'This is one of mine.' As they passed it Trelawney proudly patted a clay bust, massive and misshapen, on a wooden plinth. It appeared to resemble a Roman god.

'Oh!' Cameo searched for the right words. 'It's most…'

'Original,' Benedict supplied from behind her. Over her shoulder she flashed him a grateful grin.

Trelawney bustled away. 'I'll fetch you both some wine. Sit down, sit down.'

Benedict lightly touched her waist. 'This way.'

Her back stiffened at the slight, courteous gesture. Why did it ignite a passionate flame within her, sending tongues of warmth to colour her cheeks? *It's the fire*, she told herself. She'd just come in from the cool outside into a warm room. Yet she knew no external fire caused her inner surge of heat. What was happening to her?

Benedict led her to a red-velvet sofa and sat down beside her. She became instantly aware of his thigh only inches away. She sensed his awareness of her body, too, as he crossed one of his long legs over the other in his usual relaxed gesture. She loosened her pink-paisley shawl, a touch of frivolity she'd allowed Miss Ashe.

'French vintage, my dears. Partake.' Trelawney returned to them and held out two glasses.

Cameo murmured her thanks. Rapidly she scanned the room. She experienced a sudden anxiety that there might be someone from her circle of acquaintance at the gathering of artists. But she spotted no one she met in society.

Benedict swallowed deeply, drawing Cameo's eyes to his strong neck. She sipped her own. It tasted fruity and delicious, even if not as smooth as the wine served by Briggs at home. Her papa was very fussy about his claret.

Trelawney sat down opposite them. After a swig from his own glass he gave a satisfied smile. 'Quite the crowd today.'

'Do you have these gatherings often?' Cameo asked.

'The great days of the artists' salon are long gone, alas.' Trelawney sighed. 'All we have are my soirées to ensure those in the art world can meet each other. Artists, writers, poets, critics, sculptors akin to myself. They all come to my gatherings.'

Benedict leant towards Cameo and jerked his head towards a man on the other side of the room. 'Over by the window. Ruskin. The art critic.'

The whiskered critic met her glance and gave Benedict a nod of recognition the artist casually returned.

'He knows you,' Cameo breathed.

'Of course.' Benedict sounded amused. 'It's a small community in a way, the art world. We all know exactly what each other are up to, what we're doing, what we're trying to achieve.' He indicated a ruddy-skinned man. 'That's William Holman Hunt, one of the Pre-Raphaelite Brotherhood. And that's Rossetti, the leader.'

She stared at the artist with the curly black hair, waving his arms about emphatically. A pale, ethereal red-haired woman stood close by his side. 'That's his model, Lizzie Siddall.'

'I believe Rossetti is teaching Miss Lizzie to paint.' Trelawney chuckled. 'That reminds me, Cole, did that society matron who wanted lessons from you write to you again?'

Cameo froze.

Benedict rolled his eyes. 'She appears to have given up.'

Trelawney turned to Cameo. 'You should have heard him. My dear, he was irate. Some poor Mayfair matron wrote to him asking for art lessons. Refused in no uncertain terms, wasn't she, Cole?'

'Indeed.'

'Why did you refuse her?' Cameo found her strangled voice. 'Because she's a woman?'

'Of course not. That would be ridiculous.' Benedict shrugged. 'I simply have no desire to mingle with the upper classes.'

She gulped her wine. 'But…why?'

'Let's just say art would be a hobby, nothing more, an accomplishment to boast about. Many aristocrats claim to value art and artists, but it's all too often not true. It's an affectation, or worse, an investment.'

'How do you know? Surely you're wrong. There might be a society lady…' Cameo furiously swallowed the words with another gulp of wine '…who is passionate about art.'

'I doubt it. I refuse to waste my time finding out.'

'Ooh!' The exclamation escaped from her lips before she contained it.

Benedict quirked an eyebrow at her. 'This angers you?'

Trelawney chuckled again. 'I'm not surprised. You do sound a radical revolutionary when you talk like that, Cole. I had a German fellow at my last soirée I should have introduced you to. He's moved into Dean Street in Soho not far from you. Name of Karl Marx.'

Benedict's lips thinned. 'I'm not so radical or revolutionary. I prefer to avoid the aristocracy, that's all, as well you know, Trelawney. I had too much to do with them at one time of my life and I vowed never to again.'

So that explained the rude reply he had sent her in response to her request for painting lessons, Cameo thought to herself. He didn't merely disapprove of society ladies dabbling in art. That was an excuse. He had an aversion to mixing with upper-class society. But why? What had happened that he'd made such a vow? In any case, she couldn't reveal her real identity now. He would despise her, think her typical of her class, as arrogant as someone like Lord Warley, snatching whatever she wanted.

Cameo jerked her head away, tears smarting in her eyes. Her pleasure at being at the soirée amidst all the bohemian artists and writers vanished. She didn't belong. She'd never belong in this bright, wonderful, exciting world.

Benedict stood up. 'Will you excuse me for a moment? There's someone I need to speak to.'

'Miss Cameo is safe with me.' Trelawney twinkled. 'Fear not, my boy.'

'Are you all right, my dear?' Nicholas Trelawney enquired after Benedict had gone, patting Cameo's hand. 'You look a trifle upset. You mustn't mind what Benedict says. It's the artistic temperament. They're all the same, such passionate people. It's frightening to have them all in the same room. My dear! The fireworks!'

She offered him a smile. It was difficult to be downcast in the company of Nicholas Trelawney.

'I have great hopes for our Benedict. He's extremely talented.'

Cameo nodded. She'd known it the moment she first saw his painting in the Royal Academy and was drawn to it like a magnet.

'He's the typical artist, so focused on his work and nothing else. A tendency to be, how can I say it, somewhat *obsessed*. And now what do I see?' Trelawney leaned forward confidentially. 'If you knew how hard I've tried to get him here! My dear, what have you done?'

At what must have been her look of puzzlement, he chuckled. 'To Benedict, my dear. He's quite transformed.' She heard sincerity in the sculptor's voice. 'You're making him very happy.'

'I…I'm not…sure what you mean, Mr Tre-lawney.'

'Oh!' He jolted in surprise. 'Do forgive me. The way you both… It seemed…I thought…' The sculptor patted her hand again. 'My apologies.'

Cameo blushed. She glanced over to where Benedict stood in a group by the window. A drop of wine caught in her throat. Next to the artist stood one of the most beautiful women Cameo had ever seen, with improbably golden hair that shone bright as a beacon. She laughed up at Benedict, her head thrown back, revealing strong white teeth slightly buckled at the front. This small imperfection seemed to make no difference to the crowd of admirers gathered around her.

As if she sensed Cameo's stare, the woman revolved. She gave her a hard look, then moved closer to Benedict.

'Who is that?' Cameo asked Trelawney in an undertone.

'That's Maisie Jones. Lovely, isn't she? She was Benedict's model before you, my dear.'

A wave of jealousy soured the wine on Cameo's tongue. Of course Benedict had had other models before. She chided herself. The man was an artist, after all. She recognised the woman now. She was the model holding sheaves of wheat in Benedict's painting at the Royal Academy of Art. In real life, she appeared even more beautiful.

Another surge of envy rose up inside her followed by a dashing slump of her spirits. She toyed with her wine glass. It was unbearable to imagine the beautiful Maisie Jones in Benedict's studio, alone with him as he painted. She was just so dazzling.

Suddenly Cameo felt pale and wan. She almost wished she hadn't come. What was better, to have entered the bohemian artistic world of Benedict Cole or to never know it existed? And what was she going to do about the feelings aroused in her by the artist himself?

Trelawney jerked his head towards Maisie. 'She's a good girl really, but she isn't right for Benedict.'

'Oh?' Cameo asked in a small voice. So their relationship had been more than professional. She felt shocked at how much the information hurt.

'All over long ago,' Trelawney added hastily.

'Have you been acquainted with Benedict for a long time, Mr Trelawney?'

Trelawney sipped his wine. 'I met him when he first came to London,' he said after a moment. 'Hard times, for such a young man. He doesn't dwell on that, of course. He's not the type. But I expect you know all about that, don't you?'

At last, Cameo thought, someone who might be able to unravel the mystery that was Benedict Cole. She had to know. What was behind the anger he'd revealed against the upper classes?

'Well, I know some things, but…'

'Know what?' Benedict's deep voice startled her. 'What have you two been gossiping about, Trelawney?'

From across the room Benedict had been watching Miss Cameo Ashe. He had practically ignored poor Maisie, chattering away beside him, but he found it difficult not to study his new model constantly, thinking about the best way to paint her. It was an urge, a constant need for him. He wanted to be alone with her, hold a paintbrush and capture that beautiful visage on canvas. He realised he had felt proud to enter the room earlier with her beside him, with her engaging manner and eagerness. She obviously loved being there among all the artists, drinking in the scene with those deep purple-grey eyes.

But something was bothering him more and more. Unbeknown to her, before the soirée he'd lurked around the front of Trelawney's house, waiting until she had appeared in a black-crested carriage, the same one, he was sure, that he'd spotted around the corner of his studio the day he'd followed her. He had watched her get out of the carriage and something about the way the coach driver had sprung to attention implied more than the status of a governess.

Cameo Ashe wasn't a seamstress, or a governess. He was convinced of that by the way she told those stories, with a quick wit and imagination, but without the brazenness of a hardened liar. And why would a governess have a carriage available to her? Her story didn't ring true.

After weighing up various explanations he began to think of a reason for the inconsistencies in her story. A primitive kick in his groin told him how much he disliked the explanation, but it persisted in being the only one that added up. Was she a wealthy man's mistress? And if so, why was she modelling for him?

Now, once again he stared over to where Cameo's lovely profile was bent towards Trelawney, deep in conversation.

She wore her grey dress, the one he'd first seen her in, less plain than her usual weekday attire. He knew her blue everyday dress well now, how perfectly it fitted the subtle curves of her body. He could have drawn it blindfolded. Tonight a silk paisley shawl lightly hung over the grey. That dress had felt smooth when he'd guided her to the sofa by the waist earlier, silky to the touch. He'd been forced to get up and walk away from her as their debate became more heated, raising her temperature, making her eyes sparkle and her skin warm up, sending gentle wafts of her violet scent over him.

Beside him, Maisie had ceased talking and twisted her blonde head to see what held his attention. 'Who's that, then? Over there with Trelawney? I've never seen her before.'

His attention returned to the soirée. 'She's the model for my new work.'

Maisie's lips pursed. 'I think you'd better introduce us.'

Benedict followed her as she wove her way over to where Cameo Ashe and Nicholas Trelawney sat near the fire.

'Well?' he asked them again. 'What were you whispering about?'

Miss Ashe coloured as pink as her shawl.

'Never fear!' Trelawney assured Benedict, as quick understanding flashed between them. 'No dark secrets have been revealed.'

'I should hope not.' Benedict kept the warning light, but it was there all the same.

Maisie broke in. 'You said you'd make some introductions, Benedict.' She brushed up against him, her lush figure spilling out of her tight blue gown, the colour heightening the shade of her eyes. He saw those eyes turn as cold as the ocean as they looked upon Cameo.

'Maisie, this is Miss Cameo Ashe, my new model. Miss Ashe, this is Miss Maisie Jones.'

'Hello,' Maisie drawled. 'I don't think we've met, have we?'

'No. I don't believe so. How do you do?'

Maisie crossed her arms, emphasising her breasts even more. 'Been modelling long, have you?'

'This is my first time.'

Maisie ran a finger up and down Benedict's arm. 'And you got Benedict Cole? My, my. Not that you would have got him if I'd been still been—what did you call me, Benedict? Your muse?'

He smiled at the blonde woman who came up to his shoulder. 'I don't think I ever used the word *muse*, Maisie, though you were perfect for my last painting. I've told you that before.'

She gave a pout of pleasure but her face hardened again as she returned to Cameo. 'There's already plenty of models for all the artists round here.'

'Now, now, Maisie.' Nicholas Trelawney wagged his finger. 'Put away your claws.'

With a toss of her head the model flounced away. 'I'll see you soon, Benedict. You know where I am for your next painting.'

'I never knew what you saw in that woman, Cole.' Trelawney laughed. 'Or perhaps I do.'

'She's a good model,' Benedict vouchsafed as he sat down and tried not to stare at Cameo Ashe.

Benedict lit the lamp in his studio.

Ever since Trelawney's soirée a few nights before, sleep had proved impossible.

Mixing his paints, he brooded on the occasion when he became aware of the seriousness of his feelings for Cameo.

To put it bluntly, she fascinated him.

As they'd gone to leave the soirée, Trelawney had murmured to Benedict under his breath, 'Take good care of your new model. She's charming.'

And he'd found out more about her. It had gutted him, but he'd had to know. After the gathering he had taken a hackney cab and followed the carriage that bore Miss Ashe away. It had rolled along to Mayfair, to a quiet, stately square that spelt money and class. The carriage had stopped outside the front of one of the houses and, with a furtive look over her shoulder as though she didn't want to be observed, Miss Cameo Ashe had alighted from the carriage and hurried into the house.

By the front door.

There could be no doubt. She wasn't a seamstress or a governess as she claimed. They would have entered through the servants' entrance.

Benedict had barely closed his eyes that night or for the few nights afterwards. He had continued to work, hour after hour, not only at her portrait, but also on other sketches and drawings of her until fatigue made it impossible to continue. He fell into bed satisfied with what he'd done, though sleep usually slipped further away, into the dawn.

Her face haunted him. Her face and also the story she'd told him, the inconsistencies in it. He frowned, yet again perplexed. What was she trying to hide?

He hoped more than ever it wasn't what he suspected. But why could he assume he was the only man who found her captivating?

Damnation. This model was proving to be the most captivating of all. And the question continued to haunt him.

Who was she?

Chapter Nine

'The garden stretches southward. In the midst
A cedar spread his dark-green layers of
shade.
The garden-glasses shone…'

—Alfred, Lord Tennyson:
'The Gardener's Daughter'

Benedict threw down the paintbrush, his face
white with exhaustion. 'That's enough.'

Cameo released her pose and breathed out.
Every single muscle in her body ached with tension. 'Is the portrait going well?'

'It's hard to say at this stage.' Benedict covered it up with the sheet. 'It's absorbing me night
and day. I've never worked so quickly.'

'Oh.' Cameo's heart sank. She didn't want him
to work quickly. She wanted her days in the studio to last for ever, but they were passing all too
soon. Since the soirée at Nicholas Trelawney's

house, Benedict hadn't seemed to stop working. She worried about him, seeing the lines around his mouth and the shadows under his eyes. She knew artists could be obsessed, as Trelawney had told her. She knew from her own passion for art. 'Do you need me to pose any more today?'

'No, Miss Ashe. I think that's enough.' He flexed his shoulders in a strong, leisurely movement from which she found it difficult to turn away.

'You'll still want me tomorrow?' It was getting harder and harder for her to slip away, but Maud and George's engagement had proved to be a diversion at home. Still, it wouldn't last for ever and she wasn't sure how long she could keep it up.

He nodded.

'Where do you live?' he startled her by asking as she went to collect her bonnet and coat, hanging over the armchair by the fire.

She couldn't say Mayfair. 'Not far from here.'

'Do you walk home after our sessions?'

'Of course.' As far as the carriage hidden around the corner.

'It's a beautiful day. I could do with some air. I'll accompany you, if I may.'

Cameo choked. 'Accompany me?'

'Is there some difficulty?'

'It's just that…I'm not going straight home today. I plan to go to…Hyde Park.'

'Perfect. We'll go to the park.'

Her first instinct, of sheer pleasure at the thought of being outdoors with him, was overcome by panic. She couldn't go with Benedict Cole to Hyde Park, the place where society gathered to walk or ride, or simply to see or be seen. She couldn't risk it. There'd be a scandal if she were spotted unchaperoned with a bohemian artist. A lady with no relations such as Miss Cameo Ashe might be able to take a promenade with an unknown male in the park, but for Lady Catherine Mary St Clair: unthinkable.

Helplessly, she watched as he pulled on his long brown coat and slung his scarf around his neck. 'Come along, Miss Ashe. To the park.'

Benedict glanced at Cameo sideways as she sat on the park bench in her blue bonnet with its paler blue trimmings and her smart grey coat, cut away in a cape to allow for her layers of skirt. She appeared nervous, jumping like a frightened deer each time someone walked past.

When he stretched his legs beside her she flinched, as aware of his body as he remained of hers. She moved away from him, putting a bigger space between his thigh and her own.

He knew why. It was that kiss, still unspoken

between them, and the growing attraction he found harder and harder to resist.

Balling his fist, he focused his attention on the ducks in the water opposite. It was driving him mad, the mystery of her. His fingers itched for a pencil, to catch the swanlike slope of her white neck as she leant back slightly on the bench. Instead he forced himself to focus on the lake in front of them and the sleek feathers of a mother duck, grey-brown with a flash of turquoise-blue on the underside, with her ducklings, three balls of feathered fluff, beside her. Nearby, a boy and girl with their nanny were throwing bits of bread, shrieking in delight, with the look of joy that only came after a long winter ended and the spring sunshine seeped into the earth. The cold still bit at his skin, but a hint of warm April air hovered. Already the park lawn was studded here and there with white flowers, the kind that came first in the spring time, the grass, after the winter rains, lush and vivid.

Next to him the sun seemed to be having an effect on his model. She relaxed somewhat, her fingers less clenched inside her kid-leather gloves.

He glanced sideways at her. 'You're enjoying the air.'

As she lifted her face to the gentle sunshine, she gathered a deep breath that lifted her corset. 'Spring is my favourite time of year in Hyde Park. Did you come here for the Great Exhibition last year?'

'With half of London, yes. What were there, six million people, the newspaper said?'

'The crowds were enormous. I don't think I ever saw anything as beautiful as the Crystal Palace. I liked the way they enclosed the trees within the structure. The displays were wonderful.'

He chuckled. 'I agree with you, though John Ruskin certainly didn't.'

Cameo inched towards him on the bench. 'What did he say?'

'He created a furore. He bemoaned the fact that lesser works were being displayed at such expense in the Crystal Palace while in Venice the works of great masters were "rotting in the rain, without roofs to cover them, and with holes made by cannon shot through the canvas",' Benedict quoted. 'He had a point.'

'I still liked the Great Exhibition. Do you ever work outside?'

He laughed and quoted Ruskin again. '"In the rain without a roof to cover me?"'

She laughed, too. He hadn't heard her laugh much before, that light, musical gurgle. 'Just out of doors.'

'I do. It's essential. I did most of the work for the background of your portrait outside.'

'I thought you were working on it in the studio.'

'Yes, but I already had done a lot of the preparatory process before I found you.' He ignored his swift pulse at the memory of first seeing her. 'That's the time-consuming part. I made sketches and colour studies to make sure I got the setting as exact as possible. Nature trains the artist's eye, you see.'

He faced her squarely, his leg moving against hers, and saw her hold back a jolt. 'Your sketch. The one you did the other day.'

She took another of those corset-filling breaths as her leg stayed against his. 'What about it, Mr Cole? I told you I have an interest in art.'

'Yes, you told me that, among many other things.' He let the note of disbelief ring in his voice. 'Your sketch showed some skill. Do you only work in pencil and charcoal, or also in colour?'

'I use watercolours and oils, too. Only once or twice, of course. They're expensive,' she added hastily.

'You need to use oils to paint properly.'

She bit her lip. 'What did you mean by the correct study of nature?'

Why had she changed the subject? 'I'm not

sure I'm in the mood for giving an art lecture today.'

'Please.'

'You're most persistent.' He pointed to a single flower blooming at the base of the trunk of an oak tree nearby. 'Look at that daffodil. What do you see?'

'I see a daffodil.'

'Look again. Describe it to me.'

'It's yellow.'

'Is that all you see? Yellow? What kind of yellow?'

She swallowed hard. He guessed she was holding back one of her sharp retorts. To be honest he enjoyed them.

'There are many yellows,' she said after a moment. 'There's the more golden yellow at the centre of the flower, it's almost orange. And then there's the paler yellow of the petals. At the tip they are almost translucent.'

'Good. What else?'

Two tiny lines formed between her fine eyebrows. 'They're like sunshine. That's how to paint them. To try to capture their warmth and brightness, their golden life, not merely their colour.'

It wasn't often he shared such a sense of connection with a model. He felt strangely pleased by her answer. She'd grasped immediately what he meant. 'Very good. Artists see in terms of light and shade. Even if we paint using dark colours we capture light by layering the darker colours over paler ones so the light is revealed. Titian, one of the greats of the Venetian school, was an expert at it. He used feather-light strokes to let the light come through.'

'I think I understand.'

'By paying attention to the natural world we can see what truly is. In this I agree with the Pre-Raphaelites. Truth from Nature is their motto. I, too, paint what I see. Truth is of great value to me. If there's one thing I cannot abide, Miss Ashe, it's a lie.'

He could see he had hit home with that comment. Her lips quivered and then parted. He hoped briefly she might choose to tell him the truth about herself. It had become so important to him. Continuing to paint her with his need to discern her soul was becoming unbearable. The portrait would be a masterpiece if his passion for her was unleashed, he knew it.

Yet again she changed the subject. 'You're not a member of the Pre-Raphaelite Brotherhood, though? You seem to know them well.'

Benedict hid his disappointment at her continued deception. He had hoped she'd started to trust him. Didn't she realise he would never judge her, no matter what she told him about her circumstances? Did she realise what was happening between them? Instead he answered her question. 'I'm friendly with them. We share an interest in the same techniques, especially to do with the natural world. We aim to reproduce it as exactly as possible.'

Her lower lip took another bite. 'You achieved that in the painting of the girl with the wheat. The one of Maisie Jones.'

'You've seen that work?'

She gave a quick nod.

'You're a woman of constant surprises,' he drawled. 'I'm beginning to wonder what you'll come up with next.'

She flushed pink, always a giveaway with Miss Ashe.

'My work does draw on the Pre-Raphaelite ideas about nature, among other things,' he went on, when she said nothing more, though the colour in her cheeks continued to deepen. 'But no other painter taught me. I learnt that from my parents.'

'Your parents?'

He'd surprised himself. He so rarely discussed his family background. He hesitated for a moment. Then he said, 'Before I came to London, my...my father, Arthur Cole, was a gamekeeper on a large estate. We lived in his cottage. He knew every inch of the estate, every wood, every lake, each animal and each tree. He was also a wood carver and he taught me to carve. You have to be precise, detailed. I still carve my own frames for my paintings.'

'And your bed.'

'My bed?'

'Your bed in the studio. That's carved, isn't it?'

'I didn't realise you took such an interest in my bed.' He enjoyed making her retrieve another of those deep breaths as she flushed even rosier.

After a moment she rallied. 'Where is he now? Your father, I mean. Is he still on the estate?'

Tightness formed in his throat. 'He died.'

'I'm so sorry. And did he teach you to paint, as well?'

His mouth twisted. 'Not Arthur Cole, no.'

'Your mother?'

The warmth of her memory flooded back. He could almost feel himself back indoors in their cottage. 'My mother possessed a gift for colour. Our home was humble, but she made it beautiful. It didn't look like the other cottages on the estate. She didn't leave her furniture plain. She painted it with simple designs of flowers and fruit in reds, yellows, blues and greens.' He paused for a moment, found it hard to go on. 'Colour surrounded her. At night, before I went to sleep, I'd lie awake, soaking in those designs as they glowed bright as jewels in the lamplight, my mother, in her red dress, the most colourful sight of all. My father…my father used to tease her. He said she looked like a gypsy.'

'She sounds beautiful.'

'She was. I painted my first-ever portrait of her sitting at the door of our cottage in her scarlet gown.'

'Where is she now?'

The pain inside him became almost unbearable. He clenched his fists and forced himself to say evenly, 'She died not long after my father. Because of the way she was treated, no doubt.'

'What happened to her?'

'She was cast out,' he replied, unable to keep the rage from his voice. 'The lord of the manor forced her to leave our cottage, our home. All the loyalty…it was not returned. Just broken promises. But that's how some members of the aristocracy behave.'

She opened her mouth and closed it again, as if she meant to speak but changed her mind. She waited a moment before she asked him another question. 'That's terribly sad. Then what happened? How did you become a painter?'

He shrugged, trying to cast off the memory of those years. 'I came to London. I studied. I painted. Through my art I am determined to be accepted on my own terms.'

Terminating their conversation, he stood. 'I think that's enough air, Miss Ashe.'

Stones crunched under Cameo's boots as she tried to keep up with Benedict's fast pace as he strode away. She barely noticed her surroundings as they headed away from the lake towards the gates of Hyde Park.

While she'd listened to him talk about the way his beloved mother had been treated she had longed to reach over and erase those bitter lines bracketing his mouth. Yet ever since their kiss, he'd made it clear they needed to keep their distance.

Cameo frowned slightly. He said he had grown up in a cottage, but that didn't explain his cultured voice, his obvious education. He had vision and a God-given talent, and passion, so much passion. He was an enigma, yet there was no doubt about his hostility towards the aristocracy and their broken promises.

She could never tell him the truth about herself.

Her heart ached as he strode away ahead of her. As if sensing her gaze, he stopped and turned. Her pulse skipped a beat. His long brown coat hung open, his red scarf tied carelessly, his dark head bared, for he didn't bother with a hat. He pushed his hair from his forehead in what had become a familiar gesture as he waited for her. She stepped towards him, her heart seeming to lift—and froze on the spot.

Behind Benedict, another man approached.

It couldn't be! Her mouth dried. But there was no mistaking Lord Warley, that correct figure with his top hat and cane, out for a promenade in the park.

Cameo swallowed her shriek. Pulling her bonnet down over her face, she skittered sharply on her heel, hitched up her skirts and sped away. Fast footsteps came behind her, closer and closer. She ran on, hardly knowing where she went. Spotting a glade of trees, she dashed into them, a low branch scratching at her bonnet. She cried out as someone caught her from behind and spun her around.

Benedict Cole gripped her by the elbow. 'What is it? Tell me.'

Frantically Cameo tried to peer past him, through the trees. Where was Lord Warley? Had he recognised her, followed her? Of all the people to discover her secret!

'I must leave! I must go straight away.'

Benedict's jaw set as he twisted his head and scanned the area behind them. 'There's no one following you.'

He clenched her elbow harder. 'What exactly is it you're running from? Or should I say whom?'

'No one…'

'I don't think so. You saw someone you knew, I didn't see who it was. But you certainly didn't want them to see you.'

With a grip of fury, Benedict tugged Cameo deeper behind the trees. 'I told you not to lie to me. Do you think I can't see you're concealing something?'

'You've no right to question me!' In panic she tried to wrench free. 'Let me go! Let me go, I say!'

Benedict's eyes glittered as he released her. 'All right.' His mouth formed a furious line. 'Go. Go now. But, Miss Ashe? Don't come back to the studio until you're ready to tell me the truth.'

Chapter Ten

'The heavy clocks knolling…'
—Alfred, Lord Tennyson:
'The Gardener's Daughter'

'Your parents are in the drawing room, Lady Catherine Mary. Your mother asked for you, I believe.'

Cameo bit her lip as Briggs took her bonnet and cloak. With shaking fingers she smoothed down her dress. The hem was grass stained from her dash across the park. Hopefully no one would notice. If they did, she would have to think of another convincing lie.

So many lies. There seemed to be no escape.

'Thank you, Briggs.'

'Where have you been?' her father demanded the minute she entered the drawing room. 'Your mama tells me you couldn't be found. Lord Warley called. And you weren't here to receive him!'

'The servants looked for you everywhere, Cameo dear.' Lady Buxton was fluttering, twisting her rings. 'You've been out so much of late. Lord Warley expressed such disappointment not to find you at home.'

'Terribly rude of you, Cameo!' the earl barked. 'The son of my greatest friend came to pay his addresses to you, I understand, and you don't even do him the courtesy of being here. And he had some story about seeing you in Hyde Park.'

'With a gentleman,' her mother added in a horrified note. 'Unchaperoned!'

So Lord Warley had seen her. 'Well, I…'

'And you're not in your riding habit, Cameo.'

'Come on! Out with it!' her papa barked. 'Where have you been?'

'I've…I've…I've been…'

'With me.'

Cameo spun around to see George coming into the room.

'Sorry, Pater. Cameo has been out with me at…'

'The park.' Cameo threw George a grateful glance.

'That's it. The park. We went for a stroll.'

'Humph.' The earl grunted. 'Took your sister out, did you?'

'That's right, sir. Apologies if she was meant to be here.'

'That's all right, George dear.' The countess gave her son a doting glance. 'It was thoughtful of you.' She diverted to her daughter. 'But you simply must be here tomorrow, Cameo. We have callers on Thursdays and I've asked Lord Warley to tea.'

'But I can't be at home tomorrow morning. I've got another riding lesson,' Cameo protested. What conclusions would Benedict Cole come to if she didn't appear at the studio, after the warning he'd given her? She had to tell him the truth, beg his forgiveness.

The earl frowned, brushing his whiskers. 'You must cancel your riding lesson and stay at home tomorrow with your mama.'

Lady Buxton spoke up. 'I'll be so pleased to have you with me, Cameo dear.'

'But—'

'No more arguing.' The vein on her father's forehead popped out. 'What's the matter with you, young lady? It's high time you remembered your duties.'

'I'm sorry, Papa.' Cameo's head reeled. She must see Benedict tomorrow and tell him the truth. She must!

'Good.' Her papa nodded and turned to his wife. 'We'll go into luncheon, Charlotte. Goodness knows where Briggs has got to—he ought to have announced it by now.'

'What the devil's going on?' George muttered to Cameo, pulling her back into the drawing room before they followed their parents into the dining room across the hall. 'Where have you been?'

'It's a secret, George.'

George threw her a frown of concern. 'Secrets are never a good idea, old girl. Maud and I have noticed you've been disappearing rather a lot lately. We guessed you were up to something. We know the signs all too well. What is it?'

'I'll tell you both when I can, George, I promise.'

'Promise?'

'Cross my heart and hope to die.' She waved in the air as they used to when they were children.

'Hmm. I suppose that will have to do. I say, you're not involving Maud in one of your schemes, are you?'

'Of course not.'

'That's all right, then. Maud's not the same as you, always up to some scrape or another.' He gave her a pat on the arm as they went towards the dining room. 'I hope you know what you're doing, I really do. I get the feeling, little sister, you're playing with fire.'

'Well. This has been most pleasant.'

Lord Warley replaced the thin porcelain teacup so slowly on to the saucer Cameo nearly screamed. On the marble chimney piece, with its vast urns on either side, sat the French clock that chimed noisily on the quarter-hour. All day she'd watched the needles drag as she sat taking calls with her mama, listening to endless plans for the Season, for balls, dinners and other entertainments. She had hoped Lord Warley might be detained and she might escape. But right on time, on the stroke of four o'clock, Briggs entered the drawing room with the silver tray aloft bearing the Warley-crested calling card upon it. Now, forced to take tea with him, Cameo sat stuck in the same position, her feet crossed beneath her skirts, her hands folded in her lap, a fixed smile and falsely interested expression on her face. It was harder than modelling for Benedict.

Benedict. Under her skirts, she rubbed her shoes across the thick oriental carpet. How she longed to be in the studio in Soho with its bare boards. Would he be there now, painting? Had he already sought out another model? How long would he wait?

He would give up on her.

Her mother brought her out of her reverie. 'Aren't we, Cameo?'

'I'm sorry?' Cameo dragged her attention back to the drawing room to find Lord Warley studying her as though he were guessing at her thoughts. Her skin crawled.

'We're delighted you could come this afternoon, especially after Cameo wasn't here when you came to call yesterday.' Lady Buxton apologised. 'Her brother, George, took her to the park.'

'Who am I to deprive a brother and sister of company on a sunny day in Hyde Park? But I must admit—' Warley hoisted one leg over the other '—I didn't think it was your brother I saw you with in the park, Lady Catherine Mary.'

Cameo choked on her tea.

'Perhaps I am mistaken.' His lips pursed in a suggestive manner that told Cameo he didn't believe himself mistaken at all.

It seemed safer not to reply. Why, she'd been right about Lord Warley all along. There was something nasty about him, something unwholesome. He knew she hadn't been in the park with George. For some reason he was holding it over her.

Picking up a plate of sandwiches from the tea stand, she leaned over and offered them to him. 'Another cucumber sandwich?' she asked coldly.

'I think I've had quite sufficient.' He fingered the gold watch hanging from a chain on his blue silk waistcoat. 'It really is time I left you dear ladies. But before I depart I must say I'm looking forward to welcoming you to Warley Park.' He smoothed his hair and addressed her mama, but his eyes flicked towards Cameo. 'The grounds are particularly magnificent in the spring.'

'Lord Warley persuaded me yesterday to bring our visit forward, Cameo,' her mama explained. 'We'll travel to Sussex on Saturday.'

Why, that was in only two days. Her heart sank. It was the worst possible moment. It made it even more pressing to get to the studio and Benedict.

'I'm sure you'll enjoy it, Lady Catherine Mary.'

'It will be delightful,' the countess replied to Lord Warley with a smile when Cameo didn't respond.

His tongue darted out. 'I'll be particularly pleased to show your daughter my estate.'

'Oh, she's very happy to come, aren't you, Cameo dear?'

'Of course,' she answered politely, though she couldn't think of anything worse.

'Then it's settled.'

Lord Warley stood up and took his silver-topped cane. Why did he always carry it with him? He wasn't old. It made her uneasy.

'Charmed, Lady Buxton. Lady Catherine Mary.' He leaned over Cameo's hand. She could have sworn his tongue flicked her wrist before she snatched it away.

'Always a pleasure,' her mother said.

'How can you say that, Mama?' Cameo demanded after he left the drawing room. For once, she refrained from holding back. 'How can you say it's a pleasure?'

'Cameo!' Her mother appeared utterly shocked, fanning her face with her handkerchief. 'He's such a handsome young man and always so polite.'

No, he's not, she recalled mutinously, choking back the words. She wished she could tell her mama about the way Lord Warley made her feel, but they never discussed those kinds of matters. It just wasn't done.

'Lord Warley's a member of the same club as your father and dear George, like his father before him. Your father was always such good friends with his,' her mama reminded her. 'He won't hear a thing against that family and Lord Warley has become a most eager suitor.'

Cameo repressed a chill. 'Lord Warley is attentive to many young ladies.'

'But most attentive to you, Cameo dear. We all noticed at Lady Russell's ball. What a charming couple you made! Now, don't go disappearing anywhere in the next few days. I'll supervise the packing of your belongings. My maid will attend to it. You'll enjoy visiting Warley Park, once you get there. It will be delightful.'

I don't think it will be delightful. The desperate words almost burst out of Cameo's mouth.
She didn't desire to go to Warley Park. For her
parents' sake she would obey but, oh, how she
yearned to stay in London, in Soho, to be precise. She had to see Benedict.

'Yes, Mama. I won't go anywhere tomorrow,'
Cameo replied.

It wasn't exactly lying if she slipped out tonight.

Chapter Eleven

⚜

'So home I went, but could not sleep…'
—Alfred, Lord Tennyson:
'The Gardener's Daughter'

Cameo pushed aside the chintz curtains and stared out her bedroom window. Fog drifted into the square. Beside her window the boughs of the ash tree gleamed faintly.

Even the ash tree couldn't soothe her now. Cameo kept hearing Benedict's voice in her head over and over again: *Don't come back to the studio until you're ready to tell me the truth*.

The decision had been made. She must tell him without delay. Would he, an artist, be able to see her real self and not just an aristocrat? Would he let her continue to model for him?

For hours she had waited for the house to quieten, to grasp her chance to slip out unobserved. Before dinner there had been no hope with her parents and George about and the servants going up and down the stairs. They hadn't dined until eight o'clock, and then she had sat through three courses: a consommé, thin and clear, followed by beef in puff pastry, with new spring vegetables, and for pudding, Bavarian cream with slivered almonds on top. Briggs offered it to her with a smile, knowing the pudding to be a favourite, but it had held no taste. Then, as usual, her papa and George had drunk port, but instead of going into the drawing room with her mama as she ordinarily did she had pleaded fatigue and come upstairs to pace the carpet.

The gold-and-blue enamel clock by her bed chimed. Ten o'clock. The chime decided her. She glanced down at her clothing. She still wore a low-cut green taffeta evening dress. She might as well wear it, since Benedict must be told the truth, but she swapped her evening slippers for a pair of black-kid boots. From her wardrobe she pulled out a black velvet cloak and threw it over her dress, covering it completely.

The room dimmed to darkness as she blew out the candles. Slipping on her kid gloves, she silently turned the brass knob of her bedroom door. In the hall the candles in the wall sconces were still flaming. All seemed quiet, although it was too risky to go down the main marble staircase. Hurrying along the carpeted hall in the other direction, she held her breath as she clicked open the latch of the small door that led to the backstairs and raced down. At the bottom the kitchen stood dim and empty, the range cold, the big scrubbed pine table bare. Thank goodness the servants had all gone to bed. It struck her that Bert might have been persuaded to deliver a note, but she didn't like to involve the servants. It was unfair. What was worse, all too easily she could imagine Benedict ripping such a note up in disgust.

Holding her breath, she tiptoed across the kitchen to turn the key in the lock of the side door and hastened out into the night.

Alone in the square in front of the house she hesitated. A sudden shaft of light beamed out as a maid opened the front door of the next house to welcome a gentleman pulling up in a carriage. She shrank out of sight behind an ash tree.

The square became dark and quiet again. The fog shrouding her in a dirty mist, her boots tapped out an echo in the gloom as she made her way to Oxford Street. It was so different to travel alone at night and on foot. As it was so late in the evening, she hadn't dared ask Bert to take her, either; he'd been reluctant enough about the evening outing to Mr Trelawney's soirée. It might get him into trouble.

Shivering, she nearly turned back. But to her

relief on the main road there were still plenty of people about. She could barely see them in spite of the yellow gaslights that lit each corner, but she could hear them: the strangers' voices as they came and went in the fog, their white faces startling her as they brushed past and the noisy clatter of horses' hooves and carriage wheels on the road alongside.

Panic built inside her as she travelled further and further away from Mayfair. The streets grew darker, the gaslight more sparse. After turning off Oxford Street she suspected she'd lost her way. A policeman swinging a truncheon gave her a searching stare as she came hurtling around a corner. She hesitated to ask him for directions, knowing he might ask why. He carried on without a word, his footsteps plodding away.

The streets felt different at night, too. She hurried along past the shops, the clothing stores, bookshops and tea shops, all shut up firmly, their blinds and awnings down. The public houses were open, though, noisy and lively. A woman stood outside one of them, guffawing at a man in a dinner coat as he tried to embrace her, while in an alleyway, she could have sworn she saw another man pressing a woman against a wall.

Her heart thumped. Oh, she should never have come out alone at night. George and Maud were right—she took too many risks. They'd be appalled if they knew her whereabouts. Only the thought of Benedict in the studio, wondering why she hadn't come that morning, urged her on.

'Out you go!' Right in front of her two men were forcibly ejected from a public house.

One of them stopped and stared at her. 'Well, what have we here?' he asked drunkenly, reaching for her arm.

Cameo dodged his grasp.

'There's no hurry,' he hiccoughed, as she sped past.

'Come on,' she heard his companion say. 'Let's try to get a drink somewhere else.' They staggered off in the other direction.

Narrowly missing being hit by a carriage, Cameo sped across to the other side of the road.

Benedict set down the glass, its contents spilling over the rim.

Damnation. He still didn't believe Miss Cameo Ashe, the best model he'd ever had, hadn't come back after the incident in the park. *The best model*, he mocked himself. *Yes, that's why you miss her, Cole, not because of the way she felt in your arms.*

He'd thought she possessed more courage than that. Who had she seen? Why had she been so frightened? All he had done was frighten her further. He needed her to trust him, to tell him what terrified her, because whoever she had seen made her very frightened indeed, he had glimpsed it in her eyes. He burned with the need to protect her. Why didn't she trust him enough to tell him the truth about herself, that she had a wealthy protector? Did she think he would judge her? He didn't judge her. Not judgement, no, that wasn't what he felt. Burning, searing jealousy. That was it.

As the hours had ticked on through the day it became clear she wouldn't be returning to the studio. He'd frightened her away.

If she came back, he'd vowed to give her time to tell him about herself. He'd bite down that burning jealousy from his gullet. He was hardly in a position to condemn her—he'd had enough relationships of his own. He wasn't a hypocrite. He knew what the world was like.

All the time she needed, that's what he'd give her, to tell him what she wanted him to know, whether he liked it or not. He'd never cared if other models had been with other men before. With Cameo, he did care. But he'd wait for her to reveal herself. If he had the chance.

All day he had carried on working on her portrait, but by nightfall he'd given up and come to the Lamb. He needed the distraction, the noise. It was the public house he frequented most, not merely because of its proximity and its good meals. He enjoyed the mix of people, the work-ing men and women with their forthrightness and humour, as well the many other artists and writers who lived and worked in this less-expen-sive, not to say less-salubrious, area of London.

The Lamb was full tonight, with people pressed at the bar, clustered in groups at the ta-bles and booths. Glasses clinked amidst conver-sation and laughter and at one table a voice was raised in song.

Over the broad mantelpiece there hung a painting of a young sheep with wide surprised eyes. The animal always looked to Benedict as though it was startled to find itself in such an establishment. The painting was covered in a layer of grime and the lamb's fleece showed up yellow instead of creamy white. Benedict often ached to clean that painting, for he suspected it to be rather fine. Beneath it a fire roared in the huge granite fireplace, casting a rosy glow on the faces of those who gathered near.

At the bar he ordered whisky. He noticed other artists of his acquaintance dining at a long table in one of the rooms at the rear. John Millais, al-ways the most easy-going of the Pre-Raphael-ite Brotherhood, gave him a friendly wave and beckoned him over to join them. Benedict shook his head and managed to find a quiet corner table. He didn't feel hungry and he desired to be alone. He was not fit company tonight.

He lifted the glass and stared into it as though the amber liquid revealed some hidden truth and tossed back a gulp, feeling its welcome burn as it went down his throat.

The confrontation with Miss Cameo Ashe still rang in his ears. He hadn't been able to take the lies, the evasions any more. He had only caught the merest glimpse of the man she so evidently wished to avoid, when she'd raced away from him in Hyde Park, her elegant ankles on display under her swirling skirts. He'd been too busy chasing her to take a proper look at the cause of her alarm.

'Well, hello.' Maisie stood in front of him, the high colour in her cheeks echoing the red flowers tucked deep in her bodice. Perhaps he could paint her like that, he thought, yet the idea held no appeal.

'Hello, Maisie.'

'I haven't seen you in here for a few days. You look like you could do with some company.'

She slid down next to him, squeezing on to the tapestry-fabric seat and he smelled her fruity scent. Her breasts peeped over her tight corset and he sensed other men in the room wishing they were the ones with Maisie Jones thrust up against them.

She offered him the buck-toothed smile he once found so sensual and enchanting. Another smile came into his mind. He gripped his glass hard and tossed back another gulp of whisky.

'You're looking pretty tonight,' he complimented Maisie, driving that other smile away.

She preened. 'That's because I'm near you,' she whispered breathily, pressing her leg even closer against his. 'No one was ever as good to me as you were, Benedict.'

He sent her an amused smile. 'What about all the painting? I thought you hated that.'

'You were kind to me. You always treated me with respect. You're different from other men.' She slipped a hand inside his thigh and gave him a knowing grin. 'And we were good together, weren't we?'

He wanted to want her. To lose himself in her and forget the woman who haunted his days and nights in a way no woman ever had before. His body gave an involuntary throb at Maisie's suggestive movement. But that was all, just a reflex action. He didn't desire her, he realised, even as her fingers crept higher up his thigh.

He stood abruptly, causing Maisie's hand to fall away.

She stared up at him in surprise. 'What is it? Are you leaving?'

He nodded as he reached for his brown coat.

She pouted prettily. 'You're no fun any more, Benedict.'

He brushed her cheek with his finger. 'Take care of yourself, Maisie.'

As if sensing the finality in his voice she sat still for a moment. Then she shrugged and undulated over to one of the tables by the fire where she was greeted with raucous exclamations of pleasure, laughing as a young man pulled her down onto his lap.

Benedict couldn't have Maisie as a model again, he knew that now. He needed Cameo Ashe. With her as his model he was reaching artistic heights he had never dreamed possible. If she came back to the studio he would resist pressuring her to tell him who she was or about the men in her life. Maybe it was better not to know.

No more questions. He promised himself.

If Cameo comes back.

With a sigh of relief, through the fog Cameo spotted the public-house sign with a lamb on it.

Raindrops fell. After lifting the hood of her cloak more fully over her head, she gripped the comforting talisman of her necklace.

'I think I'll have that.'

Cameo jumped. She twisted to find a short, thickset man close behind her, his grey cap set low, obscuring the top half of his face. The lower part wore an ugly grimace.

She choked down a scream. 'What?'

Rapidly the man scanned the area. 'A pretty girl like you. Out alone?'

Her mouth went dry as she peered frantically through the fog. No one else in sight. No one to come to her aid.

'Only you and me here, lovely,' the man went on with a sneer. 'Now, what have you got there? A fancy jewel?'

Cameo backed away, the sound of her pulse thudding in her ears. 'You're mistaken, sir.'

'Sir, eh? Come on now. Can't mistake quality, even in this fog. There's no missing it. Easy does it. Pass it over.'

'No, I won't let you have it!'

The smell of ale came from his moist lips as he moved closer. His leer crawled over her, 'Hoity-toity, aren't you? And as pretty as your jewellery, I see. Now make it easy for yourself.'

He lunged.

'No!'

Cameo tried to run, but he moved too fast. Thrusting out his leg to block her flight, with greedy fingers he prised at her fist.

'No! You won't have it!'

'Be quiet,' the man hissed, his rancid breath on her face. 'Just let me have it and there won't be any trouble.' With his teeth bared like a dog, his fingers grabbed at her throat.

Benedict threw back the last of his whisky and went outside. Rain fell. He put up his collar, the cold drops a relief after the warmth of the pub. But it didn't cool his mood.

He rounded for home. He'd only ventured a few steps when he felt a tug on his coat. Pivoting on his heel, he saw the match girl. 'What is it, Becky? You're out late tonight.'

She tugged at his coat again, pulling him back towards the Lamb. She pointed urgently across the road.

'What's the matter?' he asked.

A voice cried out through the fog. In the dim lamplight opposite he made out the shape of a woman half-fallen on to the ground, struggling, a man crouched over her.

Benedict roared and began to run. 'Stop!'

Startled, the man lifted his head, his lips drawn in a snarl like an animal interrupted from his prey.

'Get off her!' With a mighty jerk, Benedict reached out and grabbed the man's rough coat, hauling him off the woman in a single movement. 'Get off her, I say!'

The man cursed and stumbled as Benedict slammed him to his feet. The other man was shorter than Benedict by a head, but he felt the smaller man's toughness as they tussled. Still holding on to his opponent's coat, Benedict shoved the man up against the lamp post, his forearm barred against his thick neck.

Wily, the man ducked. Slippery as an eel, he slipped out and under Benedict's hold. His footsteps clattered as he raced down the street, dropping something that clinked as it fell to the ground.

Benedict stared down at the woman who lay at his feet. With mounting horror he recognised the dark hair tumbling from beneath the woman's hood, the deep violet-grey eyes enormous with fear. 'My God. Cameo!'

Blood roared in his ears as he knelt down beside her.

Her head was thrown back, a pulse flickering at her vulnerable white throat.

'Benedict?' Her lips formed his name.

Anger at the man who'd got away surged inside him. Trying to contain his fury, he pushed her hair away from her colourless face. 'Did he hurt you?'

She winced as she raised herself up. 'No, you came in time.'

'What on earth are you doing here alone?'

Her lips were white. 'I came to see you. I

couldn't come earlier today. I wanted to. Please. You must believe me.'

He never dreamt she would come so late at night, alone through the dangerous London streets. Thank goodness Becky had spotted her. He peered around for the girl. She'd gone, melted away into the fog.

A muscle worked in his cheek. 'Don't concern yourself with that now. Can you stand?' He spanned her tiny waist. 'Let me help you.'

Grimacing, she got to her feet and stumbled against him, so slender he felt she might snap. She leant her head momentarily on his chest. His heart thumped as he held her.

'My necklace!'

So that was what the man had dropped. Benedict scanned the street and spotted something lying on the cobbles. Leaving Cameo leaning against the lamp post, he went to pick it up, his hand closing on the stone.

Still glaring down the street, he ached to chase the thief, to make him pay for what he'd done, but he went back to her. He refused to leave her shaking like a leaf. 'I've got it. Steady now. You must come to the studio.'

After a tottering step forward, she half collapsed against the lamp post.

Without a word he swept her up in his arms. The hood of her cloak fell back as the scent of violets rose from her hair. She was feather light, her skirt and petticoats frothing into lacy foam.

She struggled against him. 'You don't need to carry me!'

'You've been hurt.'

'I can walk!'

'Don't argue.'

With a shuddering sigh she subsided, her head dropping on to his shoulder. Holding her tight, he strode down the street and through the alley, shoved his back against the ground-floor door to open it and carried her up the stairs.

Chapter Twelve

'Love with knit brows went by,
And with a flying finger swept my lips,
And spake…'

—Alfred, Lord Tennyson:
'The Gardener's Daughter'

Moonlight shone through the bare windows of the cold studio, glittering on the bottles of paint-brushes by the easel. The studio felt different in the dark, Cameo thought with a dazed look over Benedict's shoulder, as though she were viewing part of it she hadn't discovered before. It was like a dream she'd had once, when she visited a house she knew, only to discover an unknown room.

Gently Benedict lowered her on to the chaise longue and loosened her cloak from her shaking body. There were marks on the black velvet from the muddy street. Her hands went to her neck. Perhaps there were marks there, too. She shivered.

'Rest,' he instructed. 'I'll light the lamp.'

Released from his arms, Cameo continued to shake. At the fireplace she watched him strike a match, the flame illuminating the hard set of his jaw. He lit the lamp and hauled off his coat and scarf, tossing them down on to the armchair. With lithe movements he crouched to ignite the fire and threw on some logs, his muscular body outlined in the shadows.

She knew the full strength of that body now. Benedict Cole was a man who lifted women as easily as he lifted logs, as if they were mere twigs. And the ruthless way he had thrown the thief from on top of her... It had been terrifying, seeing him take on the thief, but she had never experienced such relief as when she'd heard his voice, seen his face, through the fog.

Helplessly, Cameo tried to slow her racing breaths. She watched Benedict move around the studio, heard the crackle of the fire, the tick of the clock slower than her heartbeat. Her body continued to tremble and her speeding pulse did not abate until she could no longer explain it by her scare outside. No, a painful jolt of her heart told her. She'd been frightened out on the street, but even more frightening were the emotions raging through her now.

From between her eyelashes she stole another shaky peep across the room to where Benedict stood stoking the fire. Her mouth dried as she stared at him anew. How could she fool herself any more? Benedict Cole alone, not painting lessons, had brought her to the studio through the fog, through the dark and dangerous London streets. She came to the studio not only for art's sake, not any more. She came to the studio for the sake of the artist.

When Benedict Cole had carried her up the stairs in his strong arms, she'd known she never wanted to leave those arms, not ever again. She wanted to stay there, cradled against his chest, breathing him in, her lips close to the skin of his warm neck.

She loved him.

Benedict pivoted and saw her watching him. 'How are you feeling?'

'I'm quite all right.' Her voice made a contradictory whisper.

The smell of smoke reached her as the fire roared into full life. He prodded the logs with the poker before he reached for a whisky bottle on the chimney piece and found a glass.

'You've had a shock. I'm not sure if you drink

whisky, but I think in these circumstances it's medicinal.'

Returning to the chaise longue, he held out the glass.

'Thank you. I think I need some whisky.' Fumbling, she slipped off her gloves and wrapped two hands around the glass like an unsteady child, took a huge gulp and spluttered.

A smile played on his lips as he removed the glass and placed it on the floor. 'Perhaps not.'

He brooded over her for a moment. 'Do you wish me to call for a doctor?'

'No, I'm not hurt.' That wasn't what she felt. 'I can't thank you enough for saving me. You came just in time.'

He folded his arms. 'It certainly looked that way.'

'I'm sorry I couldn't come today.' No longer could she deceive the man she loved. 'I want to explain about what happened in the park and—'

'That doesn't matter now,' he interrupted. 'None of that matters. Not any more. What happened outside?'

'I'd just seen the public house, the Lamb, and I went to cross the road when that horrible man came up and grabbed me. I felt so terrified. He tried to get my cameo.' She struggled up. 'My necklace!'

'Don't worry. I've got it here.' He pulled it

from his pocket, dangled it on the black ribbon. He gave a faint smile. 'You don't seem yourself without it. Shall I put it back on for you?'

Her reply was a mere nod. She couldn't manage any more.

In the silence lengthening between them, her breaths grew uneven as he tied it around her neck. His fingers traced the carved stone, touched the soft hollow of her skin. His touch left her breathless.

'The stone's not damaged,' he said. 'And there's no bruising on your skin. Do you think you sustained any other injury?'

She shook her head. She felt no pain in her body, not with Benedict so close.

'But you slipped.'

'Oh, yes.' She winced, remembering. 'I hit my head on the cobbles.'

'May I examine you?' He leant over her, his fingers pressing through her hair, gentle but firm. 'It would be easier if your hair wasn't up in this—'

'Overdone style?' she broke in irrepressibly, recalling how he had described her hairstyle the first day she'd come to the studio.

Benedict had the grace to laugh. 'You're obviously not too badly hurt then, since your wits remain. But if I might loosen it… May I?'

Still breathless, she nodded. She might have heard a hairpin drop, so quiet it became between them, as one by one he removed the thin curves of metal, cupping them in his hand as the strands of hair tumbled to her shoulders.

The hairpins set aside, his fingers once again searched her tender scalp.

'There's no skin broken.' He removed his hands just as she thought she could handle no more of his firm pressure seeming to loosen every muscle of her body. 'You might have a lump in a day or so, I suspect. Do you have a headache?'

'No, I don't have a headache. I just had a fright.'

'You're safe now.' His voice caressed her with reassuring warmth. 'You're safe here with me, Cameo.'

'You called me Cameo,' she said in wonder. 'And when you saved me on the street, you called me Cameo then, too.'

He sent her a wry smile. 'I think we've strayed beyond the social niceties now you're here in my studio in the middle of the night. And perhaps you can call me Benedict from now on. You did on the street.'

'Did I?' To cover her sudden confusion she reached for the whisky glass and swallowed an enormous gulp.

'Easy. That's strong stuff.'

Carefully she replaced the glass on the table, her fingers not quite obeying.

'Lie back now.'

With the whisky running hot through her veins, she did as he commanded, her head lolling against the curve of the chaise longue.

'That's better. I think you're going to have to stay for a while.'

'For the whole night? Here? In the studio with you?' The words tumbled from her mouth as she tried to raise herself up. Her pulse thumped at the idea.

'I don't anticipate you staying all night. But you do need to recuperate.' With narrowed eyes he continued to brood over her. 'You must stay still.' With a teasing half curve of a smile he added, 'Perhaps I should paint you, keep you lying down. You suit the subject of the portrait very well tonight, with your hair loose. Yes, you suit it very well. Except for your dress, of course.'

For a long moment she stared up at him, her mind awhirl, her heart racing. With a swish of her skirts she slid from the chaise longue.

'What are you doing? I told you to rest.'

'You said you wanted to paint me.' Cameo's cheeks flamed. 'Might it be easier…if I wore my chemise?'

* * *

Benedict scanned Cameo's flushed face as he tried to find words in his dry mouth. 'You've been hurt. You should rest.'

'I'm feeling much better already,' she protested. She had colour back in her cheeks, it was true. 'It must have been the whisky. I'm well enough to pose.'

He fell back on his heels. 'Are you sure?'

'Yes…and…'

'What is it?'

'When I first came to the studio, you told me the subject of your painting wore a simple white dress.'

'That's right.'

'You said I could pose in my normal attire, but surely it will be easier to paint my form—' she swallowed the word '—in my chemise.'

His senses flared up like a stoked fire. 'Ah, yes. Your form.'

'My chemise is white, you see. I can…un-dress…if that's what you need.'

The instant quickening in his loins he forced himself to ignore. 'I don't require you to do that. The painting is coming along well. As for your form—as an artist I've studied anatomy of both the male and the female. I can use my knowledge and—' his inspection lingered over her body '—my imagination.'

Her cheeks coloured more crimson. 'Will it be easier if I undress?'

The room became still, except for the sound of her rapid breathing.

'It might,' he admitted at last.

'You'll have to help me remove my gown,' she said. 'It has buttons at the back. I can't reach all of them.'

'Cameo. Are you sure?'

In silent answer she twirled and with a graceful movement lifted up her hair.

The back of her neck appeared slender and vulnerable, soft tendrils of midnight-black hair curling about. Benedict swallowed hard as her violet scent assailed him and restrained himself from putting his lips to that tender skin. Forcing himself to focus on his task, he found the small jet-black buttons holding together the green dress. It was one he'd never seen her wear before, an evening gown of exquisite work. It confirmed his suspicions, but he couldn't think about that now. Slowly he undid the buttons, down, right down, to where they ended at the small of her back.

Clutching the fabric of the dress in front of her, she spun to face him. His pulse sped as she lifted her chin and let the fabric fall. With a rustle the gown slid down over her petticoats as it dropped to the floor.

She stepped out of the pool of emerald at her feet. Unable to speak, he beheld the hint of her breasts beneath the whiteness of her chemise on its delicate lacy shoulders, above the boned corset that cinched her waist into a perfect hourglass.

'I can do my petticoats myself.'

Before he could respond, Cameo released foamy white layers which followed her dress to the floor: a silk outer petticoat, another with a heavy-weighted hem, then one, two, three, four, five, six lighter ones, all frills and lace and silk and cotton and scalloped edges.

She turned her back, lifting her hair once again. 'Please help me take off my corset. It's tight.'

God help him if he moved now. 'Cameo…'

'It's uncomfortable,' she insisted, without turning. 'I'll be able to pose for longer without it. Please.'

She waited.

'Please.'

Cursing his stiff fingers, he found the laces of the corset and freed her from its cruel constraints. Neatly she caught it in front of her and cast it aside as she spun to face him.

He couldn't look away.

'"Gown'd in pure white, that fitted to the shape…"' he muttered, quoting to himself. Her natural, unrestrained curves were even more beautiful than when she wore a corset, the outline of her torso a slender stalk beneath the cotton.

Cameo didn't seem to hear him. 'What about my drawers?' Her lower lip jutted out doubtfully as she contemplated her legs where the cotton chemise ended beguilingly at their lace edges above her stockinged knee.

'No.' The curt command escaped him. He would lose control himself if she removed those, let alone be able paint her.

He waited a moment.

'Lie down,' he said at last, his voice husky. Then he frowned. 'I don't want you to get cold. I'll build up the fire.'

At the fireplace he threw on logs and made it blaze. Taking the iron poker, he thrust it among the flames, its tip red-hot. 'Are you warm enough?'

'Yes. I meant to ask—what about my necklace?'

'It's part of you,' he responded without thinking. 'Leave it on. I won't put it in the painting.'

Her curls went tumbling as she inclined her head. 'How do you desire me to pose? As before?'

'Almost. Let's try some changes. I'd prefer

you to recline more to appear natural. Imagine you're lying under a tree.'

In a graceful movement she curved her hip so she lay almost on her side, tucking her legs up on to the chaise longue.

Benedict frowned. Her instinctive pose seemed perfect, but there was something wrong.

'I'm going to have to undo this.' He pointed to her black boot. 'Your feet should be bare. May I?'

He witnessed her teeth catch her lip as he slid off the boot and dropped it to the floor. His hand hovered over her calf and he felt her muscles tense beneath his hold.

'And your stockings?' His fingers moved down her silk-clad leg in the slightest of caresses. 'I'll be careful. They're so fine. It's a shame to tear them.'

Permission was granted by the slightest lowering of her head. He lifted up her chemise, his whole body tensing, and forced himself to concentrate as he folded it over her thighs. His blood pumped as he pushed the lacy edges of her drawers up until the top of her white stocking lay revealed, held up by a blue-ribbon garter. He heard a sigh escape her as he brushed the tender skin of her inner thigh untying the blue ribbon. Time slowed as he unfurled the fragile stocking, peeling it down her leg, like a petal opening to reveal the interior of a bloom.

His body hardened. How he managed to repeat the process with the other slender leg he had no idea, as he seized hold of her hip, shifting her into a reclining position on her side, one knee slightly in front of the other, her head tilted. 'Can you stay in that pose?'

'Yes.'

Every animal instinct in him fought as he went to the easel. Desire raged as jealousy kicked him in the gut. Jealousy that another man had touched her, held her as he wanted to hold her. There could be no uncertainty now. She'd come to him in the dark of night, on foot, not in the carriage owned by her wealthy protector, wearing her evening gown because she had to hide coming to him. Perhaps it was fear, perhaps it was shame. Whatever it was, he disdained to make it harder for her.

Only an artist could have walked away from her at that moment, he reflected with a bitter twist of a smile. Yet he needed time to collect himself, make sense of what he had experienced outside. The way he'd found her, lying there on the street. He still yearned to find the thief and tear him limb from limb. It enraged him anyone wanted to hurt Cameo. *Cameo.* It felt right, speaking her name at last. How long since he'd stopped calling her Miss Ashe in his mind? He hardly remembered.

Not bothering with his painting shirt, he lifted his palette, squeezed some paint out on to the board. 'Damnation,' he muttered, as too much spurted out. Forcing himself to pick up his brush, he assessed her as she lay in her simple white garments. The moonlight shining through the windows transformed her skin to a pearly sheen. He had never seen her look so lovely, with a purity combined with a sensuality he could barely resist. With an inner groan he dipped the brush into the paint and began to outline her body on the canvas.

Soon the familiar focus found him in spite of his body's need. She was right, the chemise helped. He'd guessed the proportions of her body correctly, though her legs were longer than he'd first assumed and the smoothness of her arms he'd barely imagined. He worked on, faster than he had ever worked before, steady and sure.

He wasn't sure how much time had passed before he noticed her shivering through the cotton of her chemise.

The paintbrush clattered to the floor as he leapt up. 'I've let the fire go down.'

After stoking the flames, he went to her. 'I'm sorry you became cold. I lost track of time. It was coming so fast.'

A shake of her head sent dark curls spiralling. 'I just need to move.'

He felt his own body tauten as she stretched like a cat beside him, arching her back. He ran his hand through his hair. 'How are you feeling now? No after-effects from your scare on the street?'

'No, not at all.'

'Do you need to take a break from posing?' He quirked his eyebrow and added, 'Perhaps you'd appreciate more whisky.'

She laughed. 'No, I'm quite well. But I've been thinking, while you were working,' she spoke with sudden shyness, 'about the painting's subject. I'm curious. I thought you quoted a line of poetry before. Was it from the poem for this painting?'

He nodded. 'I told you, I think, this portrait is based upon a poem by Tennyson.'

'Yes, but you never told me which poem.' She smiled, suddenly mischievous. 'You were most mysterious, Mr Cole.'

'Perhaps it's time for that mystery to be revealed.'

Cameo watched as Benedict took out a battered leather-bound volume from the bookshelf by the fire. Even the stretch of his shoulder as he reached for it sent a tremor through her.

'May I?' He indicated the space beside her.

Cameo moved aside with a gulp. 'Yes, of course.' Her stomach contracted as Benedict stood beside her next to the chaise longue, her awareness of him heightened by the fact she wore only her chemise, her legs bare. She still felt amazed at her boldness in undressing for him, but she didn't regret it. It felt right, not wrong.

Watching him paint had only increased her certainty. As he worked she had made a decision. She would stay with him tonight, for as long as he allowed her to remain. Explanations, confessions, they could come later.

Not tonight.

She loved him.

With a finger Benedict opened the book. Her stomach experienced another of those tight surges, lower down.

'The painting is based on a poem entitled "The Gardener's Daughter; or, The Pictures". It's one of Tennyson's early works.' He riffled through the pages. 'It's long and I'm not using it all, but there's a description of a woman. I'll read part of it.'

Benedict's voice became a caress.

'A certain miracle of symmetry,
A miniature of loveliness, all grace

Summ'd up…she
So light of foot, so light of spirit—oh, she
To me myself, for some three careless
moons,
The summer pilot of an empty heart
Unto the shores of nothing! Know you not
Such touches are but embassies of love…
She…said to me, she sitting with us then,
"When will *you* paint like this?" and I re-
plied,
(My words were half in earnest, half in
jest,)
"'Tis not your work, but Love's. Love, un-
perceived,
A more ideal Artist he than all,
Came, drew your pencil from you, made
those eyes
Darker than darkest pansies, and that hair
More black than ashbuds in the front of
March."'

Slowly he laid the book down on the chaise
longue between them.

Cameo's pulse pounded. No words came from
her mouth. If she opened her lips now, she would
only be able to tell him—*she loved him*.

'Do you understand?' His voice was husky.
'When I first saw you I knew you were the one.
You're the girl from the poem.'

'Me?' Tears threatened to brim over her lashes.

'I didn't dare believe it.' He leant forward and touched her hair. 'You came, in the month of March no less, with your hair as black as ash buds and your eyes like the hearts of deepest pansies. It wasn't merely your likeness to the poet's description. I'm an artist and yet it was as if I never saw a woman before I saw you.'

Cameo couldn't take her eyes from his face.

Benedict hollowed a laugh. 'To think I chose that particular poem believing I could paint its subject! I don't think I ever truly painted before, because I hadn't been touched in the way the poet describes. The poem captures how everything changes, even for an artist, when we see with the eyes…'

He fell silent.

Cameo could barely breathe. 'With the eyes…?'

'Of love.' His voice seemed to brush her heart. 'I couldn't believe it and yet I fought it. Cameo.'

The book of poems slipped to the floor as Benedict's lips came down on hers, her chemise crushing against him as he explored her mouth with exquisite force. Her fingers grasped the edge of his shirt, finding his hot, muscled skin as she sought his ardent lips, his searching tongue, sensing the building of his body's hard desire.

'I yearned to do this from the moment I saw your cameo necklace,' he murmured as his mouth moved over her chin down to her neck. 'I longed to put my lips to that beautiful skin…'

With a sigh her head fell back against the chaise longue. He trailed melting kisses along her throat, around the cameo stone, finding touch points to send tremors shuddering through her core and flashing circles of light inside her head.

She slid underneath him; let his lips trace the rapid rise and fall of her breasts through the lace of her chemise. Fingers of sharp desire pierced her as his teeth tore away the delicate fabric, to tease with his tongue the delicate rosebuds of her breasts.

'Benedict.' The word was a moan.

'You're saying my name.'

With a ragged breath he came to meet her mouth, his fingers sweeping her breast, where his lips had been.

'Say it again,' he instructed, close against her lips.

'Say what, Mr Cole?' She managed to find a teasing tone amidst her shudders.

On the tip of her breast his fingers firmed, quivering her into submission.

'Benedict.'

His pressure relented. 'I find it difficult to resist you. I thought you had a lover. I thought you wanted someone else.'

'You thought I had a lover? Benedict, no. It was you I wanted. But when you first kissed me—you said you were sorry for it, do you remember?' She gave a mock pout.

Benedict smiled ruefully as he drew away and ran his fingers through his hair. 'I was sorry. I had to keep some defences raised. I knew what I'd unleashed. I didn't seek this with my model.' His lips tightened. 'I must be honest with you. I had a relationship with Maisie.'

Cameo recalled her instinctive jealousy of the beautiful blonde, tasted it on her tongue. She raised herself up on to her elbows, unable to keep the words from spilling out. 'Maisie is beautiful.'

'Yes, she is.' Benedict stroked her cheek. 'And so are you. I told you artists see in terms of light and shade. It's comparing sunlight to moonlight.' A tingle ran through her as his voice deepened. 'I like moonlight best.'

He encircled her in his arms and she nestled into them. 'Don't believe I always become intimate with my models. I'm not that sort of man. That's why I tried so hard to resist you. I knew what you were doing to me. It seemed safer to keep you at a distance.'

'So you were purposely that way?' Sternly

she sat up in his arms. 'You've been quite temperamental, Mr Cole.'

'Perhaps I was brusquer with you than I ought to have been. It was only because I desired you so much.' He curled a strand of her hair around his finger. 'I can't believe it's such a short time ago that you came into my studio. It feels as if you have always been in my mind, as if I've always been hoping for you, waiting for you to appear. I'll never forget that moment when you released your hair.'

'You seemed so angry with me then,' she recalled. It seemed long ago.

'I've told you why. It was the power of my feelings for you. When you didn't come today, I realised my feelings. I thought I'd scared you away.' He took her in his arms again. 'This is rare, Cameo.'

Dizziness engulfed her as again his mouth found hers. A diamond burst of passion exploded inside her as she yielded to him, allowing him to search her mouth deeply, her tongue passionately seeking his in return. The taste of him was known to her now, the warmth of his lips, the coolness of his tongue, the pressure that inflamed her. She clung to him, needing his kiss to last for ever, to go deeper, deeper.

'Just paint me, Benedict,' Cameo whispered in a voice she hardly recognised when at last he released her. 'Paint me.'

Chapter Thirteen

'The drowsy hours, dispensers of all good,
O'er the mute city stole with folded wings...
Love at first sight, first-born, and heir to all,
Made this night thus.'

—Alfred, Lord Tennyson:
'The Gardener's Daughter'

'Cameo—'

'Benedict.' She pressed herself almost wantonly against him.

He groaned. In a single movement he picked her up and carried her to his bed. She imprinted her lips on his warm neck, hearing him release another deep groan as he laid her against the pillows.

Benedict's eyes turned black with desire as he leaned over her. 'Are you sure?'

His index finger swept the tip of her breast, hardening it through the cotton.

Cameo's stomach contracted, low down. She knew her eyes must be giving him the same message. Her decision had been made, watching him paint. 'Yes. I'm sure.'

Surprising her into a gasp, his hands searched underneath her petticoat, sliding her drawers down over her legs in a swift, taut movement. Casting them aside, he studied her, the rippling effect on her skin even more powerful than his touch. 'I've longed to see you like this.'

'And like this?' Cameo didn't pause. Momentarily her chemise formed a veil between them as she lifted it over her head. With only the slightest sense of shyness she fell naked against the cotton sheets.

Still holding her captive with his scrutiny, he sent the dress sailing away across the wooden floor, to float into a white cloud across the floorboards.

His gaze lingered over her bare skin.

Silence shivered between them.

'You said you wanted me to paint you,' he said at last, his voice husky.

Mystified, she watched as he went to the easel. Taking a fresh paintbrush he brought it to where she lay.

'Will you let me?' His strong body silhouetted in the light, he leant over her. 'I want my brush to discover every part of you.'

At her tremulous nod, Benedict put the tip of the paintbrush to her forehead and, light as a feather, traced it over her face, down her nose, across her cheeks, around her mouth, causing her lips to circle and part. With all the attention he gave as an artist to his canvas, so he touched her now. Downwards he stroked, over her chin, along her throat, behind her ears, finding pleasure points to make her quiver as he watched. The light edge of the bristles moved along her arms to caress each fingertip, only to come back again, just as slowly, almost lazily, looping inwards towards the delicate, hardened tips of her breasts.

Even more deliberate now, a tender torture, his brush moved downwards over her stomach. She tensed as he went further still, veering at the last moment to trail up and down each thigh, along her calves. At her feet the brush danced lightly, tickling her toes, before it moved slowly, so slowly, up to the crevice between her legs.

Cameo stiffened. His brush circled, teasing her, playing with her. Instinctively, she arched her back, as deep, excruciating darts of pleasure spread inside.

'Benedict,' she murmured, closing her eyes as the room began to spin. 'Benedict.'

The feeling spread deeper still. The brush flicking. Teasing. Tantalising. A wave broke over her, in her. Then pleasure, such as she had never imagined. Waves of it. Shudders. Gasps.

Just when she thought to swoon away he stood, left her quivering on the bed. In a single sleek movement, he lifted his shirt over his head, his chest muscles flexing, to reveal his strong arms and dark-haired chest. She remembered how he'd torn one of his shirts. She knew why, now.

With a flick of his button, he released his trousers. She'd never seen a man naked before, except for a marble statue at a museum, which her nanny had hurried her away from. She hadn't realised he would be as magnificent as this.

'You…you're a sculpture,' Cameo said impulsively, awed.

Benedict grinned briefly as he joined her on the bed, his nakedness like a hot flame against her skin. 'Not one of Nicholas Trelawney's, I hope.'

A breath escaped her, ending on a suddenly nervous note she couldn't disguise.

Gently he cupped her face. 'Cameo.'

Her breath escaped again.

He kissed her, slowly, languorously, until the fluttering in her stomach unfurled.

'My paintbrush knows you now,' he whispered into her ear. 'Will you let me discover inside you? Is this what you desire?'

'You're my desire,' she whispered. She knew it then. No going back. No regrets. For a moment she'd felt a qualm, but he'd kissed it away. She would never seek a society marriage. This was her chance of experiencing love, if only for a little while, in Benedict's arms.

It was worth any risk.

Lowering his dark head, he took the pink tip of one breast into his mouth, while at the same time, between her parted thighs his hand found its way towards the most delicate part of her that no man had touched. She jerked against his searching fingers inside her, waves of desire rocking her from within with strange urgency, while his hardness pressed against her, his powerful pulse a match to the throbbing of her heart.

He came back up. 'I can't wait much longer.' His words brushed against her lips.

'Don't wait...' she breathed.

He shifted, raised her wrists above her head. Her fingers caught against the wooden bedhead, felt the carved leaves and buds as he found his mark.

A sharp pain.

A slight frown as he drew away momentarily. Puzzled.

She lifted her hips for more, needing him. Yearning for him to go on.

He shafted deeper.

Now she released her cry of pain mixed with joy, as he entered, thrusting deep inside. He muffled her cry in his mouth.

As her peak built with his, he tore his lips away.

'You're my muse.' Benedict's voice became a throaty rasp. 'Do you understand what that means?'

Cameo lifted her body to meet him as he went deeper, into her very soul. 'I know what it means. I'm yours.'

Benedict glanced over to where Cameo lay asleep, naked beside him. Her breathing sounded slow and steady, rhythmically lifting her bare breasts up and down. Yet he lay awake, still stunned by her physical response. He'd guessed she possessed passion inside her, he saw it while painting her. For him it had been impossible not to sense it, but even so...

As she slept, her hand tucked under her pale cheek, he kept watch over her. He yearned to paint her that way, of course, as he wanted to paint her in every aspect, every mood. The moonlight came in through the window, silvering her skin with its gentle light. The softness of her skin he had barely been able to believe; it was as though she had been bathed in milk and honey since birth.

He frowned. There was something else. He'd felt it inside her, that moment of surrender. She was so perfect. A bud.

The tightness, the momentary barrier he'd discovered. It had made him suspect…

No. Impossible. There were no other signs. The man in the park who owned the black-crested carriage, surely he'd touched Cameo first, though the mere thought inflamed Benedict.

Yet that moment of sweet resistance…

Unable to lie still any longer, he got up, wrapped his dressing gown around him and went to the window, frowning as he stared out. Soon the sun would streak the sky gold and below in the street there came the sounds of the first of the market carts rolled in for the day.

'Benedict.' A soft touch on his shoulder. 'What's the matter?'

At her voice, he pivoted to find her standing beside him, her slim body wrapped in a white sheet like a toga, her dark hair tumbling over one shoulder.

'You look like a Roman goddess. I should paint you that way.' He crooked a mocking smile. 'I always want to paint you, don't I?'

'Why are you awake?' She seemed to sense he wasn't as light-hearted as he tried to sound. 'Will you tell me what's wrong?'

He reached over and ran his hand down from her lips to her neck, to where her breasts disappeared beneath the swathes of sheet. 'You haven't been entirely honest with me, have you?'

She froze.

He encircled her wrist. 'When were you planning to tell me?'

A whimper escaped as she tried to pull her wrist free.

He tightened his grip. 'Your bones are so delicate, like a bird. I held a bird once. It flew into our cottage. It flapped its wings against the window, unable to break free. I caught it. I felt its tiny bones beneath the feathers before I carried it outside and released it to the sky.'

In reply he turned her palm upward, lifting it to his lips. Pure white, as soft as snowfall. But he knew the clues. 'I know your secret.'

'My secret...'

'I can tell by these. By the paint caught in your fingernails. By the way you watch me work. By the way you sketch. By the way you observe the world. You're an artist. Aren't you?'

She almost collapsed into his arms with relief. He sensed her worry that he meant to ask her another burning question. But he refused to pressure her about that, either. Not now. He didn't want to hear any other man's name on her lips. Tonight was theirs alone.

'You knew,' she murmured.

'All along. Did you think you could fool me into believing you were a mere model? But you've always been more than that.' He reached out and drew her closer, laid her palm flat against his dressing gown, so she felt his hardness. 'You standing there in the moonlight does this to me.'

She leaned over and lifted the paintbrush from the table where he'd left it beside the bed. 'Come back to bed. It's my turn now.'

Once more she surprised him, guiding him as he lay down on the bed. She let the sheet fall completely away from her and stood for a moment in her nakedness, her breasts high, her waist curving sweetly above her rounded hips. Her hair formed a curtained shadow over her face as she joined him on the bed and straddled him, her slim legs bent on either side of his hips.

'Don't move.' She dropped the paintbrush. 'Wait. Will you let me…use my fingers?'

Benedict groaned his assent. He exhaled as she plied her hand in imitation of the way he'd teased her with the soft bristles of the brush earlier, flicking her fingertips first across his brow and cheeks, circling his mouth, and then taking her hand down his neck to the swirls of dark hair covering his chest.

Shifting her body backwards caused her breasts to form two tender points over him, as with slow movements her hand strayed further still down to his darker hair below. Tentative to start, unpractised, her caress grew more confident as she stroked steadily, until he feared his strength in holding back.

Just when he thought himself in danger, he reached for her and rolled her beneath him, slid inside. Her tightness, her moistness told him she, too, was deeply aroused. She rocked her hips and he moved, too, in an instinctive rhythm to match hers, diving further, deeper, as he kissed her hard and spilled her name into her mouth as he came.

He fell away to lie beside her as her high breasts heaved with her ragged breathing. It took him a moment to catch his own breath before he said, 'You're quite an artist.'

She laughed.

'I learnt from a master,' she replied.

'It's the student who matters.' He ran a finger along the side of her face, along the profile he knew so well. 'Cameo. You're more than a model to me. Will you let me teach you?'

Her face was a glow of light, as though a sunburst had broken through a cloud above her head. 'Teach me to paint?'

'Yes. We'll have to start your art lessons,' he clarified, as he idly caressed the tip of her breast, 'among other things.'

'Really?'

'Really.'

Her smile said it all. Then she dived away, retrieved the paintbrush and dangled it in front of him.

The sheets dropped from her bare breasts as she rose up and the sight made him groan aloud.

'Perhaps I wish to remain an artist's model, after all,' she said saucily. 'I'm sure there are many other artists who might want me to pose for them, among the Pre-Raphaelite Brotherhood, perhaps?'

He grabbed the paintbrush. 'The only artist you'll model for is me,' he growled and, rearing up, pulled the sheets over their heads.

Chapter Fourteen

"'Now,' said he, 'will you climb to the top
of Art.
You cannot fail…'"

—Alfred, Lord Tennyson:
'The Gardener's Daughter'

Maud held out a swatch of blue fabric. 'What
do you think of this one?'

Leaning against the sofa, Cameo examined
the soft silk. 'It's lovely, Maud. Don't you think
it's a little soon to be planning the bridesmaids'
dresses?'

Maud giggled, her dimple appearing. 'You've
forgotten. I've been planning this for years. You
used to draw the dresses for me, don't you recall? I wish I still had some of those drawings.
They were lovely.' Maud lowered her voice and
darted a glance towards the velvet chairs by the
fireplace, where their mothers were inspecting

lace. 'Mama told me the other day that soon we'll all be wearing some kind of cage, a hoop to hold our skirts out. It's coming into fashion. Can you imagine? Now, consider this pale green. Or perhaps this violet blue—it's pretty and it suits your eyes.'

'I'm happy with any colour you choose. It will be your special day.' She gave her friend's arm an affectionate squeeze, yet as she spoke wistfulness crept over her like a climbing vine. She loved both George and Maud so much and she couldn't have been more pleased for them.

But they didn't need to lie about who they were. Or what they'd been doing.

The passion of her night at the studio with Benedict returned with a flush.

She loved Benedict Cole.

At dawn, when she had arrived home in a hackney cab Benedict hailed for her, she'd breathed a sigh of relief at managing the feat. She had worried she might not make it. She'd crept into the house through the kitchen and upstairs to her bedroom, her lips, her whole body aching for more of him. She'd tried to sleep, but instead had lain awake in a kind of blissful languor. She'd heard it whispered that lovemaking was painful. Apart from that first sting, it hadn't been, for her. She desired Benedict too much.

Even today the flicker of fire in her belly told her that her passion for him hadn't abated.

As she'd dressed in the morning she had stared at herself in the looking glass, studying her reflection. She appeared no different, yet she had given herself, completely, to Benedict Cole.

She could tell no one. Not even Maud, who loved her. Her friend would be shocked, deeply appalled to learn what Cameo had done. In the eyes of society, she was no longer chaste. But she felt no shame, no disgrace. There could be no shame or disgrace when there was such passion, such love. No, she would never regret making Benedict that gift.

Maud's gentle touch on her sleeve brought her back to the drawing room. 'Is something wrong?'

'No.' Nothing was wrong. Everything was right, in her heart.

'You can't fool me,' Maud said. 'What is it? What's happened?'

What had happened between her and Benedict was too sacred to share.

Instead, Cameo pointed to her necklace. 'Last night someone tried to relieve me of this.'

'Do you mean you were robbed?' Maud sounded terrified.

'Yes. A thief tried to grab my jewellery and he pushed me down on to the street.'

Maud fanned her face. 'I would have had hysterics! It sounds frightful. Are you quite all right?'

'Oh, yes. Someone—' her heart gave a thump just thinking about Benedict and the way he'd swept her up in his arms '—someone came to help me and luckily the thief didn't get away with it.'

'Where did it happen?' Maud glanced anxiously around the drawing room as if the thief might instantly appear.

'Don't worry. It didn't happen in Mayfair.'

It had happened in Soho, near the studio. Her cheeks burned.

'What have you been up to, Cameo?' Maud asked anxiously. 'George and I know there is something happening you're not telling us. We're worried. I have the feeling you're doing something dangerous.'

'I'm only doing what I must.' Cameo knew in her heart how true those words were. It was no longer simply a whim of hers to go to the art studio. It was an aching need, a scorching desire she couldn't fight. Benedict Cole had opened up a new world for her, as an artist, as a man. *As a lover.*

'Oh, Cameo,' Maud wailed. 'What do you mean? Where were you, out at night, somewhere so dangerous you were robbed? It's because of this learning about art, isn't it? Please tell me. You can trust me.'

Cameo hesitated. She trusted her friend, but it wasn't fair to tell. 'I'll tell you everything as soon as I can, Maud. I promise.'

After Maud had gone Cameo went upstairs and stared out of her bedroom window at the ash tree. To think she once believed she hated Benedict Cole when she had received his letter. She chuckled. That was before she knew him. She had gone to his studio with the intention of punishing him and having lessons without him knowing who she was. But now—

She must have fallen in love the first moment she saw him. Perhaps when he'd opened the door of his studio, or perhaps… She fingered the necklace at her throat, recalling his first touch, when he'd dropped the cameo stone on to the bare skin between her breasts.

She wasn't sure exactly when it had happened. All she knew was how she felt about him now.

Benedict Cole. The man she loved. The artist. That was why he was temperamental and moody and totally focused on his painting and all the other things that went with being an artist, but she wouldn't have him any other way.

She understood.

But people from her world, her kind of circles,

didn't usually fall in love with artists. Mayfair and Soho rarely mixed. What would her friends and family think? George? Maud? Her parents? They were going to be furious when they found out she'd been having art lessons. And if they knew she had fallen in love…it didn't bear thinking about.

And what about Benedict? She clenched her fingers. What would he say when he discovered who she was and the world she came from?

Cameo gulped. He knew she was an artist, but he still didn't know she was Lady Catherine Mary St Clair.

Why, oh, why hadn't she told him? She'd meant to, but the way he'd made love to her… She flushed again, remembering. She'd refused to spoil that moment, on that sacred night, and she sensed he would have sent her home, if he knew.

He wouldn't have taken her into his arms and into his bed.

'I'll tell him the truth when I get back from Warley Park,' she said aloud. The night they'd shared demanded her truthfulness. She knew that, deep in her soul.

Was it wrong, the lovemaking they had shared? she wondered anew as she ran her fingers over her necklace.

No. She refused to regret it. The passion she

had experienced with Benedict didn't feel wrong, it felt natural and right. So right.

She bit her lip. For a moment she was sure she had witnessed in his eyes the knowledge that it was her first time. She sensed that he'd felt it in her body. But that had been right, too. He was the only man for her.

It was time to tell Benedict the truth. The honesty between their bodies must be matched in words. She couldn't maintain such a barrier between them.

If only she didn't have to go away, to Sussex. If only she could rush to the studio, up the stairs and into Benedict's arms. She'd heard people call Warley Park the finest estate in Sussex, but it wasn't enough to make her wish to spend time with Lord Warley.

Far away from Benedict Cole.

Clutching her sketchbook, Cameo hurried down the long gravel drive of Warley Park, trying to avoid being seen. She'd been desperate to be alone ever since she'd arrived with her mama and papa for the dreaded visit.

Before they left she had tried to persuade George to come with them.

'Not likely, little sister!' He laughed as he stood by the carriage, ready to see them off.

'Warley's your beau. I'm staying here in London with Maud.'

'Stop calling him my beau!' she insisted furiously, making George laugh.

'You and Warley might join Maud and me at a double wedding.' He waved their carriage away, calling, 'Enjoy Sussex!'

How could she enjoy it with Lord Warley always standing too close, introducing her possessively to neighbours as though she were part of the property? That afternoon, pleading exhaustion and saying she needed to retire to her bedroom, Cameo had declined his offer to show her the grounds. 'We have some magnificent woods,' he'd said, with a suggestive lift of an eyebrow.

She shuddered. She did want to see the woods she'd noticed as they drove through the lodge gates, but not with Lord Warley. 'How kind,' she'd demurred. 'Thank you, but I'm afraid I need to rest this afternoon.'

After luncheon she had duly gone upstairs to the guest bedroom she'd been allocated, with its painted yellow-silk panels lining the walls and magnificent French furniture the colour of honey. After a quick look out the window to ensure the coast was clear she had slipped out.

The weather had turned unseasonably warm. Cameo pushed back her bonnet and lifted her face to the spring sunshine, letting it seep into her. Its golden light spilled over the undulating lawns edged by flower beds waiting to burst into summer bloom, dazzling the water on the lake, with its graceful bubbling fountain, a statue of four mermaids, sirens rising from their rock. She had to admit the grounds were spectacular. Indeed the whole of Warley Park was glorious. She'd heard its name so many times spoken with awe and she understood immediately why it was so admired. The house was simply breathtaking. Not much remained of the original building, a central 'E' that dated to Tudor times with ancient wood panelling and stonework. When the family had bought and renamed it, a Georgian front and two Georgian wings had been added, making the house enormous. The later additions could have made the proportions wrong, but instead they enhanced it. The house blended together over the decades as if it had grown there instead of being built by human hands. It was a setting that deserved better than Lord Warley. How horrible of him to have rushed to tell her mama that he'd seen her unchaperoned in the park. But there'd always been something unwholesome about him, something sly.

At last, after crunching for a mile along the drive, Cameo found the woods. These, too, were magnificent. Laying her palm on the bark of a huge oak tree, feeling its sense of rooted calm, she entered them almost reverently. They were ancient, a magical place to be sure, quiet and serene. Full of oak, willow and ash trees, wild garlic grew there, with its earthy pungent scent, along with pale yellow primroses and a glade of snowdrops, their nodding heads beckoning her deeper and deeper. She selected a dry log in some dappled sunshine and, with her back against a tree, started to sketch her surroundings.

She found it impossible not to dream of Benedict. She longed for him. Was that what love was, she wondered, this longing? Was he longing for her, too, at the same moment? Did he love her? He hadn't said the words, as such, only read from Tennyson's poem. And then, his paintbrush…

A shudder of desire coursed through her. Even as she sat there, alone.

Laying her sketch pad aside, she took out the leather-bound book she'd tucked into her pocket. She flicked through the pages to 'The Gardener's Daughter; or, The Pictures'. The full poem was much longer than the section Benedict had read to her, a narrative, a story in itself. The love and yearning in it, did he feel it now, just as she did?

A twig snapped.

'Hello,' Cameo said gently. A soft brown baby rabbit was poised near her, sitting up as though it were listening for something. The creature flopped its long ears towards her, its brown eyes bright with interest. She reached for her pencil and sketchbook, but her movement sent it leaping away further into the wood. How she'd have loved to follow it, she thought with a sigh, as she stood up and brushed off her skirt.

Reluctantly, she made her way back. At least she'd enjoyed some blissful solitude. She saw no one in the wood, though nearby she spotted two thatched cottages, with whitewashed walls. They must belong to the estate workers.

In her guest bedroom she bathed in front of the fire in a hip bath before dressing for dinner. Sponging her limbs brought yet another vivid memory of Benedict's touch, of him releasing her from her corset, peeling back her silk stockings… She bit her lip. She must halt these constant thoughts, yet the sensations of being held in his arms flooded her body: the masculine scent of him, that heady mix of soap, paint and turpentine, the strength of his flexed muscles, his lips on her… Oh, to be in the studio, in his arms. She preferred a garret to a great estate so long as Benedict was there.

The dinner bell rang as she finished dressing. Her feet dragged as she descended the broad marble staircase. Another dinner. She wasn't sure if she could face it. She paused in the central hall under an exquisitely painted cupola of gods and goddesses reclining above. After craning her neck at it she turned with a sigh towards the dining room and noticed an open door to another room, a room bright with candles she hadn't entered before. Her heart quickened. It must be the gallery Lord Warley had mentioned at the ball. She could see the paintings. Even from this distance Cameo could tell they were Old Masters. Surely there was enough time before dinner for a quick look.

Benedict measured the frame with his hands. He had no need of more precise instruments. His eye told him where to cut in much the same way a sculptor knew where to apply the chisel. *Use your hands and eyes, lad, that's what you need to carve*, Arthur Cole had told him, and Benedict followed his example.

There seemed to him something sensuous about wood. It felt warm to the touch, not cold, even when it was no longer rooted in soil. To him it felt animate, still breathing with the life of the tree from which it came.

For his paintings he only ever used wooden frames he'd made himself with individual carvings to amplify the work's subject. It was his trademark. Let others have their gilt.

He stroked the piece of wood for the frame of Cameo's portrait. He was using ash, of course, an added homage to the girl in the Tennyson poem upon which the painting was based, with her hair blacker than ash buds. The Venus of the woods, the poet Gilpin called the ash tree. With its elegant beauty and its slender grey trunk, it reminded him of Cameo as he'd first seen her in her grey dress.

Flexing his aching muscles, he stretched his stiff shoulders. His tired limbs wouldn't obey him for too much longer. He'd been locked away in the studio for days now. He barely recalled the last time he went outside for air, and not until swaying with hunger did he remember to eat.

The ash cut well as he carved the frame. He handled it with respect for its beauty, for nothing was more beautiful than an ash tree burst into leaf. It was believed by many to be magical, used for charms and remedies, and his mother had been able to predict if the summer would be wet or dry by whether the ash came into leaf before the oak. It was uncanny; she'd always been right.

He'd carve ash leaves and ash buds on the frame, too, as well as its flowers, to add another layer to the painting. He glanced over to where the portrait stood on the easel, drying. So close now to completion. He brooded over the work, more pleased than he dared to admit. The colours were the exact tints he sought, the lines were the cleanest he'd ever accomplished and the

natural detail appeared true and painstakingly
fine. He'd hoped to paint so well, suspected it,
worked towards it, dreamed of it. But he hadn't
been sure of achieving it, not until he'd stood
and studied the almost-finished portrait. Then
he'd known for certain. He'd found his muse.
She'd entranced him right from the start, with
her quickness, her spirit and her unique ability
to focus as he worked. She was the perfect model
for him, perhaps because she was an artist, too.
His smile faded, thinking of the sketch she'd
burnt. It had shown real promise. He still wasn't
sure why she had cast it into the fire.

The light shadowed. He lit the lamp, wondered where she was that night. When she'd
told him she couldn't come to pose for a few
days, he hadn't asked her why, because he hadn't
wanted to hear her answer. She had denied having a lover, but she must be with her protector,
the man who kept her in such style in Mayfair.
It slammed into him again then, the pain in his
gut. He'd never felt so possessive of a model before, of any woman. He'd practically lived with
Maisie Jones and she had been disloyal to him,
probably more than once, but he had never felt
this way.

He frowned. If Cameo had a protector, why
had he, Benedict, been the only man to make
love to her? He'd only become more certain of

it. If he'd known she was untouched, he might not have made love to her that night. But how could a night like that be regretted? It had been unforgettable.

He wanted all of her, body and soul.

Again. For ever. In front of his easel. In his arms. In his bed.

His alone.

Benedict took up his chisel. When Cameo returned it would be time to ask some questions after all.

'I thought I'd find you here.'

Cameo's skin prickled. Lord Warley slithered up beside her, silent as a serpent. Perfectly turned out as usual, he wore a black-tailed dinner coat with a maroon waistcoat. He smiled, seemingly pleased to have caught her unawares. She wasn't sure how long she'd been in the gallery, spellbound.

He broke the spell. 'You've spoilt my surprise.' He waved around the gallery. 'I planned to bring you here after dinner tonight. What do you think of them?'

What did she think of them? What did he imagine she thought of the most glorious collection of Old Masters she'd ever seen outside the Royal Academy? She stared at the pictures lining the scarlet walls of the long, elegant room with its stone floor. It reminded Cameo of the interior of a jewel box. Its walls like red velvet, the vibrant paintings—da Vinci, Titian, Raphael, Rembrandt—glowing in their golden frames as bright as coloured gems. 'They're magnificent.'

He tucked his thumbs into his waistcoat pockets. 'Of all that I inherited from my father, I think this collection pleased me most. For a number of reasons.' He smirked with satisfaction. 'An excellent investment.'

Incredulous, she swayed her head, setting her pearl earrings swinging against her jaw. 'How can you think of art merely as an investment? Surely you must appreciate it for its beauty.'

'Make no mistake, I appreciate beauty.' He bent a bow. 'I am not an art lover, but my family have been collecting art for centuries, my father in particular. He was quite the connoisseur. He travelled on a number of Grand Tours of Europe and brought home many of the paintings you see before you.'

'He had excellent taste.'

'Indeed.' He pointed to a wall of portraits. 'And these are the family portraits. That's my father, the previous Lord Warley, but you knew him, of course.'

Cameo noted Lord Warley's resemblance to his dark-haired father. The previous earl's jaw appeared stronger, firmer than his son's. It reminded her of someone, but she couldn't think who.

'And what do you think of Warley Park now you have spent some time here?'

Again she wondered what he expected her to say about such a magnificent estate. 'Warley Park is beautiful.'

'I wanted you to come here. I wanted you to see my home in all its glory.'

'Well, now I have.'

'This afternoon I spotted you coming out of the woods. So that's where you were hiding.' He lowered his voice. 'I would have enjoyed hunting you down.'

Alone with Lord Warley in the woods—it didn't bear thinking about. She wouldn't dare venture into the solitude of the trees again.

She turned away from him and pretended to study a painting by Titian portraying a girl with the red hair so famously admired by the artist. She saw the feather-light paint strokes he made, the kind Benedict had told her about. She wondered how it might have been to model for Titian.

Nowhere near as wonderful as modelling for Benedict Cole.

Lord Warley nudged up behind her. She stifled her urge to run, like the rabbit she'd seen in the woods, as she felt his breath lifting the hairs on her neck.

Her petticoats whirled as she spun around.

'I wonder if you have given any more thought to our discussion at Lady Russell's ball.'

Cameo backed up against the wall.

'I refer to my desire to pay my addresses to you. Warley Park and all these paintings can be yours, Lady Catherine Mary.'

Why was he so intent on pursuing her? Surely he realised her lack of interest in him. 'I thought you wished for more time for us to get to know each other,' she parried.

'Why wait any longer? I have only become more certain of your charms.' He stretched his arm out straight beside her, his hand flat on the wall, blocking any movement. 'Let me go to your father and ask his permission for your hand in marriage.'

Violently she shook her head. 'No.'

'Come, come. Don't be coy.' His tongue darted around his lips. 'There's no other man who has your affections, is there?'

She jerked her head away, her hair catching on the gilt picture frame.

'This is not the time for such a discussion, Lord Warley.' Pulling the strand of hair loose with a painful tug, she ducked beneath his arm and edged towards the door. 'Hasn't the bell rung for dinner?'

In the dining room, her parents were already seated. Her mama gave her a reproachful look and her papa exclaimed, 'Where did you get to, Cameo? Frightfully rude.'

A footman sped to help her into her chair. 'I'm sorry, Papa.'

'Allow me.' Lord Warley came in, waved the footman away and slid out her chair, taking the opportunity to slide his hands over her taffeta-clad hips. He assumed his own place at the head of the table, the butler standing to attention behind him.

In the light of the candelabra, the table groaned with blue-and-white china platters and tureens, ripe fruit piled high on silver stands, crystal glasses gleaming with ruby-red wine. The dining room itself, part of the few older sections of the house, was half-panelled in timber. Directly opposite her on a green wall was hung an enormous painting of a hound with a fox caught in its mouth. Disgusted, she twisted her head away, only to find her host's eyes fixed on her.

'Do you appreciate that painting? It's one I purchased myself.'

Not surprised to learn it was his selection, she made no reply.

After a moment still staring at her, he pronounced, 'I'm pleased to be able to dine alone tonight, just the four of us. *En famille*, might we almost say? And Lady Catherine Mary is looking particularly well.'

She didn't want Lord Warley to look at her that way. Only Benedict.

'I'm delighted you could all come to stay,' Warley continued as the butler poured wine and the footmen served them roasted quail with tiny potatoes around it, like eggs in a nest. 'Especially you, my lord.' He nodded to Cameo's father. 'My father would have appreciated you considering yourself an honoured guest.'

The earl grunted. 'Humph.'

Cameo threw him a sharp look. For a moment she wondered if her father was quite as impressed with Lord Warley as he always implied. But he was indestructibly loyal to his old friendship.

'We're delighted, too,' Lady Buxton gushed, 'aren't we, Cameo?'

She gave a slight movement of her head that might have meant anything.

'I desired Lady Catherine Mary to see Warley Park,' Lord Warley said meaningfully, tapping his glass. 'I've spent no time with her in London of late. I've made calls, but she's so often not at home.'

'You must make sure you always receive old

friends, Cameo,' the countess admonished. 'I don't know what you've been doing recently.'

'Spending time with her brother in Hyde Park, eh?' he queried lightly.

Cameo looked over to where Lord Warley sat expansively at the head of the table and caught a flicker of something cruel in his eyes.

She stared down at the quail's tiny, fragile bones on her plate. Sickened, she pushed the dish away.

'Cole? May I come in? I saw your light on.'

The rap on the studio door diverted him.

Benedict threw down the chisel. 'It's open.'

Trelawney entered, rubbing his hands together against the cold. Benedict realised he'd let the fire go down, as usual.

'Thought I'd drag you out for a quick drink at the Lamb. Some dinner, too. You'll need it, if I know you.' Trelawney's gaze fell on the painting. 'My goodness. So this is what you've been working on?'

There was always a difficult moment when Benedict first showed a painting, no matter how good he thought it, a moment when his stomach hit the floor.

Trelawney crossed the wooden floor to the easel and pulled an eyeglass from his waistcoat pocket, peering admiringly at the portrait. 'My goodness. My goodness.'

He turned to Benedict. 'You realise what you've done, don't you?'

Trelawney inspected it even more closely. He was surprisingly perceptive when it came to art assessment. 'You've gone to a whole new level with your new model, Cole. It's magnificent. You've cracked it this time. Marvellous work.'

'I've been like a man possessed,' he admitted.

'I can see why. You have to get it into the Royal Academy, my boy.'

Benedict's head reared. 'This year's show, do you mean? There's no time. It's too late. Entries have closed, haven't they?'

'I can get around that,' the sculptor assured him. 'I tell you, you have to get it in.'

'I'm not sure.' He'd started it as a private project, an experiment. To drive him onward as a painter, to test his skills. Then Cameo had come to him. Now Benedict wasn't sure if he didn't want to keep the painting to himself.

'Leave it all to me. I'm beginning to think you need someone to act for you. Perhaps I should offer my services, to be your agent, of a sort. I'd like to sell your work, if I may. This portrait alone is worth hundreds of pounds and someone should make sure you get it.' Trelawney chuckled as he tucked his eyeglass in his pocket. 'I won't be making my fortune from my own work, alas. I have to say, I just don't seem to get a moment these days. So many soirées, too little time.'

Benedict smiled.

'Seriously, dear boy.' Trelawney's face sobered as he clapped Benedict's shoulder. 'This is ideal for the Academy. The selectors won't be able to resist it. Let me make the arrangements.'

'Cameo should see it before it goes anywhere.'

'But Miss Ashe will be delighted to view it *in situ* at the Academy,' Trelawney pronounced, pulling out the eyeglass once again. 'How can she not? She'll be the talk of London. Just you wait and see.'

Chapter Fifteen

'Go and see
The Gardener's daughter: trust me, after that,
You scarce can fail to match his master-piece.'

—Alfred, Lord Tennyson:
'The Gardener's Daughter'

Cameo found Benedict asleep by the fireplace, his head resting against the armchair and his long legs sprawled out in front of him. She revelled in the moment to study him unawares, his strong jaw, with the slight stubble outlining it, the shadows beneath his eyes. He'd been working too hard.

The studio appeared to be in even more chaos than usual. An empty bottle of wine stood on the table next to a heel of bread and some cheese on a discarded plate. Papers with sketches all over them were scattered on the table and the floor and the fire was out, leaving only blackened embers in the grate.

She dropped a kiss on his lips. 'Good morning,' she whispered into his ear.

Yawning, he opened his eyes. 'Cameo?'

'Who else?' She smiled mischievously. 'I caught you napping, Mr Cole.'

'Never.' With one strong wrench she fell into his lap, her bonnet pushed back, his mouth on hers. His hungry kiss told her without words that longing had not been hers alone. Her hands went to his hair, her fingers running through the dark thickness, yearning for him, seeking him. Her body refused to lie, she reflected with a guilty pang.

'Now I've said good morning properly.' He drew away, leaving her giddy against his chest. 'We mustn't forget the social niceties you're so fond of. Will that do?'

'Yes,' she answered weakly, stumbling to her feet. Her knees buckled beneath her petticoats. She'd never have believed a man could make her swoon.

'I missed you while you were gone.' He caressed a tendril of her hair as he, too, got to his feet.

'And I missed you.' He'd never guess how much. Every hour without him at Warley Park had been a form of torture. She thought the visit there would never end with Lord Warley's eyes constantly on her as if he were plotting his next pounce, as if he were hunting game. Here in the studio she felt safe and secure.

Benedict jerked his head towards the easel, draped in a cloth. 'I've enjoyed an advantage while you've been away. I've had you with me day and night. I haven't been able to stop.'

'The portrait?'

'Something else I'm making. You're a distraction.' His warm fingers glided along her curves, over her waist and hips. 'I'll show you, but first I've got something important to tell you.'

'I've got something to tell you, too.' While at Warley Park she'd worried that he might become so angry with her about her deception he might cast her out of the studio. But she had to risk it. There must be honesty between them now. She was going to tell him. She had vowed it. But she'd pose first and gather her courage. 'Aren't you forgetting? I'm here to earn my shilling.'

'There's no need for you to pose.'

Her heart thumped. 'What do you mean?'

'That's what I wanted to tell you.' Benedict smiled. She'd missed his smile so much. 'It happened while you were gone. The moment I knew the work was complete. I knew I shouldn't add one more brushstroke.'

'The painting's done?' she gasped.

'I don't think I've ever worked so fast,' he explained. 'You've had a powerful effect on me. I felt a kind of anguish in finishing it, in stopping painting you.'

She clutched her cameo necklace, feeling the quick contraction of her throat as she swallowed desperately. She threw a frantic look around the studio. 'Where is it?'

'What's wrong?' He frowned. 'What's that frantic expression on your face?'

Cameo tried to relax the skin between her eyebrows and gave a hollow laugh. His artist's eye noticed everything. 'It's just that if you've finished the painting you won't need me as a model.'

'Not need you!' His voice became husky as he pulled her into his arms. 'The only thing that has kept me going is the thought of how I might paint you next.'

Quick footsteps came from outside the door, followed by a brisk knock.

Benedict dropped a quick kiss on her lips before he released her. 'Ah, that will be Trelawney.'

'Good news, Cole! It's all set!' Nicholas Trelawney appeared, dapper in a checked waistcoat and red cravat. 'Oh, hello, Miss Cameo! How delightful to see you again.'

'Good morning.' Cameo gripped her necklace. If only he hadn't come in just then.

The sculptor beamed at her. 'You must be so proud, my dear, of being *The Gardener's Daughter*. You're going to be famous!'

Cameo stared at Nicholas Trelawney in horror. Her cameo stone fell from her fingers. 'I don't understand.'

'They've taken it?' Benedict asked. There was a strange intensity in his tone.

'Of course.' Trelawney consulted his pocket watch. 'But hurry up. We've got to get over there this morning.'

Cameo put a restraining hand on Benedict's arm. 'What's happening? Where are you going?'

He seemed oblivious to her now. 'To the Royal Academy of Art, of course.'

Trelawney clapped. 'It's going to be in their annual exhibition!'

'What?' She barely stayed upright. Stumbling, she gripped the edge of the table. 'But…but it hasn't opened yet.'

'It soon will. We had to take the portrait over there yesterday, my dear. I organised it. I'm owed a few favours and the selectors have agreed to view it today. They'll hang this one in pride of place, I'm sure, well below the line.' Trelawney added in explanation, 'The line is the mark of how good a painting is. Good ones below the line, lesser ones above it. This one will hang well below. It's a masterpiece.'

Cameo's pulse thumped. She knew about the line. How could she not? Absolutely everyone she knew attended the Academy show. It formed an essential part of the London Season. She always attended, as did her mama and even her papa.

Her question to Benedict would hardly come out of her dry mouth. 'Do you mean you're planning to show the painting at the Academy?'

'Of course.' He laughed. 'Why do you think I painted it, if not to be exhibited? I started it as an experiment, I'll admit, and I didn't think to be ready in time. I never dreamed I'd be finished.'

'But…but…' Cameo floundered. 'I haven't seen it yet.'

Benedict sent her an amused smile. 'My model's turned shy on me,' he told Trelawney.

'My dear!' Trelawney came and clasped Cameo's hands in his. 'Work as fine as this must be seen. You must be aware that being shown in the Royal Academy is a great privilege, not one every artist can hope to have conferred on him. Benedict has already had one work in the Academy and to have another will make his career. This might be the turning point. If all goes to plan, he'll become a member of the Academy.' He became suddenly businesslike as he rounded on Benedict. 'Now, Cole. Let's get over there. I've got a cab waiting downstairs.'

'You're going right now?' Cameo gasped.

Benedict nodded.

'It's the best work you've done, Cole,' Trelawney said with glee. 'I can't wait to see the reaction. We're going to be just in time.'

'No!' Cameo cried. 'Please, Benedict. I must talk to you!'

Half dragging him aside, she tried to position them out of Trelawney's earshot. 'Please wait. I haven't seen the portrait.'

'I'm sorry, my darling. I'll take you to see it at the Academy.' Pride rang in his voice.

She tried again. 'I…I didn't think of the portrait being exhibited.' How stupid she'd been.

'What a strange model you are.' He chuckled. 'Most models desire to be admired. Don't you?'

'No! I don't!'

He frowned. It was almost a glare. 'You don't wish it shown. Why?'

Cameo bit her lip. It was impossible to unravel her web of lies with Trelawney in the studio. Where to begin? 'Can't you keep my portrait here in the studio? For you, privately?'

'I'd prefer to keep you here for my private enjoyment than a painting.' He lowered his voice, with a suggestive smile. Then he sobered. 'I'm a professional, Cameo, not a dabbling amateur. I'm proud of this work. It's going to make my reputation, I'm sure of it. There's something about it. It will create a sensation.'

Cameo's heart thudded to her stomach. It would certainly create a sensation, but for all the wrong reasons.

'Now, now, my dear,' Trelawney scolded, coming over and patting her benignly on the sleeve. 'You'll soon get over your nerves. I'm sure many models feel as you do at first. Now come along, Benedict. Don't miss this chance. If you want this painting to be in the exhibition we'd better get it over there.'

'I'm ready to take it now,' he said. His attention had moved away from her. He grabbed his coat and scarf.

'Benedict—'

'My dear...' Trelawney gave her another pat. 'There's no point talking to him until the painting has been viewed by the selectors. You won't get a word of sense from him until then.'

'But, Benedict, there's something I must tell you—'

He bent and whispered in her ear. His breath caressed her. 'We can't talk now, Cameo. Come back tonight when we'll be alone. There's something I need to say to you, too.'

* * *

Cameo hurried down the dark alleyway, through the red doorway and up the stairs, her fingers gripping the banister tight.

The day had been endless. That morning, after she left Benedict, she went home to Mayfair as if in a nightmare. Almost crazed, she'd made up her mind to go to the Royal Academy and find him, stop him. She had put on her bonnet and gloves before she reconsidered. No. Her appearance would only raise more questions. There was a chance, slim at best, that the selectors wouldn't recognise her in the painting immediately. People in her social circle weren't going to see it until the exhibition officially opened. Her identity might not be revealed. She had time to ask Benedict to withdraw it, though her heart sank at the thought. She would wait and tell him when they were alone in the studio.

During the afternoon, to stay calm, she had taken her folding easel and her watercolours out into the grassy square where she used to play with Maud and climb trees with George and tried to paint some pale daffodils clustered inside the wrought-iron railings. The occupation only agitated her more. '*O, what a tangled web we weave when first we practise to deceive...*' her nanny had intoned to her in the nursery. The web was more than tangled. She'd tied herself up in knots.

Packing up her paints, she had gone back into the house. Later, Briggs had carried a visiting card on a silver tray in to her in the drawing room. She picked it up and dropped it as if it stung her. Lord Warley.

'Please tell Lord Warley I'm not at home.'

'Very good, Lady Catherine Mary,' Briggs had replied, giving her a worried glance. He knew her well enough to know something was wrong. But she couldn't confide in anyone, until she'd seen Benedict and told him the truth.

After dinner with her mama she'd gone upstairs to her bedroom to wait until the coast was clear. There was no sign of George and her father must have been at his club. He hadn't appeared at dinner. When her mother retired to her bedroom with one of her headaches, she had raced down to the servant hall and begged Bert to take her to Soho. Something in her desperate expression must have convinced him even though he didn't like taking her to such a place at night. In Soho he parked the carriage right in front of Benedict's house, instead of around the corner.

Cameo gulped as she continued to hurry up the stairs to the studio. At the top landing the door was ajar, the studio dark, except for the firelight flickering in the grate. She could only dimly make out Benedict sitting beside it, a glass of whisky in his hand.

Wordlessly she tiptoed over and stood in front of him. She smelled the whisky fumes as he drained a large swig.

'I was wondering when you would arrive.' His grip tightened on the glass. 'Good evening, Miss Ashe. Or should I say, Lady Catherine Mary St Clair?'

With a smash Benedict hurled the whisky glass into the fire.

Chapter Sixteen

'Make thine heart ready with thine eyes:
the time
Is come to raise the veil.'

—Alfred, Lord Tennyson:
'The Gardener's Daughter'

The glass glittered in jagged fragments on the stone hearth as the smell of the liquor wafted through the air. Benedict got to his feet and mocked politely, 'I'm so sorry, Lady Catherine Mary. Please excuse me. Do you care for some whisky?'

Cameo shook her ringlets, trembling from head to foot. She lowered her head to avoid witnessing the fury in his face and gathered her black velvet cloak protectively around her, clutching its edges so tightly her knuckles whitened. She'd come without gloves. Not that it mattered now. Nothing mattered, except convincing Benedict to listen to her.

He grabbed the whisky bottle and splashed a large measure into a new, unbroken glass, the amber colour of the liquid flaring in the firelight. 'No? That's right. You don't enjoy whisky much, do you? You're not used to it. Not refined enough for you, perhaps. But I believe I'll have another.' He tossed back the drink, his strong throat contracting sharply as he swallowed.

She waited for him to speak again, still clutching her cloak. But he said nothing.

A terrible silence lengthened between them. 'So you know,' she said at last, her voice low. 'I came here to tell you myself.'

'Did you? I'm sure you say that now.'

'I planned to tell you.' Her voice grew stronger. 'I've come to apologise.'

'Really.'

She glanced up at him, at the two harsh lines on either side of his mouth. They hadn't been as deep before, she felt sure of it. Had she done that to him? 'I shouldn't have lied to you. You must believe me.'

He crooked his eyebrow and lifted the whisky glass, his clenched knuckles as white as hers. He took another large swig. 'You didn't think deception was a dangerous game? Was it a society joke for you?'

Tears threatened to gush from her eyes, down her cheeks. She blinked them away. 'It wasn't a joke, or a game. I wanted to learn about painting from you. I wanted it desperately.'

'So desperately you were prepared to lie,' he shot back in disgust. 'How delightful for you to have an extra diversion for this year's Season, to stop you from becoming bored, my lady. Perhaps, now—how did you put it in your letter, when you asked for painting lessons? Ah, here it is.'

To her horror he cast down the glass of whisky and from the table picked up a familiar crested sheet.

'I found this among my papers. There's an advantage to an untidy studio. Now, what did it say?'

He read aloud in a voice she hated.

'Dear Mr Cole,
Please forgive me for this intrusion when we have not been introduced. I am a great admirer of your work. I am a keen painter myself and I wish to enquire if you would be prepared to give me some private lessons. I will, of course, pay any rate you require for your time.'

He dropped the letter with a sneer. 'Well, you've had your *private lessons*. Perhaps now we might even consider ourselves *introduced*.'

She flinched as if he'd hit her.

'Your story about being a foundling,' he gritted out. 'I knew you were lying. Why didn't you tell me the truth when we first met?'

'I wanted to,' she whispered.

'My God, I... We... How could you do such a thing?' He loomed over her, seeming larger, more masculine than ever before. 'It was all a game, just pretence.'

'No, no,' she sobbed.

'When you ran away in the park. Did that have something to do with it? Were you afraid to be seen with me?'

'Yes. No. I mean...'

'You've been acting a lie.'

Cameo held out an imploring hand. 'I was frightened you'd send me away if you discovered who I really am. Everything became such a muddle. I thought you'd make me leave. I wished so much to stay here in the studio.'

'Have you never heard of having faith in someone? Trusting someone?' She almost tasted the bitterness of his words. 'Perhaps not. Your upper-class world is full of disloyalty and deceit.'

Anguished, she twisted her fingers in her cloak. 'I didn't mean to be deceitful. When I decided to pretend to be Miss Ashe and be your artist's model, I didn't realise…'

She choked. She couldn't go on.

'Realise what?'

'That I would fall in love with you.'

The clock ticked into the silence. He stared at her, his expression inscrutable. At last he shook his head and turned away, clenching his fists on the edge of the chimney piece. 'Love is based on truth. You don't know what love is.'

'I do! Benedict, you must believe me.' She gulped through her tears. Laying a tentative touch on his broad shoulders, she felt the heat of him through the cotton of his shirt. 'I love you.'

For a moment she thought she had reached him. With a twist of his neck his expression seemed to soften. Then the tenderness fled.

'Love isn't just saying the words.' He shook off her touch. 'Love is what you do. And what have you done? Lied to me from the moment we met. And now, thanks to your father—'

She fell back, aghast. 'My father? Does he know about the portrait already? But how? He wouldn't go to the Academy.' Not unless he was forced to, she knew. He was no art lover.

Benedict reached for the poker and stoked the fire with angry jabs before turning on his heel to glare at her. 'He's a well-connected man, your father the earl. It wasn't your father who saw the portrait first, I understand. I'm not sure who it was. I'm not a member of the Academy. Nor will there be any chance of that now,' he added bitterly.

It was even worse than she suspected.

He went on. 'I was with Trelawney having a drink, waiting to hear how the painting had been received. I understand someone who recognised you went to the Academy and contacted your father immediately. I'm told he's furious.'

Her knees threatened to buckle. She held on to the armchair for support. 'He'll be more than furious.'

'Your father demanded the painting be taken down,' Benedict continued, the poker still in his grip. 'And the Academy agreed to do so. They don't seek to upset such an influential man. They don't want adverse talk.'

'Oh, no!'

'Oh, yes,' Benedict mocked. 'I can't show it. I'm doubtful I'll ever exhibit there again. Too controversial. And it was a big step forward for me. It was my second showing there, as you know. There have been many painters who, after exhibiting there more than once, have become members of the Academy and had their careers made.'

With a clatter he slammed the poker into the bucket by the fire.

'The painting.' He jerked his head towards the hessian-wrapped canvas on his easel. 'Do you want to see it, my lady?'

Seizing a knife from the table, he tore the hessian down the front and ripped it away.

Cameo gasped.

Already framed in wood, with carvings of buds, fruit and flowers around its edges, it was beautiful, more beautiful than she had ever imagined. The carvings were ash buds. She recognised them from the buds on the tree outside her bedroom window in Mayfair. He'd told her he made his own frames.

And the work itself...

Cameo moved towards it as if magnetised, let the rich colours fill her veins. She hadn't fully appreciated his talent. With a rare delicacy of touch he'd painted her reclining under the bough of an ash tree, almost as if she were part of it, wildflowers and mossy grass picked out with precision at her feet. The simple dress, thin white cotton so similar to her chemise, appeared sheer and suggestive of her form beneath, yet tenderly evoked, without blatancy. Her hair was depicted tumbling in loose waves over her shoulders, her head tilted, as though she were waiting for something, or someone. And her eyes—she'd never known they could turn that deep amethyst colour. The expression he had caught in them, full of yearning, full of longing, made her head reel. He knew her better than she knew herself. He discerned her very soul.

She moved closer. The quotation from the Tennyson poem, painted in gold script, curled at its base.

A more ideal Artist he than all,
Came, drew your pencil from you, made those eyes
Darker than darkest pansies, and that hair
More black than ashbuds in the front of March.

'This is the best work I've ever done.' The bitterness in Benedict's voice seemed to scorch Cameo's throat as though she swallowed his words. 'I thought it would attract attention, as I told you. Were you laughing to yourself about that, Lady Catherine Mary, as I said those words? You knew it would attract all the wrong kind of attention, didn't you?'

Cameo bit her lip. No words of praise were adequate now. It was a masterpiece. They both knew it. 'I tried to stop you sending it to the Academy this morning, but Mr Trelawney was here. I thought I'd have time to explain tonight.'

'You didn't try hard enough.' He hurled a sheet over the canvas as if he hated to have it on display. 'The truth about you would have stopped me submitting the portrait, you can have no doubt. But, no, you kept your identity to yourself. You enjoyed making a fool of me.'

The edge of her cloak, twisted so hard in her fingers, almost cut her skin. What had she done? 'I never wanted that.'

'Who knows what you truly wanted? I'll tell you what has happened as a result of your duplicity.' He flashed a cynical smile that tore her inside. 'How simply can I put this? You've ruined my artistic career.'

'No! No!'

'Yes. Yes,' he mimicked, reminding her of the abrupt way he'd treated her when they had first met, before she'd discovered the tenderness inside him. 'My career is over. All I've worked towards for all these years. Gone. At the spoilt whim of a member of the aristocracy. You wanted your art lessons and you wanted them from me. Nothing was going to stop you.'

Horrified, Cameo stared at him. A sudden wave of nausea overcame her. Benedict was right. Nothing had stopped her. There was an awful grain of truth in what he said. She had considered her determination to have art lessons a virtue to be admired. Now she saw her willingness to lie to him to get what she wanted in

a different light. 'I hadn't thought of it that way.'
Her voice sounded strange to her ears.

'No. People from your world never do. You
stamp your foot until you get what you want.
You're spoilt, Cameo. But what am I saying?
That isn't your real name.'

'It is. I didn't lie to you about that. My family
have always called me Cameo.'

'I thought it suited you. And now I know exactly why.'

'What do you mean?'

Benedict said harshly, 'The Greek meaning of the word. You must appreciate what it is.
"Shadow portrait." How apt. I only knew one
side of you, the shadow side. I didn't know your
real self.'

'You did know it!' She moved closer, pressed
his chest. 'Benedict, please. You did know my
real self. It wasn't a shadow. The Cameo you
kissed, the Cameo you painted, that was really
me. You're the only person who has ever really
known me, ever really seen who I am.'

'I believed I did know you. How I prided myself as a painter on seeing the truth, the essence
of people. But you, I was wrong about you.'

She clutched at his shirt. 'You weren't wrong.'

Ruthlessly he pulled away. 'Who knows what
you're capable of? Who knows how far you will
go to get what you want?'

Tormented, Cameo stumbled backwards. 'I should have told you who I am. I made a mistake about that. But my feelings for you, they aren't a lie.'

'Aren't they? Well, that's immaterial now. I've spent the last few weeks painting your face, your beautiful, lying face. That's enough for me. I never want to see you again.'

Sheer shaking terror filled Cameo at Benedict's words. 'You can't mean that.'

He drawled cruelly, 'Oh, but I do.'

Her heart plummeted. The way he spoke to her, the way he despised her. He hated her! Then, suddenly, a flame of anger torched out of the darkness inside her.

She lifted her chin. 'You don't want to see me? You don't want me to come here to your studio? Well, that suits me, too, Mr Benedict Cole. Why would I desire the company of a man who is so blind with prejudice?'

An equally hot fury sparked from his brown eyes. 'You think I'm prejudiced? What do you mean by that?'

'You'd already made up your mind not to teach me when I sent you that letter and you hadn't even met me. You were already prejudiced against me because of my background, because of what happened to your mother.'

'I won't discuss that,' he flashed back.

'You forced me to lie. I had no choice.'

He gritted his teeth. 'You had a choice. You could have told me who you were.'

'What, and have you turn me away? You must admit it. You wouldn't give me a chance. Why, you preferred to believe me a kept woman than an aristocrat! You wouldn't have believed I longed to be a painter just as you did. I found the only way I could.'

'Did you?' Benedict wrenched her into his arms. 'And when I made love to you, was that all part of the act?'

Cameo struggled against his chest, his words shocking her to the core. How dare he imply she had pretended her passionate response to him? 'Of course not!'

'No? You didn't believe you could take what you wanted as usual, my spoilt Lady Catherine Mary St Clair?'

Down his lips crashed on hers, harder than before. Her furious mind rebelled, but her body arched towards him, longing for him, needing him. A small groan escaped her lips as she opened them, unable to resist his seeking mouth. His fingers dug into her waist as he wrenched her closer to him, against the telling hardness of his desire.

She tried to pull herself away. He held her fast.

'You wanted it, didn't you?' His lips moved

downwards, finding the touch points of passion below her ears and down her neck. 'You wanted this.'

'Yes...' she breathed, her body helpless to resist. 'With you. Yes.'

His lips were fierce now as they made their way further down to the crevice between her breasts, past her cameo necklace and deep into her bodice, as at the same time he dragged up the fabric of her full skirt, taking her petticoats with it. He pushed her against the rounded edge of the table so that only the tips of her boots touched the wooden floor. With one strong tear of her pantaloons, she felt his hands slide up the smoothness of her inner thigh.

With sudden force Benedict pushed her breathless against the table and slammed away, crashing his clenched fists on the chimney piece.

He rounded back to face her, his eyes glittering like the glass on the hearth in the firelight. 'That's quite an act.'

Cameo's legs trembled as she straightened her petticoats and steadied herself against the table.

'It's not an act,' she sobbed. 'Benedict, please. I never expected this to happen. I had no idea it would turn out this way. My family only have one way of living and they want me to live that way, too. They want me to marry and live as my family always have.'

'And who do they currently favour?'

'The…the man I ran away from in the park,' she stuttered.

'Then may I wish you happy,' he said, in a sarcastic tone. 'You are both admirably suited, I have no doubt.'

Tears rained down her face now. 'We're not suited at all. I hate him. He isn't an artist.'

He threw out a bitter laugh. 'Well, now, thanks to you, nor am I.'

He set his back to her, staring into the fire. His shoulders lowered.

'Just go, Cameo.' She barely heard him. 'Go and don't come back here again.'

'Please, no.' She could hardly speak. 'Please.'

'Go.' The single word formed a command. Then he spun on his heel. 'Wait.'

From a pouch on the table by the fire he grabbed a clutch of coins. 'You haven't been paid in full for *posing*.'

With a tug of her hand he forced the coins into it.

As the meaning of his words sank in Cameo tried to wrench away. 'I don't need money!'

'Take it. You've earned it.'

He slammed away again. Shaking, she flung the money down on the table, sent the coins flying.

'Benedict, please. Please.'

But he remained motionless. Tears stinging her cheeks, Cameo flung a final glance at the studio. The only sound she heard was her own sobs as she stumbled across the room and the studio door, as it slammed behind her.

Chapter Seventeen

'Yet might I tell of meetings, of farewells—
…perplex'd for utterance,
Stole from her sister Sorrow. Might I not
tell.'

—Alfred, Lord Tennyson:
'The Gardener's Daughter'

Cameo tried to stem her sobs, but they continued to gush up from deep within her.

Almost blinded by her tears, she accepted Bert's help down from the carriage. Looking up, she saw Briggs, his face impassive, opening the front door to greet her.

'Your parents have asked you to go directly into the drawing room,' Briggs intoned, when she entered the hall.

'Thank you, Briggs.'

Cameo found her handkerchief and blotted the tears from her cheeks. Her knees shook. A

warning in Brigg's tone told her that her father
was in a rage. He'd been in rages before.

But never before had she seen her father so
furious.

'Catherine Mary! What is the meaning of
this?' The earl paced in front of the fireplace, his
fists clenched, his reddened face bulging with
veins. 'I can't believe this! You've created a scandal! You've dragged our family name through
the gutter! Modelling for an artist? How could
you think of such a thing?'

Cameo struggled to find the words. 'I had to
get painting lessons and it was the only way.'

The earl's eyes goggled. 'Painting lessons!
You did this to get painting lessons?'

'Oh, dear…oh, dear,' Lady Buxton interjected,
her pretty face flushed. She lay on the chesterfield, fanning herself with her handkerchief.
George, looking concerned, stood beside her.
'I knew painting would lead to trouble, Cameo.'

She didn't appreciate half of it, Cameo
thought, hot tears welling up again. If only she
hadn't lied to her family. To Benedict! But to
never have met him…

'It was worth it,' she said defiantly.

The earl loomed over her, his palm raised.
'Worth it, was it, young lady?'

Cameo gasped. Her father had never raised a

hand to her. To think that her secrets and deception had brought them all to this!

George stepped forward to shield his sister. 'Cameo's done nothing wrong, Pater.'

'Nothing wrong!' Her father's face grew redder, but he dropped his hand. She knew he would not have struck her. 'I've spent the whole evening plying members of the damned Academy with drinks at my club. Do you know about this portrait of your sister, a portrait about to be shown to the entire population of London?'

George shook his head.

Cameo murmured defensively to her brother, 'It's a wonderful painting. It's based on a poem by Tennyson. It's called *The Gardener's Daughter.*'

Lord Buxton broke in with a roar. 'The *gardener's daughter*? You're not the damned gardener's daughter! You're the daughter of an earl!'

Cameo lifted her head high. 'It's a work of art. There's nothing wrong with my portrait. I'm proud of it.'

Lady Buxton fanned herself even faster. 'Oh, my goodness…oh, my goodness.'

'Did you have to do it, Papa?' Cameo's voice shook. 'Did you have to have the painting banned from the Royal Academy exhibition in such a way?'

'What else was I to do? Have all and sundry

leer at you? There I was, having a quiet drink at the club, when Lord Warley came to have a word with me. He'd seen your indiscretion and came to warn me.'

So Lord Warley had informed her father. She might have suspected. Of course. He'd come to the house that afternoon, left his card when she asked Briggs to say she wasn't home. He must have hastened hotfoot to break the news to her father at the club. She could only imagine his satisfaction at telling tales on her.

'I can only thank God Warley told me. According to him you were half-clothed in that painting!'

The countess gave a strangled cry. George rushed to her side and knelt beside her. 'It's all right, Mama.'

Lady Buxton clutched her son. 'Half-clothed!'

'I wasn't half-clothed!' Cameo retorted. 'My arms and shoulders were bare, that's all. It's no more revealing than if I had been wearing a ball dress.'

Her mother's eyes filled with tears. 'The disgrace!'

'By God, Cameo!' her father exclaimed. 'Have you no idea what you've done? Goodness knows how many people have already seen it or might have if Warley hadn't acted so quickly. We owe him our thanks. When I think of it…you—

modelling! And there seemed to be something else about that painting, Warley thought, something…intimate.'

Her parents mustn't find out the extent of her relationship with Benedict. She said desperately, 'Artistic skill. That's what you saw, Papa. The artist who painted it is the only person who has ever really understood me.'

'Understood you?' The vein on the earl's forehead bulged to bursting. 'What are you saying "he understood you"? What do you mean by that? Tell me, young lady, did he take advantage of you?'

She gripped her hands together. Never. She'd never reveal what had happened between them. 'No, he didn't take advantage of me. I realise now that I took advantage of him. He didn't know my true identity, you see. I pretended to be a poor woman with no family. I lied to him to get what I wanted. And as a result I've ruined his life.'

'His life! What about your life? You've ruined your reputation!'

Cameo's temper rose in a mix of despair and frustration. 'My reputation. Is that all you're worried about, making sure other people think well of us and that I don't disgrace the family?'

'Steady on, Cameo.' George stood up beside his mother, rubbing his head. 'It really does seem you've gone too far this time. And the St Clair family do have a position to uphold.'

'That's right, George. It's simply too much!' Lady Buxton added.

Cameo faced her brother. 'I thought you'd understand, George.'

He ducked from her expression. 'I'm sorry, Cameo. I don't think you should keep on with this. It's not right.'

'I had to paint. I had to have those lessons.' She had to be with Benedict, she added in her mind.

'Well, here's a lesson for you,' her father exploded. 'You're never to draw or paint again in this house. Do you understand?'

'Papa! You can't mean that.'

'I do mean it. Painting and all this nonsense led you into this. I should have expected as a woman you don't know what's good for you.'

'I do know what's good for me! Art is good for me—' she gulped and went bravely on '—and Benedict Cole is good for me.'

Cameo saw she'd shocked her father to the core. 'The artist is good for you? What do you mean? I'll ask you again—have you been compromised?'

She lifted her chin. 'My heart has been compromised, Father. I love him.'

'You love a painter?' The countess trembled. 'Cameo, what can you mean?'

'This is even worse than I thought!' In her father's eyes she saw his anger held something else. He wasn't just horrified, he was terrified for her. 'I'm going to make sure you never see that artist again!'

'You don't need to make sure of it, Papa,' she said bitterly. The way Benedict had behaved before she left the studio… 'Benedict Cole doesn't want to see me.'

Her father seized her by the shoulders. 'You're to keep to your bedroom. Do you understand? I'm going to instruct the servants to lock you in. You're not to leave this house. Somehow we have to cure you of this.'

'You can't do that. No, Papa. Please!'

'Can't you see I have to protect you, Cameo? You've lost your head. You seem to have got some strange ideas from that artist you've been associating with. I'm your father and it's up to me to look after you. This is my fault. I should never have let you take up painting. It isn't something women should do.'

'Papa! Please!'

He shook his head. 'I've heard of young women becoming hysterical over writing novels and poetry and such. Never thought such a thing would happen to my own daughter. I'm partly responsible for this. And there's something else.'

Cameo's heart thudded with fear. What could be worse than Benedict hating her and being told she must never paint again? 'What is it?'

'You're to marry Lord Warley.'

Cameo's legs buckled as she shook herself from her father's grasp and backed away. 'No!'

'Lord Warley was shocked, most shocked, at your behaviour, as any gentleman would be. But he's asked my permission to wed you in spite of the scandal you've created. You're fortunate he's prepared to marry you. No one else will take you after you've behaved in such a manner.'

Cameo clutched hold of the sofa to support her. 'Papa, please, I beg you, don't force me to marry him. He's not a good man. I can feel it.'

'He's a safe man, someone from our world. You need stability, Cameo. There's no choice. You're ruined if you don't, young lady, do you understand? You'll be locked in your room tonight, though I hate to do it. And tomorrow you'll accept Lord Warley's hand in marriage.'

Benedict seized his knife and glared at the painting. The sheet that had covered it lay crumpled on the floor like a shroud. He'd never forget the humiliation of bringing it back to the studio that afternoon when he'd received the politely veiled demand to remove it from the Royal Academy as if it were tainted.

There could be no doubt. It was his best work. There was Cameo posed beneath the ash tree, glorious in her youth and beauty. He'd painted her with such tenderness, as if his brush caressed her flesh.

His fist jerked. He had to hold himself back from running his knife though the canvas, tearing it apart. All the care, all the effort; through all the years he had possessed one goal: to paint such a work. He wanted to smash it, burn it, hurl it into the fire.

You should never destroy your work, he remembered saying to her, *there's always something to learn from it.* He'd learned something from this; that was certain. He'd learned never to trust her again.

Why had Cameo burnt the sketch she'd made of him? Yes, he recalled now. She'd been signing it and written her telltale title, no doubt.

Her sketches had been good. Very good. Unbidden, the image came to him of her by the fire, leaning over the table, sketching with the kind of focus he recognised. When he'd clasped her hand within his, he'd seen her arm begin to move in a way he knew made a good painter great. He wasn't sure she recognised it, but he had discerned it was there. He'd desired to release that talent in her, teach her, guide her.

To love her.

One after another, more pictures of Cameo began to flash through Benedict's mind. When he'd first opened the door to her, when she'd let down her hair, when she'd laughed in the park, when she'd leant her lovely smiling profile towards Trelawney at the soirée, when she'd dropped her green taffeta dress to the floor and stood in front of him in her petticoats and chemise—

Furiously he shook his head clear of those images and his grip clenched harder around the knife handle. He swore aloud. The combination of his desire mixed with his rage, the force of her beauty twisting as if the knife he held turned in his gut.

She couldn't possibly believe a mere apology covered the damage.

All the memories, all the pain of when he'd been deceived and cheated... Her deception had brought it all back.

Benedict dropped the knife and stumbled towards the fire. The smell of whisky reached him. Shards of glass lay on the hearth from where he'd smashed it. He reached for the bottle again, pulled the cork and poured himself another, slumping down into the armchair to nurse it.

He drank a deep fiery mouthful, but it didn't erase the taste of her on his lips.

Tears streaming down her face, she had said she loved him. He almost believed her, had almost weakened and wiped the tears away. But he'd hardened his heart. She'd made a fool of him. Part of him almost admired her determination to get into his studio, to learn all she could about art without him even knowing. He'd have taught her properly, if she only had trusted him.

And what he'd suspected the night they had made love, hardly daring to believe it was true.

His alone.

His body flared as he stretched out his legs, his body still throbbing from their physical encounter. The tip of his leather boot hit something hard, sending it skidding across the wooden floor in front of the fire. He leaned down and picked up one of the coins he'd tried to force on her. She'd flung them back at him. The amount doubtless resembled mere pin money to Lady Catherine Mary St Clair.

Something else lay on the floor. He laid down his glass, leant over to see. Rubbed his thumb over the white carving of the woman's face. It held a resemblance to Cameo, to her fine features, her straight nose, the pointed chin she'd lifted at him that night, her blazing passionate fury equalling his.

He groaned as his fist closed on the carved stone.

Cameo heard the metal key turn in the lock. She flung herself on the bed, sobs racking her body. Caged to an extent she never had been before, she was truly now a prisoner.

Her parents hated having to do it, she sensed that. But they were convinced what they were doing was right—somehow saving her from herself.

Should she try to escape? There was only one place she longed to run to: Benedict Cole's studio.

'Benedict,' she whispered silently, over and over. 'Benedict.' But it did no good repeating his name. She would never see Benedict again. She would never go to his studio and watch him pick up his paintbrush, and push the unruly lock of dark hair from his forehead as he focused on the work in front of him. She would never again see his sweep across the canvas in that strong movement she had come to know so well, never feel his touch on her, his lips on her, his keen-eyed gaze that made her body and soul tingle with only a glance.

Trembling, she touched her lips. Perhaps it

was preferable not to have experienced the kind of passion he aroused, to have never known a kiss could inflame her, or a touch could bring her body to the point of ecstasy. Better, perhaps, if she had only known her world and not entered his, the world in which he belonged and for which she longed. To not know what she missed out on and what she would now miss for ever. If she hadn't been awakened by his hands, she would never have to spend the rest of her life in a kind of sleep, for life without Benedict Cole would be death.

She clutched at her hair, the awful moments at the studio replaying over and over in her brain. How maddened he'd been. The cruel words he said to her, the harsh way he looked at her, the ruthless way his lips bruised her own, his rough tearing at her clothes—she juddered with emotion, remembering. And she'd been angry, too, furious he wouldn't listen to her, all the while desiring him to go on making love to her, until together their fury was spent.

At the ewer and basin, she poured cold water and splashed it on to her tender skin, her sore eyes, her swollen lips. She caught sight of herself in the looking glass on her dressing table.

Something was missing from her neck. A kind of dread overcame her as she put a shaking hand to the hollow of her throat.

Her talisman, her lucky charm: her cameo necklace. Like Benedict Cole, like the days and nights with him at the studio, like the flash of his smile, like the touch of his paintbrush…it was gone.

Chapter Eighteen

'In that still place she, hoarded in herself,
Grew, seldom seen.'

—Alfred, Lord Tennyson:
'The Gardener's Daughter'

'Cameo? I've brought you these.'

George furtively closed her bedroom door.
As if he were a conjurer he produced from his
pockets some paintbrushes, watercolour paints
and a small roll of sketch paper.

'Thank you, George. That's sweet of you.'

He threw her an anxious glance as he sat beside her on the window seat. 'Painting means so
much to you. I'm sorry about last night. I didn't
know you'd be locked in your room.'

'Papa says I must stay here if I won't marry
Lord Warley.' Her parents had discussed her case
with their doctor who had advised a total 'rest
cure'. Her papa had calmed down, but he re-

mained obstinate. There was no changing his mind. He was convinced he had to protect his daughter.

'Warley's coming this afternoon. Mama told me,' George said. 'Can it be so terrible? Warley, I mean? Can it be so bad to marry him?'

Cameo peeked sideways at her brother. She wished she could share everything with him, but she couldn't. George was the kindest brother in the world and he'd be the gentlest, most faithful husband to Maud. Even though he'd apologised to her for siding with her parents over her portrait, she still felt unsure what his reaction might be if she confided in him further. He was more set in his ways than she'd suspected, more shocked by her behaviour than she'd anticipated.

No, she couldn't tell George her plans, the ones she made as she lay awake all night in tearful despair. By dawn, as pink and gold streaked the sky, her usual optimism and resolve had returned. She refused to stay locked in her bedroom, trapped into marriage with Lord Warley. She'd find a way out, to go to Benedict and convince him to forgive her.

How to escape? She was being guarded as if she were a prisoner. All her painting tools, her oils, her easel, her sketchbook and pencils, even the half-finished copy of the portrait of her grandmama, had been removed by poor Briggs, who appeared to be a most reluctant gaoler.

No, her family wouldn't help. Not this time. She was on her own.

George pressed her hand. 'I hate you being locked up, old girl. Will you at least try and paint while you're stuck up here?'

'I will.'

After he'd gone she picked up the watercolour materials he'd smuggled in. Perhaps she would paint. She had to think, plan a way out. Painting might help to focus her mind.

The paints and paper ready, she poured some water from the bedside jug into a glass. Swirling the brush in the water, she scanned the room for a subject. The vase of jasmine in front of her on the dressing table, the blue-enamel clock by the bed—no. She'd paint the ash tree outside the window.

Crossing the room, Cameo drew aside the curtains and hauled up the sash, the air fresh and cool on her face. The ash boughs stood strong and open, as though reaching out to her. Stretching out, she stroked the bark.

The ash tree. Of course!

Jutting out her head, she made closer scrutiny. Yes, she could manage it. Hadn't she spent half her childhood climbing trees in the square? She would climb down the grey boughs of the ash tree and slip away into the night. She craned her neck towards the road below. There'd be quite a jump from the tree's lowest bough, but she could do it. She'd wrap something soft around her body to try to break her fall. Perhaps she might make a rope out of her bedclothes. She'd work it out, somehow.

At the dressing table, she picked up the paintbrush and outlined the ash tree's slender branches. She'd use her painting as a guide, a kind of map to get down the trunk of the tree. Once the evening fog rolled in it was difficult to see outside. Someone might hear her if she slipped and fell. She would wait until everyone was sound asleep, for the servants would have been instructed to keep an eye on her. They wouldn't disobey her father, not when he remained in such a towering rage. Nor would she ask anyone else, ever, to lie for her.

No more lies.

Cameo wrapped her shawl more closely around her. A strange coldness had chilled her skin ever since she'd left Benedict at the studio, as though her body had been reset to a lower, numbing temperature. Would he listen even if she did manage to escape? Would he forgive her for what she'd done?

She'd beg him to listen, she vowed, as her paintbrush sped across the page and the tree

began to come to life on the paper in front of
her. She painted faster and faster, trying to get
the proportions right, her arm sweeping across
the paper in a wing as Benedict had shown her.

She must do it. She must fly to Benedict.
Somehow she would escape to his arms.

There she was.

Benedict groaned. In his studio. Wherever he
turned to look.

At the studio door. *I'm so sorry I'm late, Mr
Cole. You're quite right. I've come to be your
model.*

Reading by the fire. Her dark head bowed
and intent on scanning the pages. *The Stones
of Venice.* Ruskin's work. That's what she read,
while he studied her. *You've been to Venice?* Her
eager question, her violet eyes alight. *Tell me
what you saw.*

*How can I describe it in words, instead of
paint?* he'd replied.

Sketching. She'd been drawing him when
he came across her unawares, as her hand tore
faster and faster across the paper, using the
strokes that told him instantly she was a true
artist. It couldn't be disguised, that movement,
that passion.

Lying on the chaise longue. Her head thrown
back. In her white chemise.

His body hardened.

And in his sketchbook. So many drawings of her. In every aspect, in every mood. Whenever she'd gone home, pattering down the stairs, he had drawn her. Some in charcoal, some in colour.

He'd become a man possessed, he discerned that now. And the sketches were good, better than good. They'd come to his hand perfectly formed.

They were the best work he'd ever done.

Because of her.

Hidden behind the dresser were the other paintings he secretly worked on at night, including the small one he'd planned to give to Cameo before he'd discovered the truth about her. The speed and precision of his own hand amazed him. The work had been inspired by the cameo stone that nestled at the tender point of her throat. That namesake jewel.

The cameo stone now in his possession.

His hand fisted around it.

Seizing the drawings and paintings, he propped them against the wall, one by one. He stood back and looked at them.

Was it possible?

Could he do it?

Yes.

Yes.

* * *

'You seem fatigued, Lady Catherine Mary.' Lord Warley settled himself in the blue velvet chair by the drawing-room fire. He propped his cane beside him. 'Your pallor becomes you.'

Cameo stayed mute.

'Our dear Cameo's not quite herself.' Lady Buxton fluttered as she poured tea from the silver pot. 'Are you, Cameo?'

She remained silent. They might lock her in her bedroom and make her come downstairs for tea, but they could not make her speak and willingly accept Lord Warley's hand in marriage.

'Perhaps you could leave us alone, Lady Buxton?' Lord Warley said after a moment, when it became clear Cameo deigned not to reply.

The countess paused in the act of pouring tea into her own cup. 'Of course,' she agreed with an uncertain smile. 'It's not quite done, of course, to leave you unchaperoned, but you are practically engaged.'

Lord Warley smiled, baring his teeth. 'Your charming daughter is safe with me.

'So.' He stood up as her mother shut the door. With a careless spill he set down his teacup and took a step closer. Instinctively Cameo shrank away from him, locking her eyes on the richly patterned carpet on the floor.

'It's time we had a chat, don't you think?'

The colours on the carpet. Cameo focused on them. Blue, red, pink and gold. *How would you paint them? What would Benedict tell you to look for?*

'I said it's time we had a chat.'

Cameo gave a yelp of pain as Lord Warley seized her coiled hair and pulled it upwards in a brutal thrust.

'That's better. I prefer you to attend to me when I'm speaking to you.'

She choked down her acrid fear. 'You don't have to manhandle me.'

'Manhandle you?' He twisted her hair tighter, bringing tears to her eyes, before releasing her. 'I think you've had enough manhandling already, if that painting is anything to go by.'

Benedict's paintbrush on her naked body flashed into her mind and she flushed, feeling the telltale heat rise up her neck and along her cheekbones.

Lord Warley licked his lips. 'Yes, you've been touched by that artist, it's clear.'

'How dare you!' Cameo jumped to her feet and faced him. 'How dare you speak to me in this way?'

'Oh, I dare.'

Before Cameo could move, Lord Warley's cold lips were prising hers apart. She tightened them, trying to repel his advance. He only moved in closer, his fingers sliding up the bodice of her dress. With shock she felt his bare hands dive down into her décolletage and squeeze hard. His palms were moist, his fingers rough. As his thick tongue forced its way down her throat she gagged, struggling for air.

Lord Warley smirked as he fell back on his heels. 'So that's what the artist's been having, is it?'

Cameo clutched the edge of a gilt side table. She wanted to be sick, to get the hideous taste from her mouth.

'Sit down, my dear.

'I said sit down,' he hissed when her shaking legs didn't move. Grabbing hold of her shoulders, he forced her into the velvet chair.

'Now.' Returning to his seat, he picked up his teacup as though nothing had happened. 'Let me tell you what's going to transpire, Lady Catherine Mary. I'm prepared to overlook what you have done. We'll forget about the scandal you've caused. Once you are married to me people won't remember this unfortunate incident as long as you behave yourself.'

'But why do you need to marry me? Why are you doing this?'

He sneered over the edge of his teacup. 'I've taking a liking to you.'

Cameo shook her head. 'I don't believe you.'

'Or perhaps I've taken a liking to your marriage settlement. You're quite the heiress. It's always attracted me to you. And your dowry price has gone up considerably since you became damaged goods.'

'You can't need money!'

'I have debts. I enjoy a gamble.' Putting down his cup, he licked his lips again. 'I enjoy...games.'

She shuddered. 'But I don't understand. You've inherited Warley Park. It's a huge estate. Surely enough income comes from that.'

'Young ladies shouldn't discuss money,' he said with a reproving moue. 'But since you ask, yes, I inherited it from my father and mortgaged it, too. That's why your dowry will come in useful. Most useful indeed.'

'So it's all about money.'

'It isn't just about money.' He leered. 'Not at all.'

Nausea threatened to overwhelm her. 'You're disgusting. I always thought you were.'

'There is one condition to our nuptial bliss.' He hoisted one leg over the other. 'I understand your father has forbidden you to paint while you come to your senses over this unfortunate indiscretion. I agree with his decision. It's most unseemly, especially in the circumstances. Indeed, I think it would be best if you do not pursue any interest in art.'

'Do you mean I can't paint ever again, if I marry you?' Give up painting for the rest of her life? Who could ask such a thing? Her father would have come round, but Lord Warley... 'You can't mean it.'

'Painting, drawing. You should put away such things.' He reached over and lifted a small sandwich from the tea tray, popping it whole into his mouth. 'When I'm your husband you'll be under my advice in all respects.'

'You mean to treat me as a child,' she said, her voice low.

'Women are little more than children, are they not?' He flicked an invisible crumb from his trouser leg. 'As you have shown through your misjudgement.'

She hadn't misjudged Warley. Her instincts had always warned her against him.

'You need firmer guidance, a much firmer hand.' His eyes flickered over her body. 'A woman should look to her husband in all things. All your pastimes will be up to me. I think sewing is an appropriate leisure occupation for a lady. Yes, embroidery. Women always look so meek and pretty bent over their sewing hoops.'

Benedict's face came again into Cameo's mind. She could almost feel the weave of his linen shirt. 'Can you mend this, Miss Ashe?' his teasing voice echoed.

'I'm very bad at sewing.'

She'd spoken aloud. Lord Warley's voice dragged her mind back to the drawing room.

'Are you?' Again his tongue darted out. 'There are many things you'll have to learn, Catherine Mary, and I'll enjoy teaching you in a way you won't forget.'

He stretched towards her and painfully grasped her wrist. 'Your father tells me you're still pure, that the artist with whom you spent so much time did not defile you. I'm not so sure of that. But let me assure you, when you are my wife you will be mine alone to do with as I please.'

Cameo drew away, her heart thudding with fear. 'Let me go.'

He tightened his grip, hurting her, and then released her. 'The law is on my side. The day we're married you'll belong to me and that will be the end of it. Every hour of your days and nights,' he added, with another slow look over her body that made her skin crawl, 'you will spend as I wish you to spend them.'

'And no painting.' The words came from her numb lips.

'Nothing to remind you of the days you spent with Benedict Cole.'

Hearing his name brought tears to Cameo's eyes. *Oh, Benedict, Benedict.*

'I think you have feelings for that artist,' Lord Warley hissed. 'Unless you marry me I have it in my power to make his life most unpleasant indeed. People don't take kindly to the defilement of young ladies from the upper classes. If I were to suggest he hurt you...'

'He never hurt me!'

'How quickly you rush to his defence. As I was saying, if I were to suggest you'd been seduced... Let's say Benedict Cole's life wouldn't be worth living. Do you understand?'

'Yes, I understand.' She kept her voice steady while inwardly she reeled. 'I understand exactly what kind of man you are, Lord Warley.'

'Do you indeed? I don't think you do, yet. But you will. Oh, yes, Lady Catherine Mary, you will.'

Instinctive terror that he would try to kiss her again drew her away, painfully jerking her neck. He noticed her movement. A malicious gleam entered his eyes as he got to his feet. He enjoyed making her frightened.

Taking hold of his cane, he ran his hand up and down its length. 'We shall be married as soon as possible. It will be a quiet wedding. There must be an end to all the unseemly talk about you. I'll tell your parents you have agreed.'

'You seem to think I have no choice,' Cameo

retorted. 'Perhaps I'll stay locked in my bedroom before I marry you.'

'I'll have to come upstairs and persuade you.' He leered. 'I shall enjoy breaking you in.'

Cameo's mouth dried. 'You wouldn't dare.'

'I doubt your parents would object, not at this stage. They want this scandal finished.'

Her eyes smarted. She'd never sought to disgrace her family. It had all gone so terribly wrong. She'd been immature, selfish. Everything that Benedict had said.

'You'll come to your senses.' Lord Warley gloated. 'You have no choice. Not if you wish to save your precious artist.'

Drawing herself up to her full height, Cameo stood. 'I do have a choice. As long as I live and breathe, I have the choice to despise you.'

She swept out of the drawing room, her head held high. His snide laughter rang in her ears. It wasn't until she was safely upstairs in her bedroom that she started to shake.

Cameo's fingers trembled as she picked up the paintbrush and examined the half-finished painting of the ash tree lying on her dressing table.

Lord Warley's threats continued to reverberate inside her head. *If I were to suggest you'd been seduced... Let's say Benedict Cole's life wouldn't be worth living...*

Nausea rose in her throat. Would he do it? Would Lord Warley carry out his threats? If he did and Benedict's name was blackened, he would sell no paintings, have no commissions and have no means to support himself. And if Lord Warley went further and attested Benedict had damaged her in some way...if he created some trumped-up charge against him...

Lord Warley would do that. She knew it in her bones. He was desperate for money, desperate and cruel. He wouldn't just carry out his threats; he'd enjoy doing so. And there was something else driving him, she sensed it.

Dipping the paintbrush into the water, she stared out the window. Outside the light had faded, the ash tree seeming to lose its colour.

Benedict's voice came to her again. *What do you see?*

Light is always the key. He'd told her that day in Hyde Park. *You have the makings of an artist if you can see that. Many people cannot. It's only by paying attention to the natural world we can truly see what is.*

Why, oh, why hadn't she told Benedict the truth when she'd had the chance? It was all too late now. She couldn't go to him after what Lord Warley had said. She would be signing his artistic death warrant. Ending his career, all he'd worked for, all his life. He lived in a garret to achieve his aims. She never suffered, never went without. She'd been cosseted and pampered her whole life. Her slightest whim had been catered for, every demand met. She had the finest home, the finest clothing, food and furnishings—the finest of everything. Even though she hadn't had the painting lessons she wanted, she'd bought paints, paper, canvas. She'd not lived in poverty.

She made no sacrifice for her art, as Benedict did.

So many differences between them. She didn't waken to the sounds of carts in the morning, but to the sounds of carriages and of breakfast rattling on a tray.

Their love for each other, the passion they shared—her pulse quickened at the recollection of touching him, tasting him, her lips on him—that had been real. But she'd idealised his bohemian, artistic world without fully comprehending the hardships it involved. She hadn't thought about the difficult days when work went badly, when a painting didn't sell.

She'd been playing. Pretending.

Posing.

The paintbrush snapped in two. She stared down at it. She loved Benedict Cole too much to destroy him. She must give him up and she must give up painting, too. Without him, what would be the point of it? Life seemed to ebb from her, along with the force driving her to paint, to capture life and beauty.

She would never paint again.

Everything had changed.

Her passion for painting had led her to another unforgettable passion. It had changed her, deepened her and made her into a woman, instead of a wilful girl.

Her eyes blurred with tears as she pushed back her chair, the snapped paintbrush falling to the floor. Agitated, she paced the bedroom carpet. It wasn't her parents or Lord Warley stopping her painting. It was her heart, her aching heart. How could she bear to paint, to be reminded of Benedict, when she had almost destroyed his career? She'd thought her hands would never stop aching to hold a paintbrush. Now there was another ache filling her, an empty, deeper, desperate ache she knew would never depart.

A talent such as Benedict Cole's must never be destroyed.

He might forgive her for lying about her identity, but he would find it hard to forgive her if she let his artistic career be further ruined. Who knew how far Lord Warley would go?

No! She couldn't risk him carrying out his threats. She couldn't let any more damage be done to Benedict's life, to his career, to himself, because of her. It didn't matter what happened to her. She had to save him.

She picked up the broken brush. Crushing the paper into a ball, she threw it into the wastepaper basket along with the watercolour paints and glanced out at the ash tree.

Never again would she experience the colour and excitement of Benedict's studio, or the passion she'd found in his arms.

There was to be no escape.

It was her turn to sacrifice, now.

When her mother came into her bedroom, her face was quite dry of tears. 'I've come to a decision, Mama. I'll marry Lord Warley.'

Wild anger.

Fury.

Passion.

Desire.

Mixed together like oil paints on his palette.

Into colours and forms he never knew it was possible to create.

Day and night Benedict worked as he had never worked before or had known he could.

Time had stopped, gone into another dimension.

Benedict refused to stop. A sense of urgency had been building in him, a force he couldn't ignore. Almost impatiently he painted, willing his body to keep up with the images in his brain.

Faster and faster.

By the pink light of dawn.

Into the grey dusk.

By the golden lamplight.

No need for sleep, just an hour or two, snatched on the chaise longue.

Barely any need for food or drink.

His hand soared, swept, flew. Powerful. Steady, sure.

On and on.

As if it was her body.

Her skin, not canvas.

His hands on her.

Wilder and wilder. Into the night.

Chapter Nineteen

'All the land in flowery squares,
Beneath a broad and equal-blowing wind,
Smelt of the coming summer, as one large
cloud
Drew downward.'

—Alfred, Lord Tennyson:
'The Gardener's Daughter'

'I'm sorry, Maud, what did you say?'

'Oh, Cameo.' Maud sighed. 'I hate to see you this way. George and I are so worried about you. Are you still thinking about him?'

'About whom?'

'Don't pretend. About that painter, the one in the studio in Soho. Benedict Cole.'

'It's been weeks since I saw him,' Cameo said flatly. Almost six weeks, to be precise, the most terrible weeks of her life, each day dragging since she'd agreed to wed Lord Warley.

'You'll be a summer bride,' her mama had said with satisfaction. Cameo wanted to get it over with as soon as possible and her father had agreed, but her mother had insisted that there were certain preparations to be made. 'There are some things that just can't be rushed,' she had exclaimed. 'There's the dress, and the cake, and the—'

'Humph,' her papa had interrupted. 'Fuss and bother.' Sometimes Cameo saw him peer at her from beneath his eyebrows as if he wanted to say something, but the moment always passed. His anger seemed to have passed, too, to her relief. Yet her determination to protect Benedict remained true.

Now Maud slipped her arm through Cameo's and slid closer to her on the sofa. 'You're in love with him, aren't you? With that artist. With Benedict Cole.'

'How I feel about him is immaterial.' Cameo's heart sank as she spoke. 'He despises me.'

'But how do you feel about him?'

'Why are you asking me all these questions about Benedict Cole, Maud? I'm going to marry Lord Warley—I mean Robert. I suppose I must call him by his Christian name now. The wedding is only weeks away. You're going to be my bridesmaid.' She realised she'd been sharp with her friend. 'I'm sorry. I haven't been myself lately.'

'You don't have to apologise. I'm worried about you. I'm sure there's something you're not telling me. You're so unhappy. You don't eat, you don't sleep. And you're not painting.'

'I will never paint again.'

'Painting is everything to you!'

'It's nothing to me now.'

Maud pressed Cameo's hand in sympathy.

On Cameo's finger sparkled the diamond ring Lord Warley had given her as a betrothal gift. It was ornate and heavy, a family heirloom, one he hadn't pawned to pay his gaming debts, she presumed. It seemed to chill her skin. She'd barely been able to slide it onto her finger. She shivered again.

'Cameo.' Maud patted her sleeve. 'You must tell me what's wrong. I can't believe you're marrying Lord Warley. You flinch when his name is mentioned and you're losing weight, and you're so pale. You always said you hated Lord Warley.'

'Please, Maud.' Cameo's eyes filled with tears. 'I have to marry him and that's that.'

Benedict stood back, almost shaking with exhaustion.

He refused to stay cooped up in the studio a moment longer. He flung a scarf around his neck, grabbed his coat, thrust the cameo in his pocket and headed out the door.

As usual he went to the Lamb, pushing through the crowds.

Maisie stood propped against the bar in a scarlet corset and white blouse. 'Hello there. You look as if you could use a drink.' Her warm breath fanned his face. 'I heard what happened at the Royal Academy, about your painting being removed from the exhibition.'

His exhalation tasted acrid. 'All around London, is it?'

'We models always hear what's going on. It's a shame, your work being taken down like that.'

He scowled and signed to the innkeeper. 'What are you drinking, Maisie?'

'Whatever you fancy.'

He ordered her a whisky and another for himself. He suddenly remembered Cameo drinking whisky, how she'd held the glass like a child, spluttering as she tasted it.

The innkeeper poured him a generous measure. He swallowed it in one.

Maisie swigged her drink. 'I knew she wasn't any good for you, that new model of yours.'

Benedict swallowed more whisky.

'It's not right,' she went on indignantly, jiggling her body. 'People of that sort, coming and taking ordinary people's work. A fancy titled lady? Why'd she want to be a model, then?'

'She didn't intend to be my model. She desired to be a painter.' Amazed, Benedict heard himself defending her.

Maisie rubbed up against him. 'Let me come to the studio. You don't need that sort. I'll model for you again.'

'I don't need another model.'

She sighed gustily and moved away, propping her elbow on the bar. Her expression became candid. 'She caught you, didn't she?'

He toyed with his glass.

'Come on, Benedict.' Maisie rolled her eyes. 'I know artists and I know men. You barely noticed me since you had her modelling for you. It's like I'm invisible or something.'

It was true. His head had been full of images of Cameo ever since he'd met her, from the moment she'd lifted her bonnet and he'd seen those violet eyes. Other women seemed to melt into the background; he barely discerned them. Only her face stood out, as if in relief, like the carving on her cameo necklace.

'I can't imagine how you're going to paint using another model. Maybe you should try landscapes or something.' Maisie waved to the innkeeper. 'Come on. Let's have another.'

He dropped some coins on to the counter

and shook his head. 'Not for me. You have one, Maisie. I need to go and see someone.'

'Artists.' She scooped up the coins. 'Suit yourself.'

With his fist clenched on the carved stone inside his pocket, Benedict made for the door.

Cameo stared around Hyde Park. Summer flowers were starting to bloom, the grass a bright emerald threaded with yellow-and-white daisies. Birds twittered in the leafy boughs above them, bees and butterflies danced across the lawn. All of London seemed to be out of doors today, soaking up the sunshine. Little girls in smocked dresses and boys in sailor suits, similar to those she, Maud and George used to wear, were shrieking with laughter at a nearby Punch-and-Judy show. Not far away in the pavilion a band played and from further away the distant sound of horses' hooves came, as gentlemen and ladies in smart black riding habits and top hats, with the occasional military man resplendent in uniform, rode through the park.

Just like she had pretended to be doing.

Desperate for some fresh air and solitude she'd slipped away from the house, avoiding the servants. She had to be alone.

She tried not to think about the time she'd sat in Hyde Park with Benedict, on a park bench as she now sat alone. She tried not to think about him at all. Yet only yesterday she'd passed a bookshop where the window display had caught her attention. In the window had been a book—the famous art critic John Ruskin's *The Stones of Venice*. She had bought it; she hadn't been able to stop herself. The second volume would be out the next year, the bookseller told her.

I must tell Benedict. The thought came unbidden into her head, before she remembered, her eyelids prickling with tears. She wouldn't be able to tell him. She'd never discuss the book again with him now. She wouldn't hear his voice grow bright with enthusiasm when he spoke of Venice, wouldn't see his eyes glow when he described to her the paintings by the great masters he saw in that glittering city of canals. He wouldn't speak to her of Ruskin, or Venice, or anything else.

It felt better to be out in the open air at least. She took a deep breath. She was no longer being locked in her bedroom in the Mayfair house, but she had spent a great deal of time there alone recently, not only seeking solitude, but also trying to avoid Lord Warley. He called regularly since she had agreed to marry him. She often pretended to be indisposed, staying upstairs feigning an illness, and he would go away. He'd bide his time, licking his lips in the way she'd begun to hate. He could afford to wait. He'd trapped her.

Terror reverberated through her body. Her fingers fumbled as she opened her lace parasol and trod slowly towards the gates. For a moment she imagined a figure walking down the path, tall, dark-haired, in a brown coat and a long red scarf.

She blinked away her tears.

A voice startled her. 'Why, Miss Cameo!'

It was Nicholas Trelawney, smartly dressed in a top hat, his red spotted cravat and handkerchief as jaunty as ever.

He halted in front of her. 'It is Miss Cameo, isn't it?'

She smiled. It was impossible not to respond to his irrepressibly cheerful face and she felt a shaft of joy, like sunlight from a cloud, at seeing someone from Benedict's artistic world. 'Hello, Mr Trelawney. It's good to see you again.'

'And you, my dear.' He bowed, tipping his top hat. 'My apologies. I've just recalled you're not a Miss, are you? A Lady, wasn't it, as we all found out? What a shock.'

'No, I'm not a Miss. I'm Lady Catherine Mary St Clair, that's my full title. But please call me Cameo. My family and my—' her throat choked on the word '—friends do.'

'I'm honoured. My dear, how can you look so sad about your illustrious full name? There are many people who would give their eye teeth for a title. I dare say I would.'

Cameo couldn't contain herself. 'Mr Trelawney. Please, tell me. How is—Benedict? He is painting, isn't he? I haven't seen him since my portrait was withdrawn from the Royal Academy of Art.'

Her stomach lurched at the memory of that terrible meeting.

Trelawney threw his hands in the air. 'He's been painting night and day. A man possessed. I'd never seen anything like it when I popped into his studio. My dear! His papers piled high, dust everywhere, and I'm not sure when he'd last slept or ate. But the paintings—well. He didn't plan to show anything this season after what happened with the Royal Academy, but it's incredible, he already has enough for a new show. They're magnificent.'

Cameo experienced a pang of longing at the description. With the amazing artistic focus Benedict possessed she could well imagine him painting on and on, regardless of his surroundings, ignoring the need for sleep or food. She felt relieved to hear he was painting still. She'd been frightened he might give up completely after the crushing blow of her portrait's ban. 'So this new show won't be part of the Royal Academy?'

'Alas, no, my dear. It will be at a small gallery, not quite as prestigious. In fact, they're showing *The Gardener's Daughter* there already. I had to practically prise it out of Cole's grip, but he needs a sale.'

Cameo's stomach lurched. She'd done this to Benedict.

Tucking his cane under his arm, Trelawney pulled a stubby pencil from his waistcoat and patted his trouser pockets. 'Now, do I have a scrap of paper…? Ah, yes, I do!' Triumphantly he unfolded a small square of paper and started scribbling. 'I'm writing down the address.' He held it out to her. 'You simply must see it hanging.'

Cameo recoiled. 'No, I can't.'

'You must,' Trelawney insisted.

She shook her head.

'Really, Lady Cameo, you must. I won't tell you why,' he said mysteriously. 'I've seen it and you should, too.'

There was no way to explain why it was too dangerous to go anywhere near Benedict or his paintings. If Robert found out, there could be a terrible price. 'I don't want to see Benedict Cole's work. He wouldn't want me to go and see it, either.'

'You need to go and see this exhibition. Trust me, Lady Cameo. Go and see it.' He folded the piece of paper into her unwilling fingers. 'Well, goodbye, my dear. I dare say we'll meet again.'

Trelawney gave her a bow before he tripped off down the path.

Cameo unfurled the scrap of paper from her clenched fingers. The Belleview, Soho. Not a name she had heard of. It was certainly a step down from the Royal Academy, she thought, feeling sick. And it was all her fault.

She tore the paper in two.

Chapter Twenty

'News from the humming city comes to it
In sound of funeral or of marriage bells;
And, sitting muffled in dark leaves, you hear
The windy clanging of the minster clock.'

—Alfred, Lord Tennyson:
'The Gardener's Daughter'

'Cameo, dear. You're the bride and you're not ready.' Lady Buxton swept into the bedroom, wearing a blue watered-silk gown with sapphires sparkling against her throat and wrists and an elaborate diamond tiara set on her piled dark curls. 'Where's the maid?'

Cameo wrapped her white dressing gown more tightly, covering her stays and chemise. 'I can dress myself without help from a maid, Mama. Many women do.'

Her mother squawked. 'You simply must

stop saying such things. You've been doing it too much of late. It upsets your father so. It's your wedding day. You must appear your best.'

'I don't care to appear my best for Lord Warley.' She felt sick with dread about what was to come. Not only the wedding, but also the wedding night.

At least she had the night in the studio with Benedict to remember. A memory to cherish for the rest of her life. It would have to sustain her through what was to come. She trembled at the thought.

'Oh, dear. I must talk to you about your husband-to-be.' The countess perched on the gilt chair by the dressing table. She wrung her lace handkerchief. 'Where to begin.'

'Mama…'

'It's hard for me to speak of such things.' Her mother kept twisting the handkerchief. 'But I must. My own dear mama came to me on my wedding morning and I was lucky enough to marry your papa, but your grandmama, well, she was not so fortunate. She married twice, the first time to a much older man and I feel I must tell you that—oh, dear!'

'Grandmama was married twice?' Cameo asked, amazed. 'I didn't know that.'

'Yes, she married very young and not very happily, I'm afraid. It was not long after her portrait was painted, the one in the drawing room. She became a widow, you see. Then she married my papa—your grandpapa.'

'Oh. But why are you telling me this now, Mama?'

'You're so similar to your grandmama, Cameo. I stood in the drawing room just now, looking at her portrait, and I had a strange feeling she wanted me to come to you... She wanted me to say...'

Cameo reached out and kissed her mama's soft cheek. Suddenly she knew what her mother was trying to say, but there was no need. How she wished she could confide in her about Benedict, about her love for him and how she had no choice but to marry Robert. She had to marry a man she loathed to save the man she truly loved. But to explain it was impossible.

'Don't fret, Mama,' she said gently. 'You don't have to speak of these matters. I shall be perfectly all right.'

Lady Buxton's relief was palpable. She released a sigh and stood. 'I'm sure you will come to love your husband, Cameo dear. I did.'

Cameo shuddered. It was impossible for her to grow to love Lord Warley. His name stuck in her throat. What lay before her was horrifying, even though she'd reassured her mother. All too easily, she pictured him standing at the altar of

St Mary's, licking his lips as she came down the aisle. And the wedding night to come—no, she refused think about it.

Benedict's arms. The touch of his artist's hands on her skin. The night of passion they'd shared. That was what she'd keep in her mind. She would never regret that night.

Her mouth dried. The way Benedict had momentarily pulled back, puzzled. He'd seemed to know it was her first time. Would Robert know it wasn't? Would he be able to tell? The thought terrified her.

She forced her panic away and changed the subject. 'You do look pretty, Mama.'

The countess gave a girlish smile as she tucked her handkerchief into her reticule and patted her hair. 'Dear George said the same thing. He's already at the church since he's standing up for Lord Warley. I expect dear Maud is there, too.' She frowned. 'Now, where is your veil? It's the one I wore when I married your father and your grandmama wore it before me.'

'Maud will have it ready with the tiara, at the church.'

'And where are your pearls?'

Cameo shook her head stubbornly. 'No pearls, Mama.'

Lady Buxton appeared scandalised. 'But you must!'

'No.' Cameo pointed to the velvet cushion on the dressing table where her black-and-white cameo stone usually lay. She hated it being gone. Tears threatened to brim in her eyes. 'I can't wear my cameo as it has been lost and I don't wish to wear anything else.'

'Your cameo? It wouldn't be appropriate to wear such a simple necklace to your wedding, even if you had it.'

'It belonged to Grandmama.'

Her mother's face softened. 'It did. But to wear no pearls, Cameo dear, it isn't done. You must wear some of the other family jewels instead.'

Cameo set her chin. 'No, I won't. I'll give up painting and I'll marry Robert, and I'll wear this ring.' In spite of trying to find courage her voice shook as she held out the diamond ring on her finger. 'That's all.'

'But...'

Cameo spanned her bare neck with her hands. Losing her necklace still seemed a terrible omen. 'Please, Mama. This is the last time I'll be Cameo, you see.'

Robert would not call her by that name.

'I don't understand what you mean.' Her mother shook her head, bewildered. 'And what will your papa think?'

'He won't even notice. Please, don't say anything.'

'Very well, then.' Her mother gave a reluctant nod. 'I won't argue with you on your wedding day. Are you sure you don't wish me to call for the maid?'

Cameo shook her head.

'I'll leave you to dress.'

The countess shut the bedroom door with a click. Cameo sighed. She loved her mama and it wasn't her fault all this had happened. She was stunned by the story about her grandmother.

Crossing the room, she retrieved from the bottom of her wardrobe the half-finished copy of her grandmama's portrait, the one she'd begun to paint before she went to Benedict's studio. Briggs had returned it to her bedroom, saying nothing. The happy time when she had painted it, the old sheet spread beneath her in the drawing room, seemed long ago.

Her grandmother wore a white dress in the portrait, she realised, just as she did in the painting Benedict had done of her as *The Gardener's Daughter*. She hadn't made that connection before. There was such a resemblance between the paintings. For a moment she imagined them hanging side by side in the drawing room. She stared at her grandmother's face, wishing she could speak. What advice would she give her, if she could?

Lingering, she went to the window and pulled wide the blue chintz curtains, staring out at the ash tree. It still hadn't come into leaf; its grey branches were bare. She wouldn't see its green leaves unfurl.

She sank on to the window seat. She'd slept badly the night before and for many nights before that. She wasn't sure which caused her more anguish, the dreams of being happy in the studio with Benedict when she woke up crying because they weren't real or the nightmares about Lord Warley that she suspected would become all too real, all too soon. Her mouth dried. They were terrifying, those nightmares. In one, she was imprisoned in a windowless room and he came in and—no, she must not think about it. How he would enjoy learning he tortured her in her sleep.

Feeling drained, she dragged herself over to the bed where her wedding dress lay spread out on the counterpane. Lightly she touched one of the sleeves. Made of ivory silk, with a fine lace décolletage and short train, it must be one of the loveliest dresses she'd ever seen. Next to it were white satin gloves and a beautiful cloak with a pearl clasp, a thick ivory satin on the outside, with a blue satin lining. Her slippers with a ribbon rosette and a tiny heel were satin, too, and her gloves were traced with delicate embroidery. Each of the garments was exquisite. She experienced no desire to put them on, but she forced herself to do so. Her limbs felt heavy as, one by one, she layered on petticoats made of silk and trimmed with Nottingham lace, each finer than the last. Finally, she lifted the wedding gown over her head, letting the folds of the skirt billow about her and fall to her feet.

With a weary sigh Cameo wrapped the white sash around her waist, moving in front of her dressing table to tie it. From a bottle of Parma-violet cologne she dabbed behind her ears and on her wrists. It used to be her favourite, but her sense of smell had lately evaporated. She lacked all pleasure in life.

In the glass she examined herself. Her coiffed hair, in a simple chignon with no side ringlets on either side of her cheeks, appeared dull. It no longer shone. In spite of her earlier efforts with witch hazel and rosewater, her normally pale skin appeared chalky, her eyes shadowed and dark, her mouth drawn. Was she the woman Benedict yearned to paint, body and soul? Would he even recognise her?

A fragment of the Tennyson poem he'd used for her portrait floated into her mind. She kept the leather-bound book from their family library tucked beneath her pillow now. Would he still think her hair like ash buds and her eyes like pansies? Would she still look like the gardener's daughter to him? She'd never know. That Benedict, the Benedict who'd read the poem to her with such passion, had left her life for ever. Instead his furious voice resounded in her head.

Shadow portrait...I only knew one side of you, the shadow side...I never want to see your face again.

Cameo covered her face with her hands.

'Ooh,' said one of the younger housemaids, 'you do look lovely.'

'Thank you,' Cameo whispered faintly. She tried to smile. Her mouth refused to form the curve.

In the wood-panelled hall at the bottom of the stairs, her parents and the servants stood waiting. Cameo descended the marble staircase, her embroidered gloves gliding over the smooth wooden balustrade, the lacy train of her wedding dress trailing after her. She swallowed her tears. 'I won't cry. I won't be afraid,' she instructed herself with a gulp.

'We wish you happiness on this, your wedding day, Lady Catherine Mary,' Briggs said, with a frown at the housemaid, who flushed for speaking out of turn.

The countess dabbed her handkerchief to her

eyes as the earl, smartly dressed in his morning coat, kissed his daughter's cheek. A flash of tenderness crossed Lord Buxton's expression. 'You're a credit, Cameo.'

'Thank you, Papa.' Cameo sighed inwardly. She refused to blame him, any more than her mother, for what he forced her to do. She knew her father loved her. He truly thought marriage to Lord Warley the best thing for her after the near scandal.

'I'm going to accompany your mama to St Mary's in the first carriage,' her father told her. 'The other carriage is for you, my dear. You'll follow behind.'

'Yes, Papa,' she replied obediently, as he took her mama on his arm and went out the front door, assisted by the butler and footmen.

One by one, the other servants trailed out of the hall. Cameo gave the housemaid one last smile.

'Good luck, Lady Catherine Mary,' she said, with a bob.

She'd need it. Cameo felt sick to her stomach. This should be the happiest day of her life, but the housemaid seemed more excited than she.

Briggs opened the door and she walked out into the square. She threw a last glance over her shoulder at the black-painted door with its glistening brass knobs and knocker, the iron-lace trim, the scrubbed marble steps. It was no longer her London home. In the future, her home would be Warley Park. She stumbled, missing her footing, and Bert, who had been standing beside the crested carriage ready to help her into it, rushed to assist. 'Let me help you, Lady Catherine Mary.'

Smiling gratefully at him, she stepped up on the box into the carriage. She settled the rug over her smooth satin skirt and adjusted her cloak, surprised to be able to function, to smile, to move, to speak, when such agonising pain seared her heart. 'Thank you, Bert.'

They set off, the horses going at an eager trot. Through the carriage window Cameo took one last glimpse at the house before they trotted out of the square.

Resting her head against the velvet-upholstered seat, she listened to the horses' hooves, feeling the vibrations of the wheels of the carriage taking her closer and closer to the church, to marrying Lord Warley and to never seeing Benedict Cole again.

A horrifying sense of confinement overwhelmed her, similar to her nightmares. Once the wedding ceremony was completed she'd be her husband's property for the rest of her life. That was the law. She'd be his prisoner, with no chance of escape.

Cameo struggled for air. The interior of the carriage seemed to press in on her, stifling her lungs.

A coffin.

She knew of people who had been buried alive. It was reported in the newspaper. There had been a case when a woman had awoken and tapped from inside a coffin just before her burial in the graveyard. George had read the macabre tale aloud at the breakfast table. It had sent their mother into hysterics and resulted in their father, irate, ordering George from the dining room.

Horror overcame her as if she, too, were on her way to being buried alive. Gnawing on her lip, she tried to draw deep breaths to still the flood of panic rising inside, but to no avail. Terror heated her skin as perspiration fell like dew down her spine.

Yet again her hands clutched at her bare neck. She choked. How she wished she still had her necklace, today of all days, especially now she knew more of her grandmama's story. How she wished her grandmama were beside her now.

Exhaling, Cameo stared out of the carriage window to distract herself from her hot skin, from the nausea rising in her throat. She focused her attention on the people in the streets going about their business, passing in and out of the shops and houses. There was a housemaid beating a carpet, a child playing with a cup and ball, a flower seller shouting her wares, but it served as no distraction. Her terror refused to abate. It grew stronger.

Oh, Benedict, Benedict, she called to him silently inside her head. *Please, help me*. His name throbbed in her brain. He would never know what she was sacrificing for him. He would always despise her.

If only she could see him, one last time. Yes, one last time, to watch as he moved the brush across the canvas in those strong stokes. One last time to remember him, the way he glanced up and down as he painted, his mouth set in a firm line until he smiled; the smile that showed he was finally satisfied with what he'd achieved. But Benedict would refuse her entry to the studio.

Her hand flew to her throat.

Bert stopped the horses. Cameo opened the carriage door and leapt. Her white satin slippers hit the cobbles and she began to run.

Chapter Twenty-One

'And if I said that Fancy, led by Love,
Would play with flying forms and images,
Yet this is also true…'

Alfred, Lord Tennyson:
'The Gardener's Daughter'

Cameo dashed away from the carriage. A gust of wind caught her silk cloak and it fluttered from her shoulders, like wings. Aware of the startled looks she drew as she raced through the mass of people in the crowded streets, she didn't dare glance to see if Bert came after her, or if he had driven on, not suspecting the bride had flown. She kept running, her breath coming faster and faster as she covered ground, dodging shoppers with packages, the hawkers on the street.

'Where are you going so fast, my pretty?' one of them called to her with a guffaw, as she sped by.

A few streets away she slowed and ducked inside the doorway of a grocer's, out of sight, panting. She couldn't stay hiding in the shop doorway. She lifted off her cloak and turned it inside out, so the telltale ivory silk was on the inside, the blue lining on the outside. It was still clearly fine, but the colour made it less obvious. She lifted her skirts and glanced at her slippers. They were scuffed, dirty with mud from her flight through the streets and barely fit for such an activity to start with.

Rapidly she scanned the street.

Across the street she spied a cab stand, where a couple of drivers were waiting for a fare. She sped over, barely missing being hit by a cart.

A driver with a wide, weather-beaten face lounged on his seat, his horse's reins slack. 'Can you help me?'

He gave a brief nod, his round black hat falling over his eyes.

'I need to get to the Belleview Gallery, in Soho.' Quickly she gave him the address. 'Do you know where that is?'

'I certainly do, miss,' he said in a reproving tone. 'I've taken the knowledge, haven't I?'

'The knowledge?' The phrase was new to her.

'That's right, miss. All London cab drivers had to learn the streets of our fair city, after all the crowds what came to see the Royal Exhibition last year. Mayhem it was, with new lads thinking they can take passengers without knowing where to take 'em. So we all have to learn the knowledge now and pass the test.' He added, boasting, 'Passed with flying colours, meself. I know my way around London. Been a driving cabs for years.'

'I need to get there urgently,' Cameo explained. 'I only need directions. I don't have any money for a fare.'

The man's eyes were shrewd as he pushed up his hat. 'Matter of urgency, is it?'

So urgent was her need to see Benedict's work, if not Benedict himself, it had sent her leaping from the crested carriage. 'Yes.'

'In trouble?'

She gave a startled nod in reply.

The driver's look softened. 'I've got a daughter about your age. I'd appreciate someone helping her if she needed it.' He paused and twitched the horse's reins. 'Come along, miss, jump in. It isn't far. Let's get you to Soho.'

The cab driver tipped his hat as he drove away. 'Good luck, miss!'

'Goodbye and thank you,' Cameo called. His unexpected kindness touched her, made her feel less alone in the city streets, which, although she'd spent every Season of her life in London, she realised now she barely knew, so sheltered had been her life in Mayfair. *You're spoilt, Cameo.* She recalled Benedict's enraged voice again and winced. He'd said so many hurtful things to her that terrible night, things which contained sharp painful jabs of truth.

She certainly hadn't realised the Belleview Gallery existed, in this grubby street, not much more than a laneway. She turned to look at it, a scruffy establishment with peeling paint and a tattered red awning. It was more a warehouse than a gallery and most certainly lacked the prestige of the Royal Academy of Art. Another pang of guilt came over her at how she'd so adversely affected Benedict's career.

Through the window she saw there were people standing about, admiring the paintings that hung on walls on both sides of the half-brick walls.

She twisted the brass doorknob and stepped hesitantly inside. No one noticed her. A gentleman wearing pince-nez, who she guessed might be the owner of the gallery, was with a group at the rear, pointing to one of the paintings and gesturing enthusiastically, although she couldn't hear what he was saying.

Avoiding the large group, she turned to her left and went to the first painting, a small work with a simple, square, wooden frame.

A sharp breath caught in her throat. It must be Benedict's work. She recognised his brush-strokes even before she noted his bold black signature in the lower-right corner. But it wasn't just the fact that it was Benedict's work that made her clutch her cloak with a trembling hand. It was the subject.

Her eyes widened in disbelief at the portrait of her, a head study. Her own face stared out of the frame, her eyes holding a sparkle of laughter, her mouth curving in the beginning of a radiant smile. Cameo glanced at the card beneath the painting. *My Lady Laughing*, it was called.

Had she ever looked like that, felt like that? It seemed impossible she had ever experienced such an obvious moment of joy, especially now, with despair her familiar shadow. She must have shown that part of herself to Benedict, in those lost, magical moments of happiness.

She moved to the next painting and gasped. This, too, was her portrait, painted in Benedict's own indefinable style. A large work; he'd captured her absolutely. This time in profile, depicted seated, she curved over a table, clutching a stick of charcoal. Cameo recalled how he'd seen her sketching in his studio. The memory must have been imprinted perfectly in his artist's brain. Looking at it was almost like being back in the studio. Her gaze went again to the card beneath the carved picture frame. *My Lady Drawing*, this portrait was named.

Next was the largest painting in the room, a full-sized life study. There she stood, as she must have looked when she'd first met Benedict, in her simple grey dress with the ivory buttons, her black-and-white cameo at her neck and her hair pulled into a bun. In spite of her simple attire, she witnessed for the first time how haughty she could appear, with her chin tilted and her head high. She also discerned the vulnerability, the loneliness in her eyes that Benedict had captured, a lost look, of being alone and misunderstood. He'd recognised that in her and balanced it with her haughtiness, making her whole.

She checked the card below. *My Lady Posing*. The title brought something between a sob and a laugh to her lips. It wasn't only a reference to her posing for Benedict as a model, of course, but also to her posing as the mythical Miss Ashe.

Dazed, Cameo moved on to the next painting. This time she cried out aloud. Her own face and figure were again depicted with such skill she felt awed. Her eyes were closed, her head thrown against the golden brocade of the chaise longue, her hair tumbling, revealing her neck as the stem of a flower, her emerald-green taffeta dress ruffled. It appeared so real she almost blushed, remembering his lips on her skin after that taffeta dress was removed. What had he called it? She alone knew the double meaning of the title *My Lady Lying*.

She went on to the next painting, and to the next. It couldn't be true. Every single one of Benedict Cole's paintings was of Cameo, each capturing a different mood, expression or activity. Every precious moment from the weeks they'd spent together had been frozen in time. There were too many to take in. *My Lady Reading* had her with her head buried in a book, while *My Lady in the Park* showed her sitting primly on a Hyde Park bench, while yet another, *My Lady Fury*, showed her clearly fuming with rage, as on that last terrible night she'd seen him at the studio, when he'd discovered her identity.

There, too, was *The Gardener's Daughter*, the painting which had caused so much trouble. A smile stretched her lips. So he had showed it after all. She might have suspected that an artist as strong-minded as Benedict Cole wouldn't let polite society tell him what he could and could not paint and whether he had permission to show it. Relief flooded her to see the portrait intact. In her worst moments she'd imagined him hurling it into the fire.

It felt strange seeing the portrait again. It was even more beautiful than she remembered, the carved frame with its ash buds, leaves and flowers, the fine way he'd painted the green leaves of the ash tree and its slender grey trunk and boughs, the delicate petals of the daffodils, bluebells and snowdrops at her feet, each blade of grass a tender pointed shoot. She appreciated once again his attention to nature in the Pre-Raphaelite style, the truth he captured by it. And the way he'd painted her—she saw even more clearly now the care he'd layered through the paint, how accurately he portrayed her in the filmy white dress—in truth her chemise, she recalled with a blush—her black hair over her shoulders, her eyes that vivid pansy shade. It was more powerful than staring into the looking glass, for he'd gone deeper, into her soul.

The loss of him tore her heart. At least she'd had those days with him in the studio, seen him create this work, she comforted herself, blinking away tears. At least she still had that night.

At the rear of the room, where the other viewers were gathered, she waited until a woman wearing a large purple bonnet stepped aside.

The painting here seemed to stop her heart. Smaller than the rest, a miniature, the wooden oval frame contained a small cameo carved in wooden relief at its top. Immediately inside the frame, on a velvety-black background, the words *A miniature of loveliness, all grace* were painted in gold, curling calligraphy. She knew that phrase, she recalled with wonder. It came from 'The Gardener's Daughter', too.

Within the curved quotation, Benedict had painted another oval shape resembling a brooch. It had a gold rim to it, in finely wrought detail. It appeared so real she almost reached out to clasp it. In the centre of the oval he'd depicted her partly in profile. Her shoulders were bare and around her neck, on its black-velvet ribbon, hung her cameo necklace: a cameo within a cameo. *My Lady: Cameo Portrait*, she read below, her eyes brimming with tears.

Her mind awhirl, she moved into the centre of the gallery and surveyed the exhibition as a whole, trying to take it all in. The effect in its entirety stunned her. There were close to a dozen portraits in all, including the pencil sketches. She'd never imagined the whole exhibition to be Benedict's work, let alone an exhibition entirely made up of portraits of her. How had he done it? His brilliance stunned her as she recognised his talent anew, a talent that could never be destroyed. He must have painted night and day to produce works of such extraordinary power and beauty. What did it mean? He'd dedicated an entire exhibition to her.

The woman in the purple bonnet nudged her neighbour.

'That's the model,' Cameo heard her mutter.

'It is you, isn't it, miss?'

She came out of her trance. 'Yes, it's me. But I didn't know the artist had painted all these.' She waved around the gallery.

'You didn't know.' The woman shook her bonnet in disbelief. 'Well, he certainly knows you.'

Cameo nodded, dazed. 'Yes, he does.'

Across the room a man she guessed to be the owner of the gallery had pricked up his ears and began to bear down on her, as through his pince-nez his eyes gleamed with recognition. 'Excuse me...'

Cameo couldn't speak to the owner, not at that moment. She couldn't speak to anyone, just then. Her cloak swirling around her, she rushed out of the gallery and straight into a man coming through the door.

Cameo steadied herself on the door frame.

Benedict stood on the street in his long coat, his red-paisley cravat tied loosely at his strong throat. She'd forgotten how tall he was, how he towered over her, how his presence filled the air around him. But his dark brown hair, with that wayward lock over his brow, and his black, searching eyes, glowing with a fierce inner light as they raked her face and body—no, she hadn't forgotten those.

He, too, had fallen silent.

'I've...' She stepped out into the street. The

gallery door slammed behind her. 'I've been looking at the paintings.'

It wasn't what she meant to say as the words tumbled from her lips.

'Now you know.' Benedict cupped Cameo's face, his thumbs caressing her cheeks. 'I cannot paint without seeing your face.'

Colour burst inside Cameo's head as Benedict's lips met hers; his kiss was a blaze of passion that told her all she needed. It told her he had longed for her, as she had longed for him, each moment, each hour. It told her every day apart had been a torment to his soul. It told her she was his, for ever.

'I knew you'd come.' His voice was husky. 'I've been waiting for you.'

Revelling in his familiar smell, Cameo leaned against his broad chest. 'I thought I'd never see you again.'

He tossed an ironic laugh into the air as his fingers tangled gently in her hair. 'Whereas you were all I could see. I couldn't hold you as I yearned to, except in my dreams, and when I awoke, you were gone. All I could do was paint.'

'You're tired.' His face seemed thinner, quite haggard, with a pallor suggesting he hadn't seen sun and air for many days, and dark stubble lining his jaw. 'You've been working too hard.'

'My intention was to paint you out of my system. That formed my plan. But it didn't work. As soon as I finished one portrait, another image of you would come to me, and I began another. Painting you—it didn't feel as if I had any choice in the matter.'

She glanced through the gallery window. 'The results are beautiful.'

His lip curved. 'So you approve of the paintings?'

Cameo rubbed a gloved finger along his hard, stubbled chin. 'Do you need to ask?'

He gave her his unexpectedly boyish smile, the one she loved. 'I didn't think anyone would be interested in exhibiting them. I just couldn't stop painting you. I felt half-crazed. Trelawney saw them and said they were the best works I'd ever done, an improvement even on *The Gardener's Daughter*. He convinced me to show them here.'

'Mr Trelawney told me about the exhibition. I ran into him in Hyde Park.'

'Is that right?' A chuckle.

'Do you mean he's been in on it, too?'

'Poor Trelawney's taken so many walks in the park he's declared himself a skeleton, he says he's lost so much weight. Not that there's much chance.'

'It mystified me why he'd been so insistent until I saw the paintings.'

'I knew you'd see them, somehow, some day,' Benedict told her huskily. 'I believed they'd bring you to me. I had a strange faith in that.'

'Then you've forgiven me?' Her heart pounded. 'For lying to you?'

'It's I who should ask for forgiveness.' His mouth was taut. 'When you didn't come back to the studio after that night we argued, I thought I'd driven you away for ever. I said things that were unforgivable.'

'Not unforgivable,' Cameo objected. 'I said harsh things, too.'

'Only because I wouldn't listen.' He breathed into her ear. 'I'm right, aren't I? It was your first time, wasn't it?'

'Yes.' Her confession was a shudder against his chest.

He pulled her closer. 'I took your maidenhood.'

'I wanted it to be you. It was all I ever dreamed,' she confessed softly.

'If I'd known, I wouldn't have, I should never have…'

'Benedict. Hush.' She laid a finger against his lips. 'I don't have any regrets. It was perfect.'

As he wrenched her closer her cloak fell from her shoulders to reveal the shimmering satin dress, the pearls and fine embroidery.

'Is that a wedding gown?' he asked, incredulous.

Cameo might have suspected his artist's eye would miss nothing. Self-consciously, she smoothed her skirts.

'Are you getting married? Today?'

'I didn't want to, Benedict. You've got to believe me,' she begged. 'My parents forced me into it. I had no choice—at least, I thought I didn't. Then, on the way to the church today, I knew I couldn't go through with it. So I leapt from the carriage.'

'My darling! You might have been hurt.'

'I'm perfectly all right. The carriage stopped at a corner.'

He chuckled. 'You never cease to amaze me. So you're a runaway bride.'

'I suppose I am.'

Benedict cast a quick glance around the busy street. 'We can't stay here. Come back to the studio, Cameo. We can discuss everything.'

Chapter Twenty-Two

'We spoke of other things; we coursed about
The subject most at heart, more near and
near.'

—Alfred, Lord Tennyson:
'The Gardener's Daughter'

Above Cameo's head the sign for the Lamb public house creaked as it swung in the breeze.

'Oh, Benedict.' She'd feared never to see this familiar place again, the crowds of people, the carriages and carts, the bakery with the smell of warm, fresh bread wafting from inside. 'It's so good to be here again. And there's Becky!'

'You know Becky?' Benedict asked with a smile.

'Do you know her, too?'

'I often give her money and food. She saw you being attacked, that night you came to me, when the thief was after your necklace. She found me and brought me to you.'

'Did she? Oh, I must thank her!'

Cameo raced ahead to where the match girl sat on the cobbles with her wares laid out beside her.

'Hello, Becky!'

The match girl's dirty face lit up. 'Hello, miss. I haven't seen you for such a long time. I thought you'd gone away.'

'Becky, Mr Cole told me how you helped me that night, when the thief tried to get my necklace. How can I ever thank you?'

'That's all right, miss.'

Cameo patted Becky's rough hand. A bump underneath her glove caught her attention. Why, it was the diamond ring Lord Warley had given her. Impulsively she slipped off her glove. Sliding off the ring, she dropped it into the girl's palm.

Becky stared down at the jewel in amazement. 'You can't give me this ring, miss!'

Already Cameo experienced a sense of release. How furious Lord Warley would be if he knew she'd given a diamond ring to a match girl. The thought gave her a certain satisfaction. It was no less than he deserved. 'Yes, I can. Take it to your mother, Becky. Don't let anyone give you less than it is worth.'

Cameo smiled as Becky grabbed her matches and scampered away.

She turned to see Benedict smiling at her. 'You gave away a diamond ring.'

'I don't need a diamond ring.' She shuddered. She could trust Benedict with her life. She could trust his love and talent against Robert's hate and cruelty. 'All it represented to me was a life sentence at Warley Park.'

His fingers pressed into the flesh of her upper arm. The rage in his eyes terrified her.

'Warley Park is where I grew up.'

Benedict pulled Cameo inside the studio and slammed the door.

'I don't understand.' She cast off her cloak. 'Tell me. What do you mean?'

'Just as I said. I grew up at Warley Park.'

'Do you mean the cottage you told me about, the one your mother made so colourful, was on that estate?'

He gave a brooding nod. Nowhere else had been as dear to him as that cottage at the edge of the woods, under the curling leaves of oak and ash trees.

'Why, it all makes sense now,' Cameo said wonderingly. 'Those grounds, the gardens and woods you described—I've seen them.'

'You've been there.'

'When you were painting *The Gardener's Daughter*. I had to go away. I went to Warley Park with my parents and I spent an afternoon in the woods. They were so beautiful. And I saw the estate cottages, too. But…if you grew up at Warley Park, then it must have been that family, who…'

He witnessed the horrified knowledge dawn in Cameo's eyes.

'Were they the aristocrats you hated so much, who mistreated your family and cast your mother out of her home?'

Pain blazed inside him at the recollection. 'Yes. It was them. Or should I say, Robert Ackland, the current Lord Warley, to be precise.'

'I can't take it in.'

Cameo collapsed on to the worn armchair by the fireplace and lifted an amazed face to him. 'Lord Warley tried to force me to wed him. He's in debt from gaming. That's why he sought to marry me—he needed my dowry, my marriage settlement.'

'I'm not surprised to hear he's so unscrupulous,' Benedict said in disgust, as he scraped out a chair to sit opposite her. 'It would have broken the late Lord Warley's heart.'

'You knew him, then?'

'Oh, yes, I knew him.' He paused for a moment as he struggled inside. For so long he'd kept it to himself. Then he spoke, his voice low. 'He was my father.'

'Your father! But I thought your father was Arthur Cole, the gamekeeper.'

'Arthur Cole did act as a father to me, when I was young.' He recalled the kind, weather-beaten gamekeeper who had taught him wood carving. 'He was a good man. He showed me care and compassion, as he did my mother. She was already pregnant when Arthur married her.'

'Pregnant with you,' Cameo confirmed.

'Yes. That's why my mother stayed at Warley Park. She was from a local family, a country girl. It was hard for her, living in the gamekeeper's cottage. But she did it for me and for my real father. She loved him, but they couldn't be married. He was already married to Robert's mother. Most unhappily, I understand, though they had Robert in the end.'

'So you were the firstborn. Did you always realise the late Lord Warley was your father?'

'I only knew him as the lord of the manor, when I was a boy.' Benedict pushed his hair from his brow. 'I went up to the house at Christmastime with all the other children on the estate. It was then I saw the paintings.' Those paintings. Their gleaming colours in golden frames against the scarlet walls of the gallery came to him, flooding his senses. 'There's a fine art collection there.'

'Benedict, I've seen the paintings in the gallery,' she broke in. 'The Old Masters, they're magnificent.'

'Many of those paintings were bought by my real father.'

'I saw the late Lord Warley's portrait in the gallery, too.' She studied his face. 'You both look like him. Dark-haired, dark eyed. You have the same jaw line, but your half-brother, Robert, doesn't. I can see it now.'

Benedict rubbed his jaw. 'Do I? I'd like to resemble my real father. He was an art connoisseur. He bought up a number of Venice's artworks at one time and took them to Warley Park.' His mind rolled back. 'At one of the Christmas parties, I ran away and hid in the house. I was a shy boy. I found myself in the long gallery, looking at Rembrandt, Titian, da Vinci, Raphael, not recognising what an exceptional collection hung in front of me. I only knew I was spellbound. That was the first day I met my real father properly. He found me in the gallery.'

Cameo stayed silent as if urging him to continue.

'That day, everything changed,' he went on. 'I think when Lord Warley first came across me looking at the paintings he wondered what I was doing there. But he was kind to me, asked me what I liked about them, and for some reason I wasn't shy with him. He soon realised I'd inherited his love of art, along with an instinct for colour that came from my mother. I spent hours with him in the gallery. He showed me different works he'd collected, too, explained their histories and the different painting techniques. He told me what the symbols in the paintings meant and the stories behind them, talked to me about the other paintings he'd seen abroad, in Venice in particular. He loved Venice.'

She nodded, still silent, her eyes fixed on him.

'He took more and more interest in me.' In his mind, Benedict slipped backwards in time. 'He was a painter, an amateur, but a good one. He taught me, encouraged me, believed in me. We went on painting expeditions on the estate. We'd paint in the woods, down by the stream, capture the trees, plants, birds, animals—all we saw. Truth from Nature was his motto, too, long before the Pre-Raphaelites claimed it. He saw my talent, arranged for me to have some lessons, and eventually had me sent to be educated here in London. When I was old enough, he sent me on a Grand Tour. He promised to join me in Venice.'

He halted. It was difficult to go on.

'What happened?' Cameo stroked his arm. 'Tell me.'

'My father died,' Benedict said bleakly. 'When I returned to Sussex, my mother was alone. Arthur Cole, the gamekeeper, had died a few years before, you see. When I returned from Venice I found my mother weak and ill. She'd been sick for some time, but Robert had insisted she remove herself from the gamekeeper's cottage. He knew how much our father loved her and yet he wouldn't let her stay on the estate. I found her living in squalor in a nearby town, sickened with a cough seeming to rack her whole body. She hadn't written to tell me of her illness. She intended me to have my tour in Europe. She wanted me to have the gift of art my father gave me.'

Rage rose up, like a knife in his stomach. 'Robert may as well have killed my mother. Her health failed. She didn't live too much longer. It was revenge, I think, for the way our father favoured me. I remember Robert used to complain about me being near the paintings in the gallery. He thought I'd harm them. Harm them! I appreciated those paintings at a young age more than he ever did.'

'He despises art,' Cameo said fiercely. 'All he cares about is how much the paintings are worth as an investment.'

'That lack of appreciation is something I can't understand, to have such riches and to not even value them. He's a philistine. That art collection, those glories in his house, they're no more than wallpaper to him.' Benedict clenched his jaw. 'But he still desired them.'

'What do you mean?'

'That was another thing I discovered when I got back from Venice. Lord Warley's will had been altered or replaced. He'd told me by then, of course, that I was his son. He said he loved my mother from the first moment he saw her, with her colourful, natural beauty, her wild gypsy heart. He told me he was going to leave me the paintings he'd collected himself. They would appreciate in value—it became a way of giving me a legacy. He knew Robert didn't like them, or understand them, and I did. But there was no mention of that legacy in the new will. For many years, I wondered if my father, who I'd believed to be an honourable man, had lied to me. Then I came to believe that perhaps Robert had engineered it when I travelled to Venice and my father was dying, unable to understand what was happening around him. Or that he'd even destroyed my father's will. But I can never know for sure.'

'Robert cheated you. That is sure. And you're his brother!'

'Half-brother.' He frowned. 'I didn't recognise him that day in Hyde Park—I barely caught a glimpse. I was too busy running after you and it's a quite a few years since I've seen him. He was never popular on the estate. He was cruel, even as a child. My mother used to tell me there's always good in people and she was kind to him. Robert's mother was a cold woman, you see. I received more warmth and affection in our cottage from my mother than he did from his, up in the grand main house.'

'I find it hard to be sorry for Robert,' Cameo interjected.

'But my mother did care about him, as the son of the man she loved, after all. It wasn't an easy situation. That's what made it worse, when he treated her so badly. She didn't suspect of what he was capable. I did. I came across him once, tormenting a rabbit caught in a trap in the woods.'

Benedict's mouth creased into a wicked smile as the recollection returned. 'I punched him on the nose. The coward ran away. Of course, I didn't realise we were brothers then and we were both away at school for most of the year.'

He swigged a draught of wine from the glass he'd just poured. 'When I got back from Venice and found he'd cast my mother out, I demanded an interview with him. I wanted to confront him about what he'd done to her and also about the paintings my father had wanted to leave to me.

I won't forget how he called me into our father's study at Warley Park. There he sat, very much the lord of the manor. He ruled Warley Park, and all the people's lives in it, including my mother's. I hated how he'd treated her the minute my back was turned.'

He felt barely in the studio now, as the memory raged back. 'I couldn't see my mother cast out of our home, no matter how humble it was. I wanted to take on the post of gamekeeper so she could keep the cottage. I offered to give up my career in art, if I had to. But Robert wasn't having that. He wanted to turn us out without a penny and I refused to beg. I had to let it go. I didn't want to create a scandal for my mother. When she died not much later, I left Warley Park and put any connection with it behind me. That's why I avoided any aristocratic circles—it seemed to be the only way. I determined to make my own way in the world. I haven't seen Robert since and I never wanted to see the estate again.'

'So you've never been home to Warley Park.'

'Never.' The word came out harshly as he slammed down his wine glass on the table. 'I still dream of those woods, though, and sometimes I dream of the paintings in the gallery.'

'They should be yours,' Cameo said with passion. 'Surely there's a case for them being your birthright?'

'I want nothing of Robert's—not his lands, not his house, not his paintings. Though perhaps there is something else I do want,' he added, with a quirk of an eyebrow, as he drew her to him. 'You.'

He pulled back. 'You do understand, don't you? You brought it all back, the way I'd felt so cheated, so deceived. I was full of rage and distrust towards what you represented, as a member of the aristocracy, who I thought you were, not who you really are. You were a direct reminder of a past I wanted to forget.'

'I understand that now, but, Benedict, I've just realised something.' Cameo flashed him a teasing look from under her lashes. 'You're the son of a lord. You're so damning about aristocrats, but you're one yourself.'

'The wrong side of the blanket.'

'I prefer your side to Robert's.'

Benedict gave a wry smile.

'I owe you an apology for some of the things I said when we first met.' His chuckle sounded rueful. 'You understand now, I hope. I'd become bitter, but I just longed to put it all behind me. The memories were too much for me, so I cut off that part of my past, tried not to think about my real father. It seemed easier to stay out of that world, to not have anything to do with it.'

'We're not all spoilt and arrogant.' Cameo sent

him a small, sorry smile. 'Well, some of us have recently learnt not to be.'

'Being spoilt and arrogant was something I hated in my half-brother—' Benedict twisted the name with disdain '—Robert.' He wrapped his finger in a curl escaping at Cameo's neck, making her skin tingle. 'Can you forgive me? And as for my unconventional birth, can you accept that, too?'

'Whether you are high-born or low-born makes no difference to what I see in you.'

'And what do you see?'

'You're an artist. You taught me.' She reached up to trace a daring finger around the brackets of his mouth. 'I see natural nobility. I see passion and pride and there's arrogance, too, Benedict. But I wouldn't have you any other way.'

A strange note came into her voice as she said, 'About Robert…'

'What is it?'

'I think Robert knew who you were.' Her eyes sparked. 'You didn't recognise him that day in Hyde Park, but…do you think he recognised you?'

The scene flashed in Benedict's mind. The distance between them. 'It's possible, I suppose.'

'But he knew your name, didn't he? It was Robert who recognised my portrait at the Royal Academy. He must have been at the private viewing. He went straight to my father, to have the painting removed from the exhibition. I'm absolutely certain. He intended to damage your career and my reputation. He meant to ruin us both.'

Faltering at the cold rage written all over his face, Cameo told Benedict about Robert's threats when he'd cornered her into marriage.

'Cameo.' Benedict drew her safe against his strong chest. 'You should never have consented to marry him, not for my sake.'

'I didn't want anything to happen to you.'

'I can defend myself against Robert. You need have no fear of that. He'd better pray our paths never cross. The thought of you, married to him. He's a bully. Thank goodness you're safe from him.'

'Your paintings saved me,' she whispered.

But what had she done, leaping out of the carriage? The realisation struck her. Her parents would have been aghast when she didn't appear at the church. Her mother doubtless would have had hysterics in the front pew while her father barked orders to have his daughter found. She winced. It hurt her to think of causing such panic in her parents.

And Maud, waiting by the big wooden doors of the church in her blue bridesmaid's dress, holding the lacy veil, ready to drape it over

Cameo's head and face, and crown it with the diamond tiara, before presenting her with the bouquet of cream roses that matched those of the bridesmaids. Would her friend understand what she had done, why she had done it? Would George, in his tailed morning coat, forgive her for the disgrace his sister had brought on their family by not turning up at the church?

And Lord Warley, standing at the altar. Her lips firmed. She could see him, too, his yellow teeth in a snarl. She felt no pity for him. He'd been so certain he'd had her caged. She could well imagine his rage at her having escaped from his clutches, but she wasn't going to St Mary's church, whatever happened. She refused to be delivered up to him.

But Benedict had picked up her cloak.

'What are you doing?'

'You can't stay here, Cameo.' He tied the bow under her neck. 'Not like this. I'm taking you to Mayfair.'

'What? But, Benedict…'

'They'll be frantic about you. I can't keep you here while they suffer.'

The honour in him. While she'd barely considered the havoc she would cause when she had leapt so impulsively from the carriage, the panic she might evoke. She hadn't fully considered what doing so would mean: leaving a crowd of guests, family and friends waiting at the church for the marriage ceremony, craning their necks to see the bride walk down the aisle, a bride who wouldn't appear. Her only concern had been running to Benedict. All she'd known had been the message of her heart, her desperate need to see his work again, to see something of him one more time. The scandal! She flushed with shame, not for what she'd done, but for the way her parents, her mama, in particular, would feel, as their family's name was whispered in drawing rooms, at balls and parties, with the horrified delight that only a shocking scandal brought. Her only hope was that her family and friends could forgive her for what she'd done. She'd try to make amends, try to make them understand, if they would let her.

'Oh, I've got to let them know what happened.' She twisted her hands with remorse. 'I've got to explain, ask them to forgive me. They're going to be so angry.'

'Their main concern will be to have their daughter alive and well.'

'I didn't stop to consider. Everything you said about me was true. I'm spoilt and selfish. Thoughtless.'

'Stop it, Cameo.' He put a finger to her lips. 'You're you. Lady Catherine Mary St Clair.

Cameo Ashe. They're both part of you. And I love all of you.'

Benedict's mouth was almost on hers when the studio door creaked open.

Robert twirled his silver-topped cane. 'Ah. My missing bride.'

Chapter Twenty-Three

"'And would they praise the heavens for what they have?"
And I made answer, "Were there nothing else
For which to praise the heavens but only love,
That only love were cause enough for praise."'

—Alfred, Lord Tennyson:
'The Gardener's Daughter'

Benedict stared at his half-brother, his fists like rocks. Robert. He hadn't seen him for years, but he hadn't changed much, though he looked heavier and his hair was receding. The prim mouth that hid his avaricious nature and the hint of cruelty in his prominent eyes were still the same.

Blood swirled in front of Benedict's gaze.

Every memory he possessed of his half-brother at Warley Park—killing the rabbit in the woods, being heartless to his mother when she fell ill, telling him he'd lost his inheritance—all seemed to clamour in his brain at once. Every nerve and sinew in his body shouted to rip the man apart for all he'd done, most of all, for what he threatened to do to Cameo.

'Allow me to warn you, Warley. Leave now, or you'll be sorry.'

'Leave?' his half-brother sneered. 'Without my dear fiancée?'

'I know all about you,' Cameo choked out. 'I know you and Benedict are brothers.'

'Half-brothers,' Robert corrected. 'We don't want to overstate the relationship.'

Benedict's nails bit into his palms. 'I have no desire to claim any greater relationship with you, Warley, than that we unfortunately possess.'

'Benedict is Lord Warley's son, just as you are,' Cameo threw at Robert. 'Don't you dare deny it!'

'Yes. This—artist—' Robert threw a disparaging look around the studio '—is my father's— what's the best way to put it, since we are all being so polite?—my father's by-blow.'

Benedict's throat clenched.

'Don't disparage our father.' No matter if his father had kept his promise about his will or not, he wouldn't hear his father's name slighted. That pain had healed, while he'd painted out all his emotions, poured them into his portraits of Cameo. He no longer felt any anger towards his father. Whatever he had done, he had done it because he'd had to. His father had loved his mother and him, too. That was enough. 'He was an honourable man.'

Cameo faced Robert. 'Unlike some.'

Benedict couldn't help taking in how beautiful she looked at that moment, coming to his defence, her dark hair tumbled over her shoulder, her pansy eyes sparking violet fire.

Robert sent her a slow, lecherous glance as she stood there. 'How fetching you look, Lady Catherine Mary, in your wedding gown. Tonight I shall enjoy stripping it off you. I do hope my half-brother hasn't already spoilt the fruit.'

Benedict leapt. He grabbed Warley by the waistcoat and pulled back his fist. 'Don't you dare speak to her that way.'

Robert bared his yellow teeth in a snarl. 'I'll speak to my fiancée however I like, you bastard…' He lifted his cane.

'Stop!' Cameo cried, rushing between them. 'Please don't fight!'

Benedict dropped his fists. Only Cameo's distress halted him from giving Robert exactly what he deserved.

Robert brushed off his waistcoat. 'Did you think I'd let you have her? She's not for the likes of you.'

'She's not a possession, like a painting to be hung on a wall,' Benedict said, between gritted teeth.

'She's mine. Just like all the paintings in the gallery at Warley Hall. I'll do whatever I want with her. Once we're married no one can stop me. It's the law.'

'It's because our father and I shared a passion for art, isn't it?' Benedict demanded. 'Something you didn't share. Is that it?'

'But I got everything in the end,' Robert sneered.

'And now you're after Cameo's money to pay your gaming debts.'

His half-brother licked his lips. 'It's an additional pleasure, of course, that she's also an object of your desire. That will make it even more enjoyable when she's under my control.'

'That will never happen.'

Robert rubbed his hand up and down his cane. 'She belongs to me.'

'You've always been jealous of me, no matter how much our father gave you.' Benedict kept his voice low. 'You always wanted everything of mine.'

'There's not much to take.' Robert cast another disdainful glance around the studio. 'Just look at this attic.'

'He wouldn't be so badly off if you hadn't cheated him out of his inheritance!' Cameo exclaimed.

'You don't know what you're talking about, Lady Catherine Mary.' Robert spoke her name in a way that boiled Benedict's blood further.

'Oh, yes, I do. Benedict has told me all about it. Your father wanted Benedict to have the Old Masters in the gallery at Warley Park, the ones he collected on his European tour. He left them to Benedict in his will—the will you destroyed.'

'Cameo—'

'I'm sure of it, Benedict!'

'You can't prove it,' Robert said swiftly.

A gruff voice came from the door. 'Perhaps I can.'

'Papa!' Cameo exclaimed.

To her amazement her father, puffing and out of breath, entered the studio with a face like thunder.

He scowled as he lifted off his top hat. 'Damned stupid place to live. All those stairs.'

'Your father's come to bring you to the church.' Robert's tongue darted out. 'I told him where we'd find you.'

The earl made straight for Benedict. 'You're Cole, I take it?' he demanded. 'I'm Buxton. So, you're the painter, eh? The one who did the portrait of my daughter?'

Cameo rushed in. 'That's right, Papa.'

'I can speak for myself, Cameo,' Benedict said.

Pride filled her as he stood his ground and answered her father steadily, 'Yes, I did the portrait, my lord. And I'm not planning to apologise for it.'

Cameo gulped as the vein in her father's forehead popped out. 'And you're my friend Warley's natural son, are you? Come on, out with it!'

'I am. I wouldn't want to deny it,' Benedict replied coolly.

'Disgraceful,' Robert broke in.

The earl glared at him. 'That's what you think, is it, Warley?'

'Well, he is a by-blow and—'

'That's enough!' The earl's voice became louder. 'Your father would be ashamed of you, Warley. He told me years ago about his natural son and his pride in him, even if he was born on the wrong side of the blanket. Happens in the best families. He asked me to look out for the lad. I'm afraid I've let my old friend down.'

As he turned to Benedict his voice turned gruff. 'I've been trying to find you for years. I thought you would use the family name Ackland, not Cole. This matter's been troubling me for some time. Only put two and two together this morning at the church when Robert let your connection slip.'

Rummaging in his coat pocket, he found an envelope. 'Ought to have got this to you years ago. It's been in my safekeeping in Mayfair. I went and collected it. Here. Take it. It's yours.'

Benedict received the envelope. Cameo saw his lips tighten as he stared at the handwriting on the front. She held her breath as he opened it, then scanned the pages inside. 'Benedict, what is it?'

With a stunned expression he looked up at her. In his eyes was a light, a flame of joy. 'It's my father's will.'

'What?' Robert lunged forward and tried to grab the paper from Benedict's hand.

'You won't be getting your hands on it this time,' Benedict warned him through gritted teeth.

Robert backed away.

'Indeed not.'

'What does the will say?' Cameo refused to hold back. 'Please tell me, Benedict. Did your father keep his promise to you? Are the paintings in the gallery at Warley Hall yours?'

'More than that.' Appearing dazed, Benedict rubbed his hand across his eyes. 'He left me Warley Park.'

* * *

As Benedict stood clutching the will, a vision seemed to rise in front of his eyes.

Warley Park. That huge, glorious estate, spread over hundreds of acres, with its woods, its lakes and fountains, and its smooth green lawns rising on a slope up to the grand house. And the house itself, with its Tudor core, and the elegant wings, Georgian, palatial; its perfect proportions had pleased his artist's eye even before he'd understood the splendour of what he saw. He'd only understood he liked to look at it—had understood instinctively it was something fine.

His father hadn't cut him out of his will. He'd never rejected his firstborn son. He'd left Benedict the home he loved.

'Benedict!' Cameo flung her arms around him. 'I can't believe it. My father had the will, all this time. Warley Park is yours.'

His half-brother's face paled. 'That will is null and void. It won't stand up in a court of law.'

'Won't it?' the earl bellowed. 'I think you'll find it might. I'll see to that.'

'Surely you're not going to support this… this…*artist's* claim over mine…'

'You don't think so? That will is legal and valid. There was enough for both of you, but you cut your brother out of what your father intended for him. You're a disgrace, Warley.' The vein on the earl's forehead appeared as if it would burst. 'I've always had my suspicions about you, and so did your papa, unfortunately. I tell you, he would be disgusted. As am I.'

'You don't understand the whole story, my lord…Cole's mother, she was little more than a peasant—to think that someone with that background should have Warley Park—'

'Enough,' Benedict broke in quietly. Beside him he felt Cameo quake at his tone. She knew how his mother had suffered at Robert's hands. 'It's time you left.'

For a moment he thought his half-brother was going to argue.

Benedict spoke again. One word, gritted between his teeth. 'Out.'

With a single glance at Benedict's face, Robert made for the door.

'Don't think you've heard the last of this,' he threatened, with a lift of his cane.

'I think we've heard the last of it, unless you want your gaming habits barring you from every club in London,' the earl inserted furiously.

The studio door slammed.

The earl glared as he turned to his daughter. 'Don't think that you're not in trouble, young lady! I've never known such behaviour! Not turning up at the church! Empty carriage! We didn't know what had become of you, Cameo!'

'I'm sorry, Papa.' She held out her hands imploringly. 'Can you forgive me? I couldn't go through with it. I knew I had to get to Benedict.'

Benedict stepped forward, with an internal chuckle. He'd pictured Cameo living in that grand house in Mayfair, with a wealthy protector. Here he was. Her father, who, beneath the bluster, obviously adored his daughter.

'I'm sure you've been worried about Cameo, my lord,' he said calmly. 'I was just about to return her to your care in Mayfair.'

The earl's brow furrowed, perplexed. 'About to bring her home, eh?'

'That's right, my lord.'

'Humph!' the earl exclaimed after a moment. 'Very gentlemanly of you. I suppose I wouldn't expect anything less from the eldest son of my friend.'

Benedict inclined his head.

Lord Buxton addressed Cameo. 'Ought to not have forced you into a wedding, I suppose. Your mother's been having hysterics, something about your grandmama. Says she wants your portrait hung in the drawing room. *The Gardener's Daughter*, is that the name of it, eh?'

'Yes, that's right, Papa.'

'Still for sale, is it?'

'It's not for sale,' Benedict interjected. 'But I

would be happy to make a gift of it to Cameo's mother.'

The earl's eyes boggled. 'Is that so?'

'That's so.'

Buxton stared at Benedict again. Benedict witnessed the respect dawning in his eyes.

'First, we'll arrange for the portrait to be displayed in the Royal Academy once more. Oughtn't to have had it taken down. Work of art like that. Acted too hastily.' He gave a cough. 'You'll have your hands full with my daughter, Cole. But my friend thought a great deal of you and it seems young Cameo does, too. I'll expect you to take good care of her, as your father would have wanted you to.'

Benedict met his gaze. 'I will.'

'Oh, Papa!' Cameo threw her arms around her father.

'There, there!' He gave her an awkward pat. 'I wanted to trust my daughter to my best friend's son. It seems I can, after all.'

The sound of footsteps and a muffled voice came from outside the studio.

'Cameo! Cameo! Are you in there?'

Cameo's mouth dropped open in astonishment. 'Why, that sounds like Maud!'

Pink bonnet askew on her blonde curls, a pretty young woman rushed past Benedict as soon as he opened the door. She was followed closely by a dark-haired young man.

'Maud!' Cameo exclaimed, as the young woman hugged her as if she wouldn't let her go.

'Oh, Cameo! I've been so worried! I couldn't wait downstairs a moment longer! I thought something dreadful had happened to you!'

The young man who could only be Cameo's brother—such was their resemblance—stepped forward and held out his hand to Benedict. 'I'm George St Clair. How do you do? You must be...'

'Benedict Cole.'

'The artist?'

'He's my friend Henry's eldest son,' Lord Buxton put in irascibly. 'Warley Park belongs to him.'

'I say.' George whistled. 'That's a turn-up.'

Cameo spoke up. 'Perhaps I should make some introductions. This is my friend Miss Maud Cartwright, Benedict.' The pretty blonde who had embraced Cameo dimpled at Benedict.

'I knew Cameo must have come to you. I waited outside the church in Mayfair, with the veil and flowers,' Maud described breathlessly, her eyes round, as she clutched Cameo's hand. 'And the carriage arrived and Bert opened the door, and, oh, Cameo, you weren't there, you'd just vanished! We looked and looked for you. I was so frightened. Then I thought, oh, no, she's come up with one of her dangerous ideas…'

'Oh, Maud!' Cameo exclaimed. 'I'm sorry I gave you such a fright. I wouldn't have upset you for the entire world. And, George—' she turned to her brother '—I'm so sorry.'

He gave her arm a reassuring pat. 'I've always said you were a strange sister. Now I know for sure. You gave us all an awful shock, not turning up at St Mary's like that. But it seems it has all turned out for the best.'

'It's so romantic.' Maud sighed.

'Romantic, eh?' The earl cleared his throat. 'I've had enough of all this nonsense for one day. It's time to go home.'

'Yes, Papa,' George said and sent Cameo a wink.

'Goodbye, Maud,' Cameo said, hugging her friend. 'Goodbye, George. Goodbye, Papa.'

At the doorway her father turned back.

'We'll expect you in Mayfair, Cameo.' He nodded to Benedict. 'Both of you.'

Chapter Twenty-Four

'Such a Lord is love.'

—Alfred, Lord Tennyson:
'The Gardener's Daughter'

'Goodness, it's like Piccadilly Circus here this morning.'

Just as Benedict went to pull Cameo into his arms, Nicholas Trelawney breezed into the studio, brandishing a newspaper in his hand. 'Sorry to arrive unannounced, but I thought you'd want to see this—why, Lady Cameo!'

'Hello,' Cameo said shyly.

'What on earth is happening here this morning? Were those friends of yours I passed on the stairs?'

'That was my father, my brother George and my friend Maud,' Cameo explained.

'Is that so?' Trelawney beamed. 'How charming they all looked. I'll have to invite them to one of my soirées. And how delightful to see you here again in the studio, my dear. So you're together at last!'

'Thank you for your help in it, Mr Trelawney.'

'My pleasure, my dear, my pleasure. Who can resist playing Cupid?' Trelawney stared at Benedict. 'Why is our artist looking so stunned? What have I missed?'

'Benedict has just found out he inherited Warley Park. It's where he grew up,' she explained rapidly.

Trelawney whistled. 'So that's the estate which belonged to his father? My, my. How strange. You don't need to tell me more, my dear. I know all about it. I just didn't know the names.'

He rustled the newspaper he held in his hand. 'Well, I bring more good tidings. It seems both fortune and fame are tapping on the door!'

'What on earth do you mean, Trelawney?' Benedict asked with a dry smile.

'Page ten.' Trelawney passed Cameo the newspaper.

Hastily she leafed through the pages. 'Why, Benedict. It's a review of your work!'

Trelawney fanned himself with his hand. 'Read it aloud for us, my dear. I'm not sure I can take the strain.'

With mounting excitement, Cameo read.

'A new exhibition by Benedict Cole at the Belleview Gallery, Soho, is certain to be the talk of the artistic season.

Mr Cole's first painting of Lady Catherine Mary St Clair appeared, albeit briefly, in the selection at the Royal Academy of Art before it was unfortunately withdrawn. That this was in error is made clear by this new exhibition, made up entirely of portraits of his muse, Lady Catherine Mary.

By painting one woman in different guises and occupations, Mr Cole has shown that he is an artist of the first order and a premier painter at this time. Not every painter can capture, as he has, the diverse and ever-changing moods of a single woman, making each more enchanting than the last.

He is to be celebrated in this achievement and long may his muse inspire him. Mr Cole fully comprehends the artist's greatest calling: in the words of the great poet Tennyson, *"'Tis not your work, but Love's."'*

Cameo dropped the paper on to the table and clapped her hands together.

Trelawney piped up. 'Every artist in London would give their teeth for such a review,' he added, a trifle wistfully. He clapped Benedict on the back. 'Congratulations, my dear boy.'

Benedict sounded gruff. 'A good response, I suppose.'

'Good? It's wonderful!' Cameo exclaimed.

'It's only the start,' Trelawney crowed. With a flourish he reached into his pocket and pulled out a small folded piece of paper, passing it to Benedict. 'I took the liberty of popping into the Belleview this morning on your behalf. They've sold three works already and the others are sure to be snapped up. And then there's the commissions, my dear boy, the commissions.' He rubbed his palms together. 'London's finest folk are all going to want a painting by Benedict Cole on their wall.'

Benedict stared at the cheque. 'It's unbelievable.'

'Believe it,' Trelawney told him, clearly delighted. 'I asked the Belleview Gallery to raise your prices, too, as soon as I realised people would be starting to flock in.'

Benedict's mouth tightened. 'Hmmm.'

Cameo experienced a sudden chill. 'What's wrong, Benedict?'

He moved away from her, stretched his hands across the wood of the chimney piece. His broad back expanded as he took a deep breath. 'There's nothing's wrong.'

He pivoted on his heel, dropped the newspaper on to the table and faced her. 'I don't consider canvas and paint more valuable than flesh and blood, that's all. My paintings doing well, my inheritance, I'd even let Robert keep Warley Park if that was the price I had to pay.' He burned her with a look. 'He doesn't have what I have. I have you.'

Cameo's heart pounded as in a smooth movement Benedict knelt down on one knee in front of her and lifted her shaking hand to his warm lips.

'Marry me, Cameo.'

She couldn't speak, not a single word. Not with his eyes holding hers, the love in his them deep and infinite.

'Ahem.' Trelawney coughed. 'My dears, I think it's time for me to slip away. I do feel *de trop*.' He pulled his spotted handkerchief from his pocket and dabbed his cheeks. 'But how affecting.'

Benedict ignored the sculptor's pantomime beside him.

'Well?' he asked her, his eyes coal black, still locked to hers. 'Will you marry me, Lady Catherine Mary St Clair?'

'Yes,' she replied. Joy bubbled up inside her like champagne. 'Yes. I will marry you, Benedict Cole.'

He stood and pulled her into his fierce embrace. The feel of him, the strength of his powerful arms, would be home to her now. Deep within her, she knew he would hold her like this for the rest of her life; his kiss, sure and loving, was a portrait of passion, never to fade.

The studio door slammed.

'Trelawney's gone,' she said, startled.

'He'll be back, you don't need to worry about that,' Benedict assured her with a grin. He ran his finger around her mouth and down to rest on her neck. He frowned. 'I'd forgotten.'

He reached into his pocket. 'I found this on the floor by the fire the night I found out who you were.'

'My grandmama's cameo!' she exclaimed with relief. It meant even more to her now that she knew her grandmother's story. 'You've had it, all this time?'

'I kept it with me. It's haunted my days and nights, as you have. I got a new ribbon for it, in the hope I might one day do this.' His hands caressed her neck as he tied it and dropped a kiss in the hollow below. 'I want you to wear it always.'

'I always will.' It was definitely a talisman, now.

'Along with the ring I don't have for you yet,' he added, with a regretful grin. 'Alas. I may now own Warley Park, but I don't have a diamond ring for you.'

'Not diamonds.' She shuddered, remembering the ring Robert had given her that chilled her finger. At least Becky would benefit from it.

She barely breathed by the time Benedict finished tying the necklace around her neck, where it belonged. He tucked her smaller hands inside his large, warm clasp, as though making a pact. 'I shall give you an amethyst, to match your eyes like deepest pansies.'

She smiled at the words he used from Tennyson's poem, the subject of the painting which had brought them together.

'I don't need a ring. I just need you,' she whispered.

His voice caressed her. 'I hope we'll always need each other, and more.'

'More?'

'I've always wanted children.' He smiled. 'I believe I'd like a daughter.'

'I'd like a son, with dark hair. He shall be called Henry, after his grandfather.'

A shaft of pain flashed across Benedict's face, followed by joy.

'We have so much still to discover about each other, so much to learn. I'm going to take you to Venice for a honeymoon. You're going to have a Grand Tour, as every aspiring artist should, to study the great Renaissance masters—Titian, Bellini, Giorgione. And I shall be your guide.' His voice deepened. 'It's the most romantic city in the world. There's a hotel I'll take you to, not far from St Mark's Square. The days we shall spend studying art and the nights we shall spend studying each other.'

Her stomach somersaulted as he lifted her clasped hands to his lips. He groaned, catching her fingertip between his teeth and nipping it gently. Slowly, finger by finger, his gaze never leaving hers, he removed her satin glove and threw it on the table, before reaching for the other. Again, ever so slowly, he slid it from her hand.

'I never wanted to see these hands become calloused, and careworn. Now I can keep you in the manner to which you were born.' He frowned as he stared at her fingers. 'You haven't been painting.'

She pulled her hands away. 'I don't think I'll need any more painting lessons.'

His brow creased. 'Why not?'

'I'm not painting any more.' She shivered, remembering the awful moment when the paintbrush had snapped in her hand. 'When I was locked in my bedroom, my brother, George, smuggled me in some watercolours and I tried to paint the ash tree outside my window. I planned

Albert Museum at www.vam.ac.uk/page/
0-9/19th-century-fashion/

For all things Victorian, from teacups to
jewellery, homeware and accessories, try:
www.victorianeralovers.com/topsites/in.php?id
=40

Or why not play dress-up in some romantic
Victorian outfits? Visit romanticthreads.com/
index.html

The Romantic Poetry of Tennyson

Interwoven into Cameo and Benedict's story
is the poetry of Alfred, Lord Tennyson, a favourite poet of Queen Victoria. While Tennyson's
works have gone in and out of favour, he was one
of the most fashionable poets of his day.

One of the most romantic writers who ever
lived, Tennyson was writing—and falling in
love—during the time of Cameo and Benedict's
story.

One of his lesser-known works is the poem
'The Gardener's Daughter; or, The Pictures'
(1842). Full of passion and longing, it's the inspiration for Benedict's painting in which Cameo
features as the model.

5_ST19

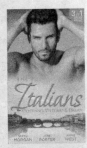

to climb down it and escape here, to you. But when I knew I had to give you up, I vowed to give up art, too. I haven't tried since.'

His lips tightened. 'You should never have been imprisoned like that.'

'My father was just trying to protect me. Even if it was misguided.'

'That's true,' Benedict agreed.

She laid her palm against his chest. 'It's all right now. I'm free.'

'You're free to paint,' he corrected her as he held out his hand. 'Come and see. I've got a surprise for you.'

'What is it?' Cameo followed him across the studio and stared at the shape beneath the sheet Benedict dragged out. He placed it next to his easel. 'Is it a frame?'

'Not a frame. It's something I made for you.' He smiled tenderly. 'To summon you back to me.'

Her heart thudded. He'd never forgotten her, even when she had despaired.

Tearing the sheet away, he ran his long fingers over the wood. 'This is ash, like the frame of the first portrait I did of you. I used it to make this.'

It was an easel, smaller proportioned than his rough-hewn one, more elegant, but with the same sturdiness. At the top of it he'd sketched a cameo profile of a woman to be carved into the wood.

Benedict pointed to it. 'Your symbol.'

'It's beautiful!' she said in wonder.

'I want you to paint,' he said seriously. 'I want you to become the painter you're meant to be.'

'I'm afraid to try again.' Tears prickled her eyelids. 'I'm scared it's gone.'

'Such a gift is never gone. You just need to let the passion rise in you again.'

Benedict dragged out the wooden chair. Holding her by the waist, he sat her down in front of the easel and she tucked her legs underneath it. 'I'll help you. I'll teach you.'

His arms enclosed her from behind as they had the day he'd caught her sketching, his breath tickling the hair on her neck as he chuckled. 'After all, that's why you came to me, isn't it?'

He picked up the charcoal, closed her fist around the stick. 'No.' He removed it. 'Let's try oils.'

In quick strides he crossed to his easel. He seized a couple of pots of paint, a bottle of brushes and a palette and was back beside her.

'Here.'

'I'm not very good with oils,' she protested.

'Then its time you learnt to be.' Behind her again, Benedict squeezed cobalt-blue oil paint on to the palette, dipped the tip of a paintbrush into it and slipped it into her hand. It was a larger brush than she'd ever used before, strange to her fingers; fingers that didn't seem to want to move, clumsy and stiff.

'You can do this, Cameo,' he urged her, the warmth on her neck making her tingle all over.

She moved the brush. Nothing came. All the happiness she'd known before whenever she painted or sketched had vanished. The marks she daubed on the paper seemed meaningless, a mess of oils, no better than that of a small child. It was over. Her spark, her passion for art, had gone.

He sensed her despair. 'It doesn't matter what you paint, my darling. Don't try to paint anything in particular. Just feel it.'

She closed her eyes, melting into him. She'd try for him, but she knew it was no good. His fingers tightened around hers as he guided her, the brush swishing thickly across the paper. Unexpectedly, something released, soaring within her as if she were flying, gliding through the air like a bird on a wing.

'That's it,' he whispered.

A joyous laugh rose within her as her hand glided, faster and faster, surer and surer. Still encircling her within the safety of his arms, his hand dropped away and suddenly she painted alone, the way she always dreamed she might, the way Benedict painted, liberated, free at last.

She opened her eyes. 'I can do it!'

Behind her, she heard him laugh as he released her from his embrace. He came around and lifted her chin. 'And I've got other things to teach you.'

Benedict seized a paintbrush. 'It's time for your lesson, Miss Ashe.'

Epilogue

'Shall I cease here? …
Might I not tell of
…vows,
where there was never need of vows…'

— Alfred, Lord Tennyson:
'The Gardener's Daughter'

'I want you here.' Benedict beckoned. 'Come over by the window. I need to see you in a proper light.'

Cameo smoothed down her dress, surprised to find her hands were trembling, just as the first time she'd come to the studio. She walked over to the window, on legs that were once again unsteady. She stood, self-conscious, the afternoon light streaming in behind her. It was the only night they'd spend there. Before they moved.

To Warley Park.

But her honeymoon night had to be spent in

the studio. It was all she'd ever wanted. It was where it all began.

'Take off your bonnet,' Benedict said huskily. 'Let me see your face.'

She removed the pearl-tipped pin that held her silk bonnet with its white lacy trimming. Slowly, she undid the white-satin ribbons tied under her chin. With a shake of her head she set her ringlets free.

She heard his sharp intake of breath, but his expression appeared inscrutable.

'And now your hair.'

One by one, Cameo took the pins from her hair. As she dropped them on the table beside her, he watched each move in a way that made her stomach lurch. She slowed her pace, tantalising him as she let each long black strand free.

He didn't shift an inch as finally she released the last hairpin. Her long black curls loosened from their ringlets and loops, until she felt them tumble about her shoulders and foam down her spine.

He stood silent for a moment. He pointed to her white gown, with its lacy collar. 'Undo your dress.'

She sought for a gulp of air. Her heart thrummed as she fumbled to untie the fine French lace around her neck. The invisible connection flared between them, as with taunting precision she undid the tiny crystal buttons at the front of her smooth bodice. She undid the top button. He stayed silent, observing her. When he made no sign, she undid the next.

'Is—is that enough?' she asked him, as she had that first time, her voice low.

'Almost.'

Cameo undid the third button, and the fourth, and then fifth. She looked over to him.

His eyes darkened to their unfathomable black. 'Let me help you.'

He came close to her, so close the heat burned from his body.

The flame she'd recognised in his work, before they'd even met.

He reached over and put his fingers to her bodice. She held her breath as he undid the remaining buttons. She released a gasp as he opened the dress to reveal the ribbon and lace trim of her silk chemise, and the top of her stays with her breasts pushed up over them.

'Will you let me...?'

'Yes...' she breathed. 'Yes.'

Cameo's mouth dried as Benedict turned her hands palms up. His fingers played against the sensitive skin of her wrists as he undid the buttons at the cuffs where her billowing silk sleeves tightened. Still not speaking, he eased the top of the dress over her shoulders.

With a sudden movement that brought a cry to her lips he put his arms around her waist, pulling her close to him, his mouth almost against hers. She longed for his lips, but he did not kiss her. Instead, with expert fingers he unclipped the waistband at the small of her back. The dress dropped in a pool of pale silk on to the floor.

He held her hand as she stepped out of the circle of silk as daintily as if she were waltzing with him. With a leather-clad toe, he casually pushed the garment aside, never taking his eyes from her.

Cameo shuddered.

'There's that draught again.' She heard the smile in his voice.

Benedict spun her around, his grasp on the laces of her corset now, releasing her from their sharp confines. With each loosened lace the fullness of her body expanded in his hands, her breasts falling and then lifting as she braced against the air, their pink tips tightening underneath her chemise.

The clatter of her corset as it hit the wooden floor. The warmth of his fingers through the thin silk barrier was all that remained between them as he twirled her to face him.

She bit her lip as he edged a finger inside her garter, before taking a flimsy silk stocking down each leg, balling them into his fists before dropping them to the floor.

Wordlessly, he untied the white ribbons of her chemise, eased it down over her shoulders and slid it over the curves of her hips. She wore no pantaloons today.

He retreated. With his gaze never moving from her naked body, he lifted a wooden chair and placed it at an angle by the window. 'Sit down.'

Against the straight-backed chair, Cameo arched slightly. He backed a step away, his gaze unwavering. Her body went taut as he gently folded her hands in her naked lap.

'Now, turn to the right.'

Remembering, she gave him a glimmer of a smile. She turned marginally on her seat.

'No, not like that. Turn some more.'

She shifted her body an inch to the right.

'More.'

She shifted again.

'Now lift your chin.' Leaning forward, Benedict held her chin, tilted her head upward and forced her to stare directly into his burning expression.

The charge shooting between them burned as hot as the fire in the grate. Would it always be like this? she wondered dizzily as he removed his hand, his fingers running lightly against her bare skin.

'There's another thing.' This time, she didn't move as he lifted up her cameo necklace from where it lay against her skin, twisted on its velvet ribbon. Lifting it high, he dropped it down again into the soft dip between her breasts.

He backed away further, still scrutinising her. 'Now, you must hold still while I do my preliminary drawings. Can you do that?'

'Yes.'

He seized a large sheet of paper and propped it against a board on his easel. Taking a stick of charcoal, he made strong, bold strokes on the paper, glancing back and forth.

Cameo hid an inner smile. *You think you're watching me, Mr Cole, when in fact I'm watching you.*

'Benedict.'

He looked up, the familiar lock of dark hair falling across his forehead.

'I just wondered—what will this painting be called?'

He smiled, his white teeth flashing. 'Well, surely it's obvious, my darling Cameo. This painting is for my own, private collection. It will be called *Portrait of the Artist's Wife*.'

A thrill ran through her body. 'On her wedding day?'

'On her wedding day,' he confirmed. Dropping his paintbrush, Benedict crossed the room and took Cameo in his arms.

> '"The secret bridal chambers of the heart,
> Let in the day." Here, then, my words have
> end.'
>
> —Alfred, Lord Tennyson:
> 'The Gardener's Daughter'

* * * * *

Historical Note

The Art of the Pre-Raphaelites

Cameo's story is inspired by the Pre-Raphaelite artists and models of Victorian England. The
beautiful, romantic Pre-Raphaelite paintings are
some of the most familiar artworks in the world
today. Just like Benedict Cole, the art and love
lives of the Pre-Raphaelite painters, a group of
brilliant, free-thinking young men, were considered scandalous, as featured in the BBC televi-
sion series *Desperate Romantics*. Their artistic
milieu was in complete contrast with the strict
conventions of the Victorian upper classes.
 Ladies like Cameo, Lady Catherine Mary St
Clair, lived in a controlled, stifling world, and
they were often trapped and unhappy. It would
have been considered unthinkable for a young
aristocratic woman such as Cameo to pursue art
seriously and even more unthinkable to be an

artist's model. Cameo's story celebrates every woman who ever challenged convention for the sake of art, and for the sake of love.

To learn more go to the Metropolitan Museum of Art: www.metmuseum.org/toah/hd/praf/hd_praf.htm

See Pre-Raphaelite images on Pinterest at www.pinterest.com/tategallery/pre-raphaelites/

Or meet the Pre-Raphaelite Sisterhood at: preraphaelitesisterhood.com

There's even a T-shirt!

The Beauty of Cameo Stones

A cameo is a small carving in relief on a semi-precious stone. Usually, the lighter-coloured layer is chipped away to reveal a darker background. Cameo stones were produced as far back as ancient Greece and Rome.

The relief image is produced by carefully carving the material with a plane, to the point at which the two contrasting colours, light and dark, can meet. The technique, used mainly for jewellery making, has gone through a number of revivals, during the Renaissance and into the nineteenth century, when cameo jewellery was popularised by Queen Victoria. At that time cameo portraits were often made of well-to-do young women to adorn jewellery, for a keepsake or to give to a lover. Glass and shells were also engraved. The word *cameo*, with an original Greek meaning of 'shadow portrait', today more commonly describes the unique style of carving or engraving, and is also used in plays and movies to capture the fleeting dramatic appearance of a character: i.e., to make a 'cameo appearance'.

Enjoy some cameo appearances on Pinterest at www.pinterest.com/elizaredgold/

Find out more about Victorian cameos at www.victorianbazaar.com/cameos.html

The Fashion of the Mid-Victorian Era

The clothes Cameo and Maud would have worn in mid-Victorian times were extraordinary. Getting dressed would have taken a while. At the time this story is set, around 1850, layers of frothy petticoats were just giving way to daring hoop skirts. Corsets and bodices, bonnets and gloves were part of daily life, and for high society, beautiful ball dresses made of silk and lace, complete with flirty fans, were an essential part of the Season. Today, Victorian-era fashion, style, homewares and decor continue to enchant. Take a peep inside a Victorian room or closet. Be inspired to add some Victorian decorative touches to your own home or fashion style.

Make a virtual visit to the Victorian and